Finally Moore

Frankie Page

To Brucey,
The most loveable, lost kitty to stumble on my doorstep...

Contents

Prologue

Scott

Amanda Erickson, 35.

She enjoys cooking, specifically with ingredients from her home garden. Loves hiking, fishing, and skiing. Her favorite movies are *Moulin Rouge* and *Bride Wars*. One day, she hopes to backpack and do a *Taste of Asia* tour.

She's perfect.

Almost too perfect...

My eyes graze over her dating profile for the hundredth time. Hopefully this app doesn't track views, or at least saves me the embarrassment of reporting them. I'd hate for her to think I'm a stalker.

Fuck, is that why she's late?

No, she's not late. I'm early. But who could blame me? This could be it. She could be the one, and I couldn't just sit around waiting to meet my soul mate.

Damn it, Scott. You're getting ahead of yourself again.

Soul mate? You haven't even seen her yet, and you're already planning the rest of your lives together. Not that I really care about her looks. They change. I'm living proof of that. The geeky kid who spent high school hiding in his best friend's shadow, then filled out his lanky frame and can now talk to a girl without the aid of a wingman.

At this point, I'd just be happy if this date goes well enough that she might consider joining me at my friend's

New Year's Eve dinner party. It's couples only, and I learned my lesson embarrassingly fast that holidays don't make good first dates—Thanksgiving was proof of that. But that's a story for a different day.

Not to mention, the upcoming event is in Chicago, so it's probably best we meet beforehand. I dread the idea of a six-hour car ride, filled with awkward silence because we have zero ability to converse with each other.

I tuck my phone into my pocket. If she hasn't already caught me studying her information like she's going to give me a pop quiz, it would be best for her not to see just how anxious I am either.

I rub the velvety crimson pedal of the rose lying on the table. The calling card of the Red Rose Blind Date program so that she knows I'm *me*. It's a cool concept, but right now I hate it. What if she saw me and already decided that I wasn't what she wanted? While looks aren't at the top of my list, maybe they are on hers?

"Scott?" an angelic voice asks. She smiles and my heart skips a beat. "At least I really hope you're him. Otherwise, this is super embarrassing."

My chair scoots across the hardwood flooring as I quickly stand and extend a hand to greet her. "Yes, sorry, I'm Scott." I grin as her espresso eyes widen at my towering height.

As she assesses me, I use the opportunity to drink in her deliciously curvy figure that's accentuated by her form-fitted dress. I know I said looks aren't everything, but *fuck* are they an added bonus. And right now, I feel like I just hit the jackpot.

She lets out a relieved sigh. "Thank god." I pull out a chair and help her sit before reclaiming my own. "I'm not sure what I was thinking. Blind dates are so stressful." Amanda peers up at me through a pair of perfectly fanned lashes.

"Tell me about it," I empathize with her.

"I thought it would be easier. This is my first date in a long time and, well, I thought getting to know you first would make me less anxious. But I think it's made it worse."

"How so?"

"The expectation." She worries her glossy lip between her teeth. "You're going to think I'm crazy and maybe I am? But it feels like I've known you my whole life. So I kept thinking things like... what if when we finally meet face-to-face, I'm not your type or... I don't know... you don't think I'm pretty or something?"

I laugh. She narrows her eyes at me, and I realize she probably thinks I'm being a dick. "No, sorry. I was just terrified of the same thing."

Her shoulders loosen as she settles in. "Really?"

"Yeah, I mean, you're perfect." Her round cheeks flush at my compliment. "And I haven't had the greatest luck when it comes to dating. So, I've honestly been waiting for the other shoe to drop, and figured you'd get one look at me and walk away without a word."

All the awkwardness magically disappears, and everything is back on track. *Perfect.* I know I keep saying it, but I can't think of any other way to describe it. The conversation flows as smoothly as the bottle of wine we ordered. It was nice being able to discuss the menu with someone, analyze the dishes, commiserate over the struggle of choosing just one out of several amazing options. The only thing that could've made our evening better is if we would've shared our plates.

This doesn't feel like our first *blind* date—no, it's like we're celebrating our twentieth anniversary. After all the ups and downs in my dating life this year, I can say without a doubt that this is how it's supposed to be. Which really proves when it's right, it's right. Simple as that.

"Sorry." Amanda frowns as she picks up and vigorously texts on her phone.

"Everything okay?" I risk asking this time.

She hasn't been on her cell *all* night, but I have noticed how her entire demeanor changes the few instances when she's had to reach for it. With how wonderful everything else has been going, at first I ignored it, figuring it's not really any of my business. I know. *Bad Scott*. But I can't help myself. This girl is incredible and I don't want to put a damper on what's been a great evening by asking a question I'm sure I don't want to know the answer to. Yet it also seems like I'm a glutton for punishment.

"Yeah... I mean, no." She grabs her half-full glass of pinot noir and swallows it down. "I swear I never go out—like ever. I've basically been locked in my home for the past ten years."

Oh my god, was she being held captive? is my immediate thought before I tell myself to calm down. This isn't some episode of *Dateline*.

"And it figures that the first time I go out, my daughter spikes a fever."

"Daughter?" I spit out my drink a little. Not enough to be noticeable but enough for me to have to reach for my napkin and swipe at my mouth.

"Yeah, Meghan, my youngest. I love her, but she's famous for terrible timing."

"Youngest?"

In all our conversations, Amanda hasn't once mentioned—even *hinted* about—being a mother of one child, let alone multiple *children*. Alarm bells sound in the back of my mind, as the gong dings and common sense throws down a major red flag. I have nothing against kids. I love them and hope to have many one day, even if they aren't biologically mine. So, the fact she has children isn't a deal-breaker for me. No, what's got the hair on the back of my neck standing on end is the realization that she didn't tell me. I thought she and I were looking for the same thing, a relationship. The only reason I can think of to not tell someone that you're a parent is if you're just looking to get laid or for something casual.

Amanda pulls up a picture on her phone, smiling when she turns the screen to me as if there is nothing wrong with this situation. "Yup, I've got three amazing babies." She points to each one. "Meghan, Amber, and my eldest, Nolan."

"I can see why you don't get out much." I pour myself another glass of pinot, thankful that the waitress had the foresight to leave the bottle—maybe she knew something I didn't.

"Yeah." Amanda lets out a nervous chuckle. "I'm sorry... I should've mentioned them. This is all new to me and I don't exactly know the protocol. Based on you looking like you just saw the Ghost of Christmas Past, I clearly see I missed the mark on this one. But I truly thought it would be better to meet you first and tell you face-to-face. Gauge your reaction in person, rather than try to interpret it over text. I know it was a risk. Most guys probably wouldn't want to date some middle-aged woman with not just one, but three kids. That being said..." She reaches across the table and takes my hand. "I got the sense you were different." She smiles, and I find it hard to not return the gesture.

"That makes sense." *I mean, I get it.* Guys, well, people in general can be assholes. Most would either ghost her the second she told them or get in her pants and hightail it the next morning. I can't even imagine how hard it must be for a single mom to get out there and try to connect with someone.

Amanda resumes her angry texting, huffing at the screen before peering back up at me. "Sorry, my husband is just worthless without me. First, he panics because our daughter has a fever and asks if he should bring her to the ER. So I ask him what her temperature is, and it's only like ninety-nine degrees? Which is nothing to worry about, especially when she has no other symptoms, so I tell him to give her some Tylenol and see how she's doing in an hour. You'd think that would solve it. But, nope, next it's questions about where the Tylenol is located and if Motrin would be better..."

I stare, a little dumbfounded. It's almost as if she was swapped out with a stunt double the moment I stepped off to find the restroom.

Red flag number two. Though this one is waving a little more vigorously.

"Husband?" Out of her entire rant, it's the only word that resonated with me. *Husband?*

"Ex..." she corrects herself. "Well, almost."

Damn it. And there it is. The one thing I can't ignore. Strike three and she's out of here.

"I mean, we're separated and all. Mostly. The kids don't know yet. He still lives in the house. We thought it would be easier if we—"

"Can I bring y'all the dessert menu?" our server asks, oblivious to the shitstorm she just stepped into.

"Check please," I say before Amanda has a chance to respond.

The server looks between us, then smiles. "Sure, I'll be right back."

"Is there a problem?" the woman—who I thought was the girl of my dreams but instead crushes them—has the audacity to ask.

"Look, Amanda, you're great... Really..." I start, and she smiles at me. "But this isn't going to work for me."

"It's the kids, isn't it?" Her eyes drop to her phone as she fiddles with the case.

"No, it's the still being married and living with your husband. I won't pretend to know anything about what your situation is like. Honestly, I'm not judging you. But I meant what I said in my profile. I'm looking for something serious... long-term—hopefully forever. It feels like you have a lot on your plate, and I'm not sure dating is the best idea right now. At least not for me."

Her shoulders sag. "I know. I'm sorry."

"Don't apologize. Like I said, you're great... perfect. But our timing doesn't feel right. Who knows? Maybe when things are a bit more settled on your end and if we're both still free... we can try this again?"

"I'd like that." She grins. We both stand, and I'm probably going to regret this but I feel compelled to hug her, then press a soft kiss on her cheek. This time, when she gazes up and smiles, it doesn't quite reach her deep-brown eyes. "But it won't happen. You're amazing, Scott. There's no way someone doesn't snatch you up."

I laugh as my thoughts wander to all my failed dating attempts over the past year. "I promise... the chances of me finding someone as great as you... are slim to none."

"Just wait. You'll see. 'Tis the season for miracles." She sighs, and I really wish I could believe her.

1

Scott

"So..." Great, it's not even nine in the morning, and based on the glimmer of mischief in my little sister's eyes, I can tell she's here to drive me insane. "I've got this friend..." Tilly says.

"Not interested," I dismiss her, but as usual she ignores me.

"Well, friend of a friend. Okay, more like a friend of a friend's stylist—"

"No." I cut her off before she can elaborate more.

You'd think that between running a business, having six-month-old twins, and being pregnant with a new baby on the way, she'd have better things to do than obsess over me and my beyond pathetic dating life. Nope, her last name might have changed but my sister still has that stubborn Moore blood pumping through her veins. Ever since Jake, her twin and the guy voted least likely of us siblings to ever settle down, announced his engagement to her best friend the other week, my sister has been dead set on me following in their blissfully married footsteps.

"But I hear—"

"No, Tilly. I'm done."

"Done?" She frowns. "You can't be done, Scott. The right girl is out there. You just need to find her—"

"I thought I did. But guess what? She's married."

"Seriously, not this again. How can she be the *right one*, if she's married?" Tilly shakes her head.

"I love you, but given I've become an expert at shitty dating, I can tell you without a doubt that Amanda is perfect for me. One date or a hundred more won't change the fact that she's the one. So, instead of wasting any more of my time on pointless, dead-in-the-water romantic rendezvous that are going to leave me feeling empty, I'm going to wait. Be ready for when she leaves her husband and is able to give us a real shot."

"Believe me, I understand the gesture, waiting around because you think no one else will measure up to the person you think you're meant to be with. I really do," she says, and I know she's talking about her now-husband Jax. "But, Scott, let's be real. It's been what? Almost three weeks? And you haven't heard a single word from this girl."

I shrug off her concern. "Divorces take time, and with the holidays coming up, I'm not worried about it. I'm sure she'll reach out after the new year."

"True, but don't you think it's strange that she hasn't sent you a single message since that seemingly *magical* date you shared? Because if I were in her shoes, I'd be reaching out to you, getting whatever motivation I could grasp on to, to push forward with what is likely one of the hardest moments of my life. Look for my silver lining in what I can only imagine is a nightmare of a situation that I pray I, nor anyone I love, never have to go through."

"Here." I slide over my sister's usual order. Peppermint tea and a cranberry scone. Hopefully this will distract her long enough so that she'll get on with her day and leave me alone.

Tilly takes a bite of the flaky pastry, and her eyes roll in the back of her head as she savors it. "These are so good. Seriously, I used to kind of hate Cassie when she was pregnant and constantly drooling over everything she ate. Like, I thought it was faker than the orgasms those porn stars have. Because when I was pregnant with the twins, I was always sick. Nothing tasted good or, heck, even sat well. But this one." She pats her small baby bump. "*Sooo* much better. If I could feel this good all the time, I'd let Jax keep me knocked up. It's fantastic."

I ignore the graphic image of what it would involve for my best friend to keep my little sister pregnant. I'm an adult and have been provided with the proper sex education offered by the Minnesota public school system. But for my sanity, I choose to be blissfully ignorant and pretend Tilly ate a watermelon seed and that's how babies are made. It's what Jax and I need to do for the sake of our friendship.

"Are you going to find out what you're having this time?" I ask, in hopes of steering this conversation away from me as far as possible, until I'm nothing but a small dot on my nosey sister's rearview mirror.

Taking another bite of scone, Tilly shrugs. "Haven't decided yet." Her reply is barely audible around all the chewing. "Maybe." She shoves the rest of the pastry into her mouth before adding, "I mean, on the bright side, this happened before we started to phase out of all the newborn stuff. So, probably not. Worst case, if it's a girl, we'll have to run out and grab a few things."

"Or just tell Robbie to keep all of Nova's stuff aside for you." My older brother and his wife Cassie had their daughter not even a month ago and the twins just turned six months. So, right now, the Moore family is overflowing with the latest baby gear.

"Good idea." Tilly licks her fingers clean, not letting a single morsel go to waste. "Wait... How dare you, Scott Edmund Moore! We were talking about you growing old and dying alone. You're not getting out of this conversation that easy."

I laugh. "I'm not going to die old and alone."

"Old, alone, *and* waiting for some girl you had *one* date with, who in the middle of it revealed that she not only has three children she never told you about but is still legally married, not even officially separated, and living in the same house as said husband." When she's pissed, Tilly can be about as blunt as Robbie, who is grumpy on even his best day of the week.

"Look, our timing was off. But Amanda is it for me. She's everything I've been looking for: smart, funny, loves the same movies, has the same passions about food..."

"That's swell and all, but you need to get back to reality, Scott. None of that crap matters. Do you know how much Jax and I truly have in common? Almost nothing. Finding your true love isn't about having similar interests or hobbies. It's about that spark that once it's lit dims everyone else out from your view."

We had that spark? Didn't we? Fuck, thinking back now, I honestly can't remember.

"And let's not forget the fact that she was out on a date when she wasn't even officially separated from her husband. I bet you a hundred bucks they still sleep in the same bed too. If that isn't a major red flag, I'm not sure what is."

"Amanda isn't like that," I'm quick to insist. *At least I hope she's not.* My sister crosses her arms and gives me the eeriest *mom* stare. "Can we just drop it... please?"

"Just... what if she doesn't leave him? They have children—they're still living together. Which means there's a chance they will work out their problems."

My heart drops to my stomach at the thought, but I pick it back up. "No, not her."

"Don't be silly, Scott. Marriages aren't that black and white, especially when children are involved. As happy as they were, I know Mom and Dad had their ups and downs. It wasn't as Hallmarky as people around town like to pretend. Remember that year Dad slept in the study, and they thought none of us noticed? After they got over whatever that was, it was like they were newlyweds all over again."

I shiver at the memory of the sounds we heard coming from their bedroom. I get what my sister is trying to say, but I have to believe. Because if not, what the fuck am I waiting for?

"Love, *true* love, has trials. You and Jax—" I start to remind her, and she holds up a hand.

"That was a hundred percent different!"

"No, it wasn't. He's my best friend, but he fucked up. Avoiding you like that for ten years, it was wrong. But as shitty as I thought it was of him to do, look at you both now. Who's to say what would've happened if he stayed?"

Tilly opens her mouth but holds back whatever counterargument she had on the tip of her tongue. "Okay," she huffs. "But promise me you won't wait forever. I hate to think that the girl of your dreams is out there, just around the corner, and you're going to miss her because you're holding out for some married woman who may or may not leave her husband someday."

"Fine." I roll my eyes and continue wiping down the counter. My sister's lack of a poker face makes it clear she's not happy with my response but is dropping it... *for now* at least. Knowing Tilly, I'm sure she'll have a folio of eligible bachelorette's to comb through by the end of the day. My sister doesn't do anything in halves.

"What are you going to do about New Year's Eve? Didn't you say it was a couples only thing?"

I stop what I'm doing to peer up at my sister with a lopsided grin and a single brow raised in silent question.

"No, Scott, I'm not going to some fancy couples party with you, in *Chicago* of all places. I hate going to the Twin Cities as it is, so that's the last place I ever want to visit."

"Come on, you're eating for two, and you know whatever Zach makes is going to be phenomenal."

Tilly considers my proposition, because she knows I'm right. Zach is an old friend of mine, and this event is sure to have top-notch service along with hors d'oevres cooked up by one of the greatest chefs I know.

"No, I'm going to spend New Year's Eve with my family, kiss my husband at midnight... not my brother. You're going to need to find another date," Tilly finally says with a satisfied grin spread across her lips. "I still have that friend of a friend's stylist I could set you up with."

"No thanks, Tilly. I'll figure it out." As much as I don't want to show up alone, I'm not interested in traveling and spending a romantic weekend away with another of Tilly's especially terrible match-making attempts.

She pouts. "Fine, well, I better go open the shop. Do you have—"

I hold out the little to-go bag. "Yes, like I'd forget your second breakfast," I scoff.

"Thank you." Tilly snatches the bag from my outstretched hand, hovers her nose over the top, and gives it a big whiff. The additional baked goods will be devoured before her first customer arrives.

"No problem. Got to make sure my new little niece or nephew is well fed."

"Oh, we are. I'll be back over for lunch. In the meantime, think about what I said. It breaks my heart imagining all of us growing old with the loves of our lives, watching our children and grandchildren go off to school, college, get married themselves. Then there's poor old Uncle Scott, sitting in the corner—bitter, jaded, and alone with a storage unit full of regrets—cursing some woman he had *one date* with for preventing him from finding his one true love." Tilly sure knows how to make an exit when she wants. She doesn't give me a chance to reply before she wanders off to her half of the business.

With that gloomy thought rattling in the back of my head, I try to focus on work. I'm hopeful that there was that *spark,* and that Amanda felt it too. And if I'm patient, she'll show up and we can explore what this is. But if not, is Tilly right? Am I just setting myself up for the biggest disappointment of all?

"Can you cover the front?" I ask Gia, my second-in-command. "I'm going to take out the trash." In reality, I just need to get some fresh air and my sister's ominous warnings out of my head.

"Are you sure? I can take it out," Gia offers.

"It's fine. No need for you to freeze." We went from a record-hot summer to another record-setting winter, not because of the warmth though. No, the chill came early this year. It's been decades since we've had a blizzard in October.

"You got it, boss."

I grab the pile of bags and bring them outside to the dumpster. I'm about to go back in when something brushes against my leg. I glance down and am relieved to see that it's a giant cat and not a rodent. The last thing we need to worry about is an infestation.

The little guy—or girl—seems friendly enough when it greets me with a loud, "Meow."

"Hey there. Are you keeping those pesky mice away?" I reach down and pet her. Well, I assume it's a *her*. Though I don't have much—any—experience with felines. Actually, pets in general. Grandpa had a few barn cats that lived around the salvage yard, probably still does, but they stayed outdoors and only came around for the food he put out. I pat her big belly. "Clearly, you're eating well."

"Stray?" Jax asks as he strolls up the back alley.

"Nah, she seems clean. At least I think she's a little too groomed to be a stray."

Jax watches from a distance as the cat continues to purr and snuggle against me. "It seems to like you."

"It probably smells food." I love cooking but the downside is that everything I wear smells like whatever I've been prepping for the day.

"Or maybe this is the universe's answer to you quitting dating."

I roll my eyes for the second time this morning. "Seriously, I told her that like an hour ago."

"Yup, and I've spent the past sixty minutes listening to her cry that you're going to die a lonely, grumpy, old man while waiting for some woman to leave her husband. Guess we can add crazy cat dude to the list?"

"It's not mine," I remind him.

"No, but it sure seems convenient that you declare you're throwing in the towel, then BAM! This cat shows up. One that clearly loves you."

"I'm not throwing in the towel, just waiting." I pick up the furball in question. I expected it to try to bolt, but instead it curls up in my arms.

"See?" Jax waves a hand in my direction.

"It's cold," I attempt to justify, because I refuse to believe that the universe is condemning me to become the crazy cat dude in town. I mean, it would kind of be nice to have someone to come home to after a long day...

Nope, don't go there, Scott.

I'm not letting my best friend and his dramatic wife get into my head. This is not some destiny thing. Besides, as a chef, owning a cat is unsanitary. I shiver at the thought of being constantly covered in pet hair, having this furball crawl all over my counters...

Maybe a dog? At least that solves one of two problems. Can't do much about the hair but my counters would be safe.

No. I'm not getting an animal to replace the human companionship I'm obviously lacking.

"Yeah, speaking of cold, where's your coat?"

I shrug. "Kitchen's hot. Besides, I was just running out the garbage. Wasn't planning on building a snowman," I tell him, and Jax bursts out laughing. "What?"

"It's fucking perfect."

"What is?" My brows knit in confusion. It's official. The back-to-back pregnancies have caused my best friend to go insane. It's the only viable explanation for his sudden hysterics.

"Well, your sister has always said if you're lonely—"

"I'm not getting a fucking cat," I grumble.

"No?" He arches a brow. "Because it sure looks like you are."

"Fuck off. It's freezing. Obviously this thing is too clean and friendly to be a barn or stray cat, so it must belong to someone. Go inside, grab my jacket and keys, and tell Gia she's in charge while I'm out."

"Where are you going?"

"To the vet. See if this giant fluffball has one of those chips or something that says who owns her. Or, hell, maybe the staff will recognize it."

Jax eyes the cat for a moment. "I doubt it. It looks like your average, fat house cat."

"Still, it's worth a shot." As a bonus, it gets me out of this annoying conversation.

When it comes to my surface-deep brothers, Robbie and Jake, I expect this. Those two nitwits wouldn't know romance if it bit them on the ass—it truly is a wonder they found women willing to put up with their shit. But to hear my sister and Jax, individuals who value and appreciate romance just as much as I do, completely dismiss what I'm doing... well, it's making me wonder if I'm just a big fucking lovesick fool...

No. This is just temporary. I'm not sure how long it'll take, but when Amanda is free, I'll be right here waiting for her. I've spent the past year going on enough shitty dates to know this particular woman is worth the effort.

"And if they don't know who the owner is?" Jax asks, returning my attention to the furry task at hand.

"I'll figure it out." I shrug. It's just another benefit of living in a small town. If she has an owner, I'll find them.

"Whatever. Better start picking out names and grab yourself a litter box. You're about to have a fur baby." Jax strolls inside, still laughing at his lame joke as the door closes behind him.

"Can I help you?" The woman at the front desk smiles as I enter our local veterinary clinic.

"Yeah, I found this cat in the alley. I was wondering if you might know the owner or if they have one?"

"That's so sweet of you to bring them in." The receptionist stands and extends her arms to take the cat from me. "Aren't you just a big ol' lover?"

"Yeah, it seems a little too nice to be a stray." I reach a hand over to scratch my new friend behind the ear.

"Well, let me see if he's chipped."

"*He*?"

She inspects the cat a second time. "Yup, he's definitely a big boy. I'm going to get the scanner and see what we can find." A few seconds later, the woman returns with a device, which she waves along the cat's spine, then up to his neck and back again. "It looks like you're in luck. This little guy has a home."

"Oh, that's good. Are they in town? I can drop him off."

"Let me see." She plops the cat back into my arms and writes down some code before returning to her computer. "His name is Bruce."

"Bruce?" I look at his face. Seems like an odd name for a pet. Then again, now that I've heard it, it also seems oddly fitting.

"You wouldn't believe some of the names we hear." The woman chuckles. "Let me call the number on file and see if I can get in touch with the owner." Bruce remains content, purring against my chest, as the receptionist dials the phone.

"Hello, Scarlett? This is Mavis with Tral Lake Pet Hospital. Bruce was found and brought into our clinic. If you can please return my call as soon as you get this. My number is 507-555-2287."

I quirk a brow at the name. There is only one Scarlett I know in town. "Does he happen to belong to Scarlett Valentine?" Though Mavis doesn't answer me right away, the way she glances at the screen tells me I'm right. "She's a friend," I add.

The receptionist still doesn't seem convinced, so I reposition Bruce into one arm, shove a hand into my pocket, and pull out my phone. I unlock the screen and scroll to the name in my contacts before passing the device to Mavis.

"Correction: she's actually friends with my younger sister. So I guess we are more like acquaintances." My fingers tap along the counter. I'm not sure why I'm so nervous... or insistent on seeing that this little guy makes it home safe.

I tell myself it's because it's the right thing to do, and not because I've grown attached to someone else's pet in a matter of minutes. When Mavis continues to glare at me like cat-napping is my favorite pastime, I ramble on.

"Scarlett, she runs the inn... She stops by my coffee shop religiously, for her daily fix of a death-by-chocolate muffin that she chases down with a large dark chocolate and oat-milk mocha, with two extra shots of espresso." Mavis's jaw drops as I rattle off Scarlett's usual order, and I can only assume the woman is impressed by the extreme caffeine intake. "If you think that's impressive, sometimes she comes in for a second."

That earns me a smile. Mavis glances around before leaning forward. "Look, we're not supposed to do this," she whispers. "But given I know your family, and it seems you really do know Miss Valentine, I'll break the rules this *one* time."

"Thank you. I appreciate it."

"But, if anyone asks, you didn't hear it from me."

I make the motion of zipping my lips shut, turning the lock, and throwing away the key. Then I glance down at the bundle of fur cradled in my arms. "All right, Bruce, let's get you home to your mama."

2

Scarlett

"ROOM TEN CALLED AGAIN. They say their heat still isn't working right," Hannah, my night manager and absolute savior, informs me as soon as I step foot in the back to grab towels for the couple in eight.

"Room ten, got it."

This spring, I really need to look into replacing windows, getting better insulation, new HVAC? Maybe all the above. Lord knows while Grandpa kept this place up and running over the years that, prior to my arrival, there hadn't been any improvements since the 1950s. Not that he was making much of a profit to do so, according to his books. At least not for the past fifteen years.

It's fine. I'm not worried. I can already say that since I've been here and began applying the skills and trade I know, the profit margin has already begun to move in a positive direction. It'll just take time, which I have plenty of.

"Don't forget, Mommy Dearest—"

My eyes snap to Hannah's, giving her a silent indication to not remind me. "I know," I grumble. "But my sanctuary isn't scheduled to be invaded for another couple of hours. Until then, I'd like to remain blissfully ignorant of her arrival."

Hannah shakes her head with a chuckle. Fortunately, she has a fair share of family issues and doesn't judge. "Oh, some good news. The honeymooners requested to extend their stay by a few extra days. Lucky for us, seeing as the suite isn't booked again until after the new year."

"Honeymooners, check," I say, then offer a silent thank you to some higher power for the extra income, as I continue to hurry around and grab additional supplies. I'm sure someone is going to need them along the way.

This would typically be done by one of my housekeepers, but winter is our slow season. Ice fishing doesn't bring in nearly the same crowds as wakeboarding does. Needless to say, it's not easy to afford the extra staff. Then, when school is back in session, it's hard to find affordable help during the early hours. Which means I'm left with a skeleton crew until the ground thaws.

"I still don't understand why anyone would want to spend their honeymoon in Minnesota, during December no less?" Hannah shivers at the thought. "I'd much rather be in one of those little huts where you can step out into the ocean, or at least somewhere warm. But Minnesota? When the best we have to offer is mosquito bites and poison ivy."

"Aren't they from Texas or something?"

Hannah looks at the screen. "No, Florida."

"See? That's why."

She scrunches her brow as she stares at me.

"Sure, the weather here can be cold and inconvenient. But when I was living in LA, I envied everyone who got to experience a white Christmas. Seriously, the first winter I spent in Tral Lake blew my mind. The snow-covered trees, being able to curl up next to a fire without the AC going... Lights on a pine tree look so much better than on a palm tree."

"They sound like sociopaths to me."

"Thanks." I roll my eyes.

Hannah shrugs. "Whatever... All I'm saying is if I ever get married, I don't give a rat's ass about the wedding. I'm gonna invest every penny on our honeymoon, so that I can spend it getting railed on the beach. Speaking of." She glances down at her watch.

"Have a scheduled dicking to get to?"

Hannah bursts out laughing. "With any luck. It's date number five, and if he doesn't fuck me after this one, I'm convinced he doesn't have much in his pants. Which, given his big dually, I already suspected small penis syndrome. But now, I'm convinced he doesn't have much motion in the ocean—I mean, that's the only reason I can think of that a man would ignore the signals I've been dropping."

"Yeah, good luck with that."

"Says Miss *All I do is read about love but refuse to date.* At least I'm out there. How long have I been working for you? Over a year? And not once have I seen you with a guy, not even a basic Tinder hookup. Like seriously? How do you survive?"

"Smut and a variety of excellent vibrators."

"Your poor pussy. She must be so lonely without a real dick to play with."

I chuckle. "She's perfectly satisfied. Speaking of pussy, have you seen Bruce around?"

"No, sorry."

I tap my chin. "Weird. Haven't seen him since yesterday morning." I shrug. "It's fine. He probably got locked inside one of the closets again when I was turning a room or something." At least that's what happened last time. "I'll make the rounds and hopefully hear him howling."

"Shouldn't be hard to locate him. He cries if he doesn't eat every three hours."

I laugh and gather up all my supplies. My apron pockets are packed to the brim. I stop when the phone rings.

But Hannah raises her palm and answers. "Tral Lake Inn... Would you mind holding one moment while I check?" She listens to their reply. "Thank you."

"I can handle it," I offer.

"It's fine. I'll get them booked, then clock out."

"Are you sure? Don't want you to be late for your *date*."

She waves a dismissive hand and resumes the call. I mouth "*thank you*" before rushing off to do the last little bit I can before *she* arrives. I manage to get through my list of chores, including unclogging a toilet, but don't hear Bruce anywhere. It's just so unlike him. I hope he's okay.

Once I'm positioned behind the main desk again, I pull out my cell, prepared to post a notice in the local Facebook group, asking everyone to keep an eye out for Bruce, when the chime above the door sounds. And in walks the most fabulously dressed woman I've ever had the misfortune of seeing. Very *winter chic*. It's like she stepped out of one of those fashion magazines, with her expertly fitted, puffed jacket and knee-high, fur-lined boots. Despite the wardrobe change, she's just as I remembered, with her salon-perfect, platinum-blonde hair and glowing, sun-kissed skin.

"Hello, Mom," I say with about as much enthusiasm as being told I need a root canal. Correction: that *would* be more fun than having Mommy Dearest invade my sanctuary.

"Is that any way to greet your mother? The one you haven't bothered to come visit for two years."

I plaster on my best customer service smile. "Hi, Mom, welcome to my inn."

She approaches the desk and pinches my cheek. "That's more like it." Then she takes a step back and studies my appearance. "You look good."

In less than two seconds, her eyes dart to my waistline, forcing my arms to wrap around my midsection in an attempt to shield myself from her inspection. Her gaze burns a hole through the layers of clothing as she's able to size me up with a single glance. It's just like high school all over again.

"At least it isn't anything a good fasting can't fix. Have you tried any of those videos I've sent you? Feel this." Mom turns to show me her butt. "Wall Pilates. An absolute game changer. You can't buy an ass as tight as this."

"I'm so happy you're here," I say through clenched teeth, praying she's blind to how much her words hurt me. Part of me knows she doesn't mean it and that, as stupid as it sounds, her nitpicking does come from a place of love.

My mother lowers her enormous designer sunglasses and finally takes a real look around. "Wow, it's like I never left."

For once, I can't tell if that was meant to be an insult or a compliment. My mother never talked much about living here, only mentioned that it was dreadful and she'd never return. A decision I believe she regrets but won't admit.

"I've been working on improving the place, but my goal has been to maintain the integrity of its rustic charm." I turn to the cabinet and grab her keys. "Here. I'll show you to your room, then I can give you a tour and go over some of the improvements I've made."

"About that... There's been a slight change of—"

She doesn't get to finish her warning before a raven-haired ball of energy rushes through the front door. "Auntie Rea-Rea!"

I push past my mother and run over to the only person I regret leaving behind when I moved. "Oh my god." I kneel down and wrap my arms around the young girl. "Brittany, you've gotten so big. I've missed you so much."

"I've missed you too. You didn't visit like you promised." My niece's reminder is like a sharp stab to the chest.

"I know, honey, but I've been very busy," I tell her. Which is true. Though it doesn't make it right.

"Mommy said to wait in the car, so Nana could talk to you. But I just couldn't."

Her statement pours a bucket of ice water over what should be a joyous reunion. Of course, my mother wouldn't have brought Brittany here on her own. *Grandma* is always ready to hand the kid back over within an hour. Basically, as soon as Brittany needs food, water, or any actual care...

And with the simple chime of a bell, this holiday season goes from bad, to awesome, to the absolute worst in a blink of an eye.

"Long time no see, sissy," Trish sings the moment she steps through the door. Someone who, if I went the rest of my life without seeing, it wouldn't bother me the least bit. So having her here in general sucks. But the shittiest part of this surprise drop-in isn't my stepsister. No, it's the man holding her hand... and the giant rock that's glistening from where it's perched on her ring finger.

"Hey, Rhea," Kasey greets me with the name I left behind two years ago, followed by that million-dollar smile, as though nothing ever happened between us.

Like an idiot, I pat down my hair, attempting to smooth whatever flyaways I can while praying that this isn't the blouse with the faded coffee stain down the front. I should get rid of it, but I refuse to buy new clothes until I lose the last fifteen pounds I've been struggling to shed.

My mother wasn't wrong with her assessment. Moving to Minnesota did a number on my waistline. The food here is delicious and—unlike Cali where everything is gluten-free—people here love their carbs. Let's just say it only took one winter to lose my beach body, and I've been trying to get it back ever since. I probably would've by now if I could stop going to the coffee shop five mornings a week to get the most sinfully delicious dark-chocolate muffins my tongue has ever had the pleasure of tasting. It has these gooey chunks of chocolate; then it's drizzled with another layer of chocolate. It's like experiencing a mini-orgasm every time I bite into one.

I'll never admit it to Tilly, because I do value our friendship. But the truth is, I only really started hanging around because of her brother. Well, his amazing cooking. Not that Scott isn't a snack on his own. But seriously, the treats he makes for our book club rival any award-winning restaurants I've frequented on the West Coast. It might have started with me being a whore for carbs, but it didn't take long for us to become amazing friends. I'd call Matilda Moore my *best* friend, but I have no intention of trying to get between her and Letty.

Taking a deep breath, I get out of my own head and try to refocus my attention on the matter at hand. *If I survive, I'll reward myself with two muffins today.* I have a little bit of time before the obligatory new year diet I'm so going to flake on starts.

Kasey raises his Tom Fords as he studies me with his icy-blue gaze—the one that used to make my heart melt. Who am I kidding? Based on the way every fiber of my being is tingling, he still does.

"You look great." Trisha elbows him, and he quickly corrects himself. "I mean, the place does. The pictures you've posted are amazing. But seeing it in person, really, it's incredible."

"Thank you." I ignore those little fuzzy butterflies that take flight in my stomach. It doesn't matter what he says or does, Kasey and I are over. Done. He made his choice... and, well, it cemented mine.

Steeling my wavering resolve, I pray for a miracle to save me, help me get through what is stacking up to be the worst Christmas ever. Then, as the front door chimes again and a familiar face comes into view, it seems like a higher being must be listening because my saving grace marches in like the gallant knight he is. I smile as an idea starts to form, and quickly rush over to greet him.

"Perfect timing." It's as if thinking about his muffins somehow manifested the man himself. I wrap my arms around Scott's neck and press a kiss to his scratchy cheek. "It looks like we have a few more guests than we originally planned."

Mom immediately perks up, with her signature sultry Valentine smirk on display and her manicured cougar claws out. "Who's this delicious-looking tall drink of water?"

"Mom, this is Scott Moore." I take a deep breath, because once I say it, there's no turning back. "My fiancé."

"Fiancé!" Her expression quickly morphs from a woman on the prowl to that of a relieved mother, who's grateful that her daughter isn't going to die a spinster, in a small town, in the middle of nowhere—her words, not mine. "I didn't even know you were seeing anyone."

"It's newish." The lie falls easily from my lips. "When you told me you were coming for the holidays, I thought it would be the perfect surprise." Then I turn to Scott, nudging him in the ribs while silently begging him to say something. I can't help but pray I'm not wrong, and that he'll go along with my increasingly stupid idea.

"I found your cat..."

3

Scott

I FOUND YOUR CAT?

Seriously, Scott? You walk into a room full of people where some girl you've never dated, let alone kissed, suddenly announces that you two are engaged and you say... I found your cat. That is not the appropriate response. Then again, what was I supposed to say?

Yup, that's me, the fiancé! Or *what the hell are you talking about?*

Now that I think about it, maybe my awkward reply was the safest. At the very least, it gives me a second to assess the situation.

Scarlett finally notices the feline in my arms and snatches him from my grip. "Brucey!" Then she turns to me. "Scott, you found him. You're my *hero.*"

While her reaction seems genuine, something tells me she's talking about a lot more than her cat. It's weird to think about how this woman has attended the majority of our family events over the past year, and yet I know almost nothing about her. Only that she's from California and loves my food—not that she's told me. It's just one of those things I've been able to pick up on. But I definitely don't know enough to pass as the man she's supposed to be marrying.

"Yeah, he scared the crap out of me. He was hanging out in the dumpsters behind the café. I brought him—" *Shit...* I can't exactly say I took him to the vet and found out he was yours. I'd like to assume I'd know what my fiancée's cat looks like. "...back to you as soon as I could."

"Oh, did you miss Daddy?" Scarlett baby-talks to the content furball in her arms while puckering her lips. I give her a look that tells her she's laying it on a bit strong. At least I hope it tells her that. Once again, it's not like we've had time to learn each other's social cues.

Okay, now, I've watched enough rom-coms to recognize a setup when I'm in the middle of one. Clearly there is some sort of issue with her family and she needs me to play along.

God, can this day get any stranger?

I look past Scarlett's mom and study the other couple in the room. The guy looks familiar, very familiar. "Wait, are you—"

"Kasey Dawson," he verifies.

"Like the same Kasey Dawson who starred in *Artificial Lover* and *Boyfriend for the Weekend*?"

"The one and only." Kasey extends a hand to shake mine.

"Holy shit! Jax is going to lose it when I tell him that I met *the* Kasey Dawson."

Scarlett bumps me with her hip. *Holy shit.* I bite my tongue. I've always thought there was something different about my sister's friend, almost as if I recognized her from somewhere. Then again, when you're looking at a bombshell like Scarlett Valentine, it's hard not to picture her as the girl who stars in your dreams. But as soon as I see them in the same room, I realize where I know her from. In the tabloids, early on in Kasey's career.

I glance in Scarlett's direction, my eyes widened in shock while hers plead with me to not let her down. *Crap, that's right.* She's in trouble, and I highly suspect this show is more for my idol and not her mother. I swallow back my excitement over meeting one of my and Jax's favorite movie stars, and the fact that I've learned the dirty little secret she's been hiding in that vault of hers, and rest my hand on Scar's hip, pulling her tight next to me.

"I'm Brittany," a small voice pops out of nowhere.

"Hello." I squat down and shake the girl's hand. "It's nice to meet you."

"Auntie Rea-Rea never told me about you." Auntie, okay, so the other woman must be Scarlett's sister. The little girl eyes me skeptically. "She tells me everything."

Shit... I swallow hard and tug at the collar of my shirt. It's as though the kid can read my mind as her large chocolate eyes see through me.

"Brittany," the woman I assume is the girl's mother scolds. "That's not very polite."

"Yeah, pip-squeak. Adults don't tell kids everything. Sometimes we have super-special adult secrets." Kasey ruffles the girl's hair. I've gathered that he's supposed to be the enemy, but *fuck*, I'm having a hard time hating him. I mean, he's so cool. Even the kid has mellowed out.

"Speaking of," Scarlett says. "Scott, don't you need to get back to work?"

"Fuck... I mean, fudge... yeah, I better get back before Logan burns down the kitchen." I did not intend on being gone this long. Granted, I hadn't planned on *any* of today happening. "Well, it was nice meeting everyone. I'm sure I'll see you around." I wave as I do my best to make a quick but polite escape.

"Of course you will, silly." Scarlett laughs, the gesture more nervous than amused.

Oh, that's right. Crap, in the panic about the impending lunch rush, I kind of forgot about the whole being engaged thing.

"We'll see you when you get home tonight," she reminds me, and we do an awkward shuffle of me going in for a hug and her going in for a kiss. After a few attempts, she lands a peck on my cheek.

"Yeah, I'll see you both when I get home tonight." I pat Bruce on the head, and even he gives me a look that says: *Really, dude? You're not fooling anyone.*

"I can't wait to learn all about you, Scott," Scarlett's mother calls after me. Despite the nice tone, there is something ominous about the way she says it.

I slide into my car, and when I park a few minutes later, I'm relieved to find that autopilot has kicked in and guided me back to the café safely. Because, I honestly have no memory of driving here. Instead of checking in on Logan and Gia and making sure that my business is running smoothly, I turn down the hall and lock myself inside my best friend's office.

"Are you okay?" Jax looks up from his computer. When I don't immediately answer him, his mouth drops into a frown. "Scott? What happened?"

"I returned the cat."

Jax lets out a sigh. "Dude, you had me scared for a second. Not cool, man." I continue to stare at him, my shoes cemented to the spot and my mind in overdrive. "Did it go okay? Returning the cat, I mean?" he prompts, and I nod yes. "Okay, then why do you look like you just walked in on me and your sister having sex?"

Under normal circumstances, the imagery would be as effective as smelling salts and wake me from the deepest of comas. But these aren't normal circumstances. So I utter the only words that come to mind. "I'm engaged."

4

Scarlett

COULD TODAY GET ANY worse? *Probably*, but I really don't feel like testing the fates any more than I already have. If Scott wouldn't have gone along with my insanity, I'm not sure what I would've done. *Scratch that*. I know exactly what I would've done. I would've dropped dead from embarrassment with my epitaph reading: Here lies Scarlett Rhea Valentine, died due to her own stupidity. But let's face it, according to her Kindle history, she didn't have much hope of dying with dignity.

Good job putting that out in the universe. Especially since it's still early enough in the day that it just might happen. Because after I pull up my big girl panties and gather up the courage to step through my most-loved establishment to beg a man I hardly know to pretend to be in love with me, I might as well call the county coroner and give them a heads up that there's a fresh body to collect.

It's eight in the evening and based on the near empty Main Street, I assume Scott's dinner rush is over and they're in the process of cleaning up. Hopefully, he'll be up for chatting after he closes. Much like me, I know he wakes up at the ass crack of dawn to get his day started, and with the expanded restaurant, he's been working later.

For someone who claims to not really know the man, you seem to know a lot about his schedule, my inner voice chimes in.

What can I say? I'm observant. It's not like I went out of my way or anything to learn it. He's usually my first stop in the morning, and on book club nights, I've noticed what time he wraps up for the day. Pre-restaurant, he would be out the door shortly after we started, but since opening, he's been hard at work long after we're done.

Taking a deep breath, I fill my push-up bra with all the confidence I can muster and enter the café.

"Scarlett!" Tilly shouts from a nearby table.

"Oh, hi." *Crap,* I wasn't expecting her to be here. Okay, I was *hoping* she wouldn't be. But I swear she and Jax never leave this place. "You're out late."

"Yeah, Uncle Jake and Aunt Letty have the boys, so we got an impromptu date night," she says. I look around but don't see her husband anywhere. As if reading my mind, she clarifies, "Oh, he's in the kitchen teaching Scott some new recipe or something."

"Isn't the point of a date night to be on a date *together*?" I tease.

Tilly shrugs before taking a bite of her dinner. "Yeah, but I see him all the time anyway. Besides, have you tasted *this*?" When I shake my head in response, she gasps, "Oh my god, come here! You have to try it."

I glance back to the kitchen. I came here with a certain mission in mind, but if Scott's helping Jax with something, it doesn't really feel like a good time to discuss our current... *situation.*

"Sure." My butt hardly hits the chair before she shoves the fork in my face. I take a bite and the flavors immediately explode on my tongue. "Holy fuck, that's delicious. What is it?"

"It's this new special Scott's trying out. He says next year he's going to do this whole around-the-world theme. This one's from Spain. It's called..."

I steal her utensil and proceed to eat her meal as Tilly attempts to pronounce whatever she thinks the dish is called. Yeah, I know. It's pretty shitty to steal a pregnant woman's dinner. But this is seriously one of the best things I've ever put in my mouth—and I do mean *ever.*

"Shoot, it's like papaya or something. Scott!" Tilly hollers across the restaurant.

"Oh, that's fine." My heart races at the thought of him coming out here. Whatever courage I had deflated the second I saw my friend in the audience. "You don't need to—"

"Don't be silly. This is my brother. His favorite thing in the world is hearing about how much someone loves his food." She waits a moment. When he doesn't appear, she shouts louder. "SCOTT!"

Ouch, I think her yelling might have popped my eardrum. I try to rub it and see if it'll make the ringing stop.

"WHAT?" Scott calls out, swinging the kitchen door open before stopping dead in his tracks. "Oh..."

Jax, only a step behind him, runs smack-dab into Scott's back. "Dude, what the hell? You don't just stand in a doorway like—" Jax smiles when he notices me sitting next to his wife. And, no, it's not a smile that's meant to be a friendly greeting. It's a smile that says: *My best friend just got done telling me all about the mess you roped him into. I think it's hilarious, and I can't wait to see it blow up in your faces when your family finds out you're a workaholic spinster.* One of those smiles. "Oh, why hello, Scarlett. How are you today? Anything interesting happen?"

Yeah, he definitely knows, and considering his wife hasn't already hounded me with a million questions, my guess is he hasn't told her yet.

"Were you two drinking?" Tilly asks. "You're acting weird."

Scott continues to look at me a little dumfounded, and Jax all but bursts out laughing while Tilly's eyes flick between the three of us.

"Okay, what's going on?" She snatches her fork back and takes a bite of her dinner. "I'm being left out of something," she says with her mouth full. "And I don't like it."

"Shall I?" Jax grips Scott's shoulders. Scott frowns, but his friend ignores him and continues before anyone can stop him. "Oh, what the heck? Scarlett and Scott are getting married!"

Tilly's fork clanks as it drops to her plate. Squeezing my eyes shut, I turn to face someone who has been a great friend, included me in not only her book club but her family events, made sure I don't spend the holidays alone... I risk opening one of my eyes to find her amber gaze wide and her jaw dropped open.

"What?" she hisses.

"I'm sorry." I wince, then quickly clarify, "I mean, we aren't actually getting married." Tilly remains silent. "You know how I told you my mom was coming for Christmas this year, which was a surprise in of itself since she said she'd drop dead before returning to this shithole? *Her words, not mine*," I make sure to stress that fact to the group of homegrown locals presently glaring at me. "Anyway, the point is... she showed up today, which is stressful enough. But then my niece ran through the door a few minutes later. At first, I was super excited because I haven't seen her for so long, followed by my stepsister—AKA her mother—on the arm of my ex. And well, there is a lot of history there and I panicked. Scott walked in carrying Brucey, and the next thing I know, I announced to everyone that he's my fiancé."

Crap, that was a lot of word vomit. I grab a nearby glass of water and chug it back.

"Brucey?" Jax questions Scott, who shrugs.

"Yeah, I know... weird name for a cat. But believe me, it fits him." Jax nods as if that makes sense to him before Scott adds quietly, "Oh, and I forgot to mention her ex is *Kasey Dawson.*"

Jax pushes his friend aside, rushes forward, grips my shoulders, and shakes me. "You seriously used to date Kasey Dawson? As in, star of *Yours for the Weekend* and *Second Time Around*? That Kasey Dawson?"

"Oh, that was a good one," Scott appears to mumble to himself.

I ignore the question because it's not important, nor is it anything I want to discuss—like ever. No, the big issue right now is the fact my friend hasn't said a single word.

"Tilly?" I urge.

With a high-pitched scream, she grips my shoulders and shakes me. "You're marrying Scott!"

"Not actually," I try to correct her, but she's too excited to hear me.

She turns to Scott. "Oh my god! See! I told you! I told you waiting for this Amanda wasn't worth it because the perfect woman was out there waiting for you. And, *bam*, she falls right into your lap. Why didn't I ever think of hooking you two up before? Oh yeah, I didn't think two workaholics would ever clock out long enough to make something of it. But that doesn't matter now, because this is perfect!"

"Amanda?" I ask Scott. I'm such a terrible person. I hadn't even considered the fact that he might have found a girlfriend. I mean, I've heard all about his laundry list of terrible dates, pretty much everyone has. But if he found someone, I can't interfere with that.

"It's not real." Scott misses my question or he chooses to ignore it as he combs his fingers through his dark, slicked-back hair.

But Tilly hears me loud and clear and attempts to wave off my hesitation. "Technicalities. I have a good feeling about this," she says, as if by putting it into the universe, it will become a reality.

"That makes one of us," I grumble under my breath, then push to my feet. "Look, I didn't mean to interrupt your evening. I just thought..." I shake my head. "Honestly, I'm not sure what I was thinking." I carefully back up towards the door, prepared to make my exit. "Can we just pretend this never happened? It's bad enough my mother and stepsister aren't going to let me ever live it down. But at least they are usually thousands of miles away and I can ignore them—for the most part. So, if you guys could just..." I wave my hand in front of my face. "...wipe this from your memory, I'd appreciate it. More than you can ever understand. Scott, good luck with Amanda, and, again, I'm so sorry for pulling you into my insanity."

With those parting words, I slip through the door before they can say anything else—because clearly I've lost my mind—and run to my car. I step down from the curb, my feet slide out from under me, and I tumble back. Closing my eyes, I prepare for the impact of my ass hitting the icy ground, only to be surprised when a pair of strong arms reaches out to catch me.

I tilt my head back and look up into the eyes of my knight in shining armor. I don't miss the fact that this is the second time he's come to my rescue over the course of a few hours. "Thank you for saving me... again."

"Seems like the theme of the day," Scott says with a smoldering, half-cocked smile. He helps me stand and maneuver to softer ground. I grab my door handle just in case I feel like doing something else embarrassing tonight. At this rate, I'm due for a good swooning moment.

"Thank you... not just for now, but for earlier. You could have thrown me under the bus, outed me right there. But you didn't. Not that it won't be humiliating when I have to tell them later, but at least I have a little time to gather myself. So again, thank you." I open my car door, prepared for take two of my escape.

Scott frowns. "What if we don't tell them?"

My feet almost slip out from under me again, but thankfully I catch myself. "What?"

"I mean..." Scott rocks on his heels with his hands tucked in his pockets. "It's a week, right? What's the harm?"

"Are you serious?" I will my heart to not burst out of my chest. He still has a grin on his face, and I think I might need that fainting couch after all. Until something else comes to mind. "What about Amanda?"

"Things with her, they're complicated." I wait for him to elaborate. He sighs. "We went on our first and only date a few weeks ago. She's married and going through a separation..." When my eyebrows shoot up, he stops me from commenting. "I know! It sounds lame, and believe me my sister has made sure to tell me what a dumbass I am. But I'm waiting, and I guess I'm also hoping that when it's all final, she'll reach out."

"That doesn't sound very lame to me. It's romantic."

"See! You get it. Now if only my sister and best friend could understand..."

"Scott, I appreciate you being willing to help me out and all, but if you're waiting for her..."

"Look, your family already thinks we're engaged and, well, I might need a small favor in return?"

"Really?" I press, unable to believe what I'm hearing.

"Don't you want to know what my favor—"

"Unless you're asking for my firstborn, I'll do whatever you need me to do if you help me survive this week."

"Okay." He sounds relieved. "Thank you."

"Oh my god." I rush forward and wrap my arms around him. "No, thank you. You have no idea how much you're saving my ass right now."

"No problem," he says as he rests his hands on my back. "But we do have a few things to figure out. I wasn't exactly sure what *home* I'm expected to return to tonight."

Crap... I did totally imply that we lived together. "Um..." I take a step back. "You're already doing me a huge favor, so feel free to say no, but I was hoping that maybe we could stay at my place. I'm short-staffed, and it's nice to be onsite in case I'm needed. Hannah usually has the nights covered pretty well, but I don't want to risk having to rush out at two in the morning if something happens that's above her paygrade. Again, this is my problem, not yours. So, if that doesn't work—"

"Breathe." Scott tilts my chin, forcing me to look at him. "It's fine. It makes sense."

"It does?"

"Yeah, I get it. Besides, I'm not sure Bruce would be happy with the temporary relocation."

"Oh my god, you're the best." This time, when I hug him, I don't think and press a quick kiss to his cheek too. I feel like an idiot the second I do and he tenses up. Not wanting him to change his mind, I take a few steps back to put some distance between us.

"I have a few things to wrap up here, then I'll need to stop by my place for some clothes..."

"Okay, yeah, no worries. I'll be up. I have a list of things I need to prep for tomorrow myself. Do you know where the groundskeeper cabin is located?"

"Yeah." He quirks a brow at me. "Don't you remember—?"

"Oh, yup." I back away slowly as the memory of the night he walked me home returns. "So, you know it's just down the path, on the south side of the property?"

"I remember." He smiles.

"Good, here." I dig out my keys and take off the one for my room. "Use this. I have a spare in my office."

"I guess I'll see you in a little bit."

"Again, thank you. I'm not sure I can ever repay you."

Scott smiles. "That's what friends are for."

5

Scott

Scarlett escorts me inside the cabin. "Home sweet home," she says as she gestures around the tiny space. "I know it's small. It was my grandfather's, and as you can tell, he was kind of a minimalist. But it works since I don't spend a ton of time here—it serves its purpose. Plus..." She smiles. "It's kind of cozy."

Small is a generous description. I mean, from the outside, it's obvious this isn't some grand mansion. But once you're inside, it feels one step short of a studio apartment and one step above an insulated shed with plumbing. My lips tip up at one side as my eyes flick around the interior. Besides the... *coziness,* as she called it, there's also something about this place that screams Scarlett. A sort of hominess that definitely has nothing to do with the old man who lived here before her.

"Um, so, yeah. Let me give you the grand tour. Behind this curtain is the tub." She opens the heavy floral drape and reveals an old claw-foot basin with a wall-mounted showerhead. "You might not think it, but these black-out curtains are great at keeping the heat in while you shower. Oh, and over here is the toilet." She opens the door to what I initially assumed was a coat closet. "If you go number two,

"

just make sure to flush twice. But sometimes you might need to let it settle and try again later." She shrugs as if indoor plumbing should be this unreliable, then shuts the door and turns to face me with a fresh flush spreading across her cheeks.

I've never discussed finances with Scarlett, and unless absolutely necessary, my siblings and I rarely discuss ours with each other either. Still, I have to wonder how much money she's losing with this place. It's public record that her grandfather's house was auctioned off by the bank over a decade ago. Which is why I'm guessing he moved in here. It's tiny and cost-efficient—a bonus when you are putting the majority of your earnings back into your business. I've seen the improvements that have been made to the inn since Scarlett took over. She's done a lot to ensure it's the perfect wedding venue and vacation spot. So the businessman in me says that there's no way she's still that deep in the red.

I can't help but wonder why she hasn't looked into improving her own living conditions? Surely, she's turned enough profit to do a few upgrades by now...

Scarlett rushes over to her kitchen area, drawing me from my thoughts as I watch her gesture to the appliance in front of her. "It's probably not the state-of-the-art setup your used to, but it works."

My jaw drops as my eyes take in the small mint-green Chambers stove. I can't believe I didn't notice it the moment I walked in. "That thing is awesome." I inspect it more closely. "My pops used to have one just like this. His was an off-white, but these old things are incredible. No joke, the griddle makes the best pancakes I've ever tasted."

Scarlett chuckles. "Well, feel free to make whatever you want on it. As you can tell, it's hardly used."

"Seriously?"

"Of course. *Mi casa es su casa.* There are a bunch of old cast-iron pans and stuff in that cupboard right over there."

I scurry over to the cupboard in question with as much joy as a small child on Christmas morning. She's right. There's an entire set holed up in here, just begging to be used.

"The place was pretty neglected when I moved in. It didn't appear as though my grandpa had used any of the cookware in years. But don't worry, I made sure to wash them up. It took me a whole bottle of Dawn and a lot of elbow grease, but I got them looking as good as new."

I pivot on my heel and stare at her, my jaw dropped and my mind reeling. "You what?"

"Oh my god." She lifts a hand to cover her smile. "The look on your face." Then she doubles over with laughter. "Totally worth it."

"So, you didn't—"

"God, no. I might not be a professional chef like you, Scott Moore, but even I know better than to use soap on cast iron."

I let out a relieved sigh as Scarlett continues to enjoy my short-lived misery.

"Anyway," she sings. "Here's my room." She slides another curtain aside, this time to reveal a small bed surrounded by a mountain of books. The walls are insulated by additional bookshelves, nearly as overflowing as the piles on the floor.

"You really like to read," I comment as my fingertips glide over the titles within my immediate reach. Mostly various genres of romance. I can't help but think these don't seem to be the kind of books her grandfather would keep. No, these are all Scarlett's.

"Yeah." She shrugs. "I need something to pass the time. Plus I love the escape."

"You sound like Tilly."

"It's why we became fast friends." She grins as she lowers herself onto the creaky mattress, which brings me to my next thought...

"Um, Scarlett?"

"Yes." She wrings her hands together, likely knowing what my next question will be before I even ask it. I've had a full tour of the place, so unless I'm blind—something that's entirely possible seeing as I'm not wearing my glasses—there's only one bed.

"Do you have a basement? Or some attic that you plan on stuffing me into?" I reach a hand behind my head and rub at the back of my neck while I wait for her reply.

"No." Scarlett's palms shoot up to cover her face.

"Okay? Well, where am I sleeping?" My gaze bounces around the room as if some hidden door will suddenly appear out of nowhere.

"Honestly, I don't sleep well. I'm up and down all night. You can have the bed. That way, you'll get some privacy, and I can take the couch. I pass out reading there most nights anyway."

I glance between the two potential options, before closing the distance and plopping my ass down on the couch. "It's fine. I'll sleep here," I tell her. It might be old, but it's comfy, probably softer than that springy mattress. Then again, maybe she prefers the couch for that exact reason. I'm struggling to figure out what's the right thing to do here. It's not a situation I've ever found myself in before.

"No, I couldn't. You're already being so nice and—"

"Really, I don't mind. You forget I'm one of four children—well, five after Jax joined the brood—and my parents' favorite family vacation was going to our cabin up in Round Bay. Robbie had the benefit of being the oldest while Tilly was the only girl, which meant it was a good day if I was lucky enough the score a spot on the couch and didn't have to resort to using a sleeping bag on the floor."

"Are you sure?" Scarlett gnaws on her glossy bottom lip, and something about the action has me pausing to watch her.

I shake my head of all the improper thoughts of my little sister's friend, telling myself it's because I haven't gotten laid in a while, and smile back at her. "Positive." I lean against the armrest and kick my legs up on the other side of the sofa to prove my point. Until, out of nowhere, a giant furball emerges and plops his ass down on my stomach. "Hey, big guy." I let out an audible *oof*. Bruce purrs as I pet him.

"Brucey," Scarlett scolds, like a mother correcting her small child. Then she turns back to me. "Sorry about that. Once I lie down, he should follow me. He's my foot warmer."

"It's fine." I continue to stroke the cat's soft fur. "Honestly, it's kind of cool having him here. We didn't have many pets growing up, nothing more than the occasional goldfish or something like that. Tilly brought up getting a kitten all the time, but Dad claimed that he was allergic. Honestly, now that I think about it, I don't even know if that was true. I think it had more to do with no one wanting to get stuck with cat box duty."

Scarlett glances at her phone. "I know it's getting late, and I don't want to inconvenience you more than I already have. But this might be a good time to get our stories straight?"

"Sure, so whatcha thinking?"

"I guess we should try to not stray too far from the truth. You know, we met and have hung out a lot via Tilly and my frequent visits to the coffee shop...."

"That makes sense. But when did we actually start dating?"

"Halloween night."

"Halloween?" I sit up a little straighter, and Bruce meows his displeasure at the shift in position.

"Yeah, well, technically the next day. But, basically, we were both at Harper's—dateless—one drink turned into a whole night of talking, drinking, and dancing. I might have hit the candy corn Jello shots a little too hard and you were a total gentleman, of course. Insisted on walking me home. Then, before either of us knew it, we were standing at the front door. I wasn't sure if it was liquid courage or just everything finally clicking into place, but I leaned up on my tippytoes and I kissed you."

Fuck. I mean, *shit*. Or maybe *fuck* was right the first time...

I know exactly the night she's talking about. Her story, for the most part, is true. Well, everything but the kissing. Not that I hadn't thought about it. There were these moments between us when I could've sworn something was there. But I dismissed it. Mostly because Scarlett was really, really drunk. Like so much so I'm actually surprised she remembers any of it. Not to mention, the fact that she's close with my little sister. While I know Tilly would be ecstatic over the idea of me dating her friend—which she made very clear today at the restaurant—it was the thought of everything that could go wrong that gave me pause.

I mean, I'm the first to admit that I have the worst dating luck in history. And given how much Scarlett and I see each other, it didn't seem worth risking the fallout. Though now I'm left wondering if she wanted me to kiss her that night. She was in this sexy Little Red Riding Hood costume, and when I dropped her off at her door, she had this look in her eyes that hinted at her wanting me to play her Big Bad Wolf and devour her.

Scarlett blushes but quickly shakes it off. "Anyway, you know how it goes. From there, we decided to go on a date. And since we spent so much time together as it was, we already knew each other and the falling in love part happened quickly and naturally." She claps her hands together as if to put a hold on that thought. "Okay, we should get some sleep," she announces before trying to escape what just became a very eye-opening conversation.

"Wait."

"Huh?" Her cheeks are even more flushed than they were a second ago.

I nudge Bruce off my lap and stand. Scarlett looks up at me, her eyes wide. I'm not sure if it's the lighting or if I just really never noticed it before but her eyes aren't just blue. One of them has an almost orange ring surrounding the iris. It's one of the coolest and most beautiful things I've ever seen. I clear my throat and she flutters her lashes.

"There's one problem with your story," I tell her.

"Oh, yeah? What's that?" she asks, her voice hardly above a whisper.

"I don't actually know anything about you." I brush a loose strand of her honey-colored hair out of her face and tuck it behind her ear.

"Oh, um." She bites her lip again, and now I'm wondering what she tastes like. "There isn't much to know really."

"I beg to differ, *Rhea?* Let's see... Ah, for starters, you were dating a major A-list celebrity and let's not forget the tiny little fact that you're the daughter of one of the greatest directors of this generation. You're pretty much Hollywood royalty. I think those are some major details you left out."

Yeah, I finally went off and Googled her.

"Just to be clear, my dad was famous, not me. And Rhea was an identity I wanted to distance myself from as much as possible. You know how people in this town are, and I didn't want it to be a big deal."

Unfortunately for her, I have a feeling that the cat won't remain in the bag too long with a celebrity like Kasey Dawson roaming around town.

"Don't get me wrong, I love my dad, but that lifestyle was never for me. And, well, I don't think talking about your exes is necessary." She slowly backs away, but I take a step forward.

"I do. If I'm marrying someone, I want to know everything about them. The good, the bad, and the *extremely awkward*. All of it."

"Seeing as we aren't actually engaged, I think we know enough about each other to fake it for a week."

I pause and add a little distance between us. "You're right."

Shit, and so was Jax. This is going to be a lot harder than I thought.

I figured it would be easy, considering Scarlett and I are just friends... acquaintances? Two people connected by one nosey sister? Whatever you want to call us, it doesn't really matter. Especially since I'm still hoping that Amanda will contact me when she's finally no longer a married woman. Except, now, I can't help but look back at our interactions over the last year and a half. Scarlett and me. And those dozens of little side-glances and sly smiles.

Was something there? Did I miss it or, hell, flat-out ignore it?

"It's getting late." I take another step back and remind myself that I'm just doing her a favor. "I should get a few hours of sleep before I open the café." I return to the couch, where one very unimpressed cat is waiting for me.

"Scott," Scarlett calls out, causing me to look her way as she glances over her shoulder with one hand curled around the room divider. "Thank you."

"No problem. I'm always happy to help my sister's friends whenever they're in need."

6

Scarlett

"I THINK I'M IN love," Hannah says, rolling up beside me in her office chair.

"Sounds like a Tuesday," I murmur sarcastically as I continue to focus on my weekly audit. "Did *Big Dually* fuck you into commitment?"

"Oh, I'm over him. After our *fifth* disappointment, I decided to call it quits. The chemistry just wasn't there. But you wouldn't believe the guy I met on the way out of the restaurant. He's about two hundred pounds of solid muscle. I spent all night dreaming about him tossing me around like a little rag doll."

"So, you didn't go home with him?"

Hannah frowns. "No, he had his own date."

I roll my eyes, because of course he did.

"But I could tell he was bored with her. So I made sure to slip my number under his windshield wiper, telling him to call me when he's ready for a good time."

"You're shameless, you know that?"

"Cunt." She playfully swats my arm. "What's with you? You seem a little testy this morning. What happened? Did you forget to charge your vibrator?"

"No."

"So, what? Little bean wouldn't poke her head out to play? Because seriously, babe, your shoulders are tense." Hannah proceeds to knead her fingers against the base of my neck to prove her point. "Screaming that you have an itch that needs to be scratched."

"It's fine." Sometimes I hate how well she knows me. Hannah arches one of her perfectly waxed brows. "Okay, you're right." I sigh and drop my head on the desk in defeat.

"I told you!" she hollers. "Self-love will only satisfy you for so long. You need to go out and get yourself some hot-blooded dick. Your pussy is desperately in need of some good loving. Okay, that settles it." I side-eye her as she throws her arms in the air in dramatic fashion. "Tonight, me and you are going out. Make Sheila do her job for once and cover the desk. Then we'll drive up to the cities and find you some grade-A peen. Oh, we could always hit that bar? You know, the one Cassie's brother runs. I mean, I've heard rumors..." She spaces out her hands to indicate the size. "And I've been told it's pierced. That's one thing on my bucket list I wouldn't mind checking off."

"First off, no. I'm not going to sleep with Cassie's brother. Secondly, I can't go to the cities. Remember? My family's here."

"So what? Bring your mom with us. I bet she'd love to go out on the prowl."

"It's not just my mom. It's my niece, stepsister, and... her fiancé."

"You're fucking kidding me, right?"

"No." I drop my head to the desk again. "I had no idea they were coming."

"I can't believe she brought that fucking cunt with her, especially after what she did and *with him*." Hannah cracks her knuckles, ready to throw down.

Ugh, I'm definitely regretting that night a few months back when we decided to do shots while folding linens. Besides the fact that the bedding looked like crap the next morning and had to be redone, I might have shared a bit more than I intended about my life before Tral Lake.

Apparently, tequila works better than any truth serum...

"My mother doesn't know." I sigh. For all her faults, this isn't one of them. I mean, I'm sure she'd still take their side. Trisha is the daughter my mom always wanted, and Kasey can do no wrong in her mind. But still, my mom bringing them along wasn't done in malice or to rub their relationship or my failures in my face.

"No, but that step-bitch of yours knows exactly what she did. Then to bring that jackass with her, flaunting him in front of you with her picture-perfect family. Fuck them. Now, we have to go out tonight. Show them all the great dick you're getting by not being tied down to that asshole."

"He's not an asshole."

"He cheated on you with your stepsister. If that doesn't make him the biggest asshole of a century, I'm not sure what does."

"I told you we were on a break." It still stings, but the level of betrayal is different.

"What world do you live in? Unless it's friends with benefits or a one-night stand, sisters—even stepsisters—don't sleep with each other's boyfriends. No, wait, I'm sorry... *fiancés*."

"I didn't officially say yes. It was why we were on a break." God, I wish I never would've told her. It's not nearly as black and white as she's making it sound.

"Scarlett, I love you, but what they did was wrong. You said that you needed time to think and then your grandpa died. Then while you were halfway across the country, settling his affairs, that bitch sank her claws into your boyfriend or fiancé... whatever you want to call him. At the end of the day, he was yours and she betrayed you."

I know I used to feel that way. There was a time I hated them both. Now... I guess I'm not so sure. "Technicalities aside, I can't—"

"Bullshit. You're a grown-ass woman. I don't care if they're visiting. You need to show that cunt you've moved on. That you're not some lonely workaholic who lives off smut and top-of-the-line vibrators."

"I can't go and cheat on my fiancé." Hannah's jaw drops, so I clarify, "Fake fiancé." I wave her off. "It's a long, stupid story. But the point is, if we go out and flaunt my hooking up, I'd be *cheating* and that would look bad." I take a deep, calming breath. "They're going home the day after Christmas. I just need to make it through the week, then I'll never have to see them again." At least, not those two. Brittany is getting old enough where she can come stay with me and escape the West Coast while on break from school.

"Um, back up, fiancé? When did this little arrangement happen?"

"It's fake," I remind her.

"Fake or not, you need to fill me in. Who are you *not* getting married to?"

"Scott Moore," I whisper.

"SCOTT MOORE!" She stands, grips my shoulders, and shakes me. "As in *Moore Books and Coffee* Scott Moore. The guy you've been low-key stalking for over a year now?"

Fucking tequila. "I have not been low-key stalking him. He happens to be friends with Tilly and runs the *one* coffee shop in town."

"You know damn well the only reason you trek across town almost every morning to get your muffin and coffee isn't because of how delicious they are. Nope, it's because of how damn *scrumdiddlyumptious* the man behind the counter is."

"Yeah, well... I didn't go this morning. So there." I stick out my tongue.

"And why's that?" She leans back and crosses her arms over her chest in challenge.

"I made my own coffee." When she doesn't appear satisfied by that answer, I add, "Fine. It seemed awkward to go there this morning."

She waves a hand, urging me to continue.

"I couldn't sleep last night. It was hard. He was being so sweet, even agreed to stay with me in my little hermit hole. There was even a point when we were discussing how we fake fell in love that I thought he might kiss me. But then my foot slid right into my mouth and I totally killed the mood. It sucked. I was so horny all night but didn't want to risk him waking up hearing me take care of business. The curtains aren't exactly soundproof, you know. Anyway, when I got up in the middle of the night, I saw him sleeping on the couch—if you can even call it one. He's so tall his legs were hanging off the edge. Bruce was sprawled out on top of him. And I felt like shit because he's doing all this for me. And what's he getting out of the deal? Back problems."

"Oh, Scar, you're so naïve." She shakes her head and chuckles.

"What? Why?"

"There is only one reason a guy would offer to be your fake soon-to-be husband and agree to sleep in that fire hazard of yours."

"It's not a fire hazard," I'm quick to counter.

"It's insulated with books, and you have a space heater. It's a death trap waiting to happen. But that's not the point."

"Then what is?"

"Scott wants to fuck you." She shrugs as if it's so obvious. "And based on the living conditions he's willing to endure to get there, he wants it bad." She grips the air and humps it before giving her imaginary partner a little spank.

"He does not." I laugh.

"Really? Come on, I know he's one of the golden boys of this town but he's still a man. They're sharks and you reek of virgin blood."

"I'm far from being a virgin."

"Twelve months without dick resets the clock." She shakes her head like this is some set-in-stone rule. "And what? You're going on at least twenty-four, am I right? There was a time when you could have been a one-woman red-light district. But now, you're as pure as fresh snow and Scott Moore wants to be the first one to get a taste before someone else pisses on it."

"Ew."

"What? Don't get mad at me because it's true. No one wants to eat snow that's been walked on."

"First of all, I'm not snow. Secondly, make up your mind. Am I getting pissed on or walked on in this analogy? Because I can assure you, the answer is neither. Besides, Scott is just nice. I'm friends with Tilly. He's doing it as a favor for her *and* he has a girlfriend."

"Scott has a girlfriend?" she asks, as though that concept is completely out of the realm of possibility.

"Well, not technically. They had some magical date at the beginning of the month and he's waiting for her to get a divorce. I guess she wasn't exactly single... yet."

"Okay, so back to my point: he just wants to fuck you."

"No, he told me he needed my help with something."

"Is it hard and hanging between his legs?"

"He didn't specify and I didn't ask. But I assure you Scott's not like that. I was just so thrilled that I didn't have to spend Christmas listening to my mom and stepsister ridicule me for trying to pretend I have a life. And he made it very clear he was just helping his sister's friend. It sounds like this is a favor he'd do for anyone."

"Did you ask Tilly? Run this plan past her?"

"I mean, she knows." I shrug.

"Who knew first, Scott or Tilly?"

"Well, Scott. He walked in with Brucey in his arms at the same time my family showed up. And before I knew it, I was telling everyone we're getting married, and he kinda just went with it."

"See? He's just hoping to get laid."

"I already told you Scott's not like that," I remind her.

"Scott's not like what?" My mom startles us with her presence.

"Um…" I stumble over my words. Hannah and I look at each other, trying to come up with something reasonable to say. The last thing I want *or need* is for my mother to think there's a problem. I may not value her opinion all that much anymore. But I definitely don't want my stepsister or Kasey to think anything's amiss.

"Wedding plans!" Hannah shouts. "Scarlett is worried about the small, intimate ceremony they're planning. She's concerned that Scott wants something bigger and is sacrificing his dreams to make her happy. But I keep telling her Scott isn't like that."

"She's right. I hate showy weddings."

Speak of the devil. *Is my bell broken? Or could I not hear it over the sound of my heart thudding in my chest?*

Scott deposits a bag on the counter before setting a cup beside it. The smell alone tells me it's my usual. "Didn't mean to interrupt." He smiles. "But when you didn't stop in this morning, I knew you must've been busy."

"Oh, thank you." I glance down at the generous offering, in search of the strings Hannah is convinced are attached to it. But as Scott continues to smile at me, I'm struggling to see them.

Or maybe I just don't want to?

"Well, I better get back and prep for lunch service." He presses a kiss to my cheek. "I'll see you tonight." Scott winks at me before turning towards my gawking employee. "Hannah, pleasure as always. Mrs. Valentine, you look lovely this morning." Mom's ego visibly inflates at the compliment as she stands a little taller. "Excuse me, I'd love to stick around and chat, but if I don't get back soon, chaos will ensue." With that, he exits.

"Oh my." Mom fans herself. "I thought men like that only existed in movies."

And books...

"Told you," Hannah leans over and whispers in my ear.

I frown at her. I get what she's saying, and if it were anyone else, I'd believe her. But this is Scott Moore, a member of the Moore family, and genuinely one of the nicest people I've ever met. I have a hard time believing he's doing this simply to get laid. I mean, I doubt he needs to work too hard to get girls in this town to spread their legs for him.

Then again, considering everything he's done for me, sex is the least I could offer him in return. Right?

7

Scott

I USE THE CROOK of my arm to wipe my brow as I continue to work the dough, pulling it towards me, then using the heels of my hands to push it down and outward. The feel of the gluten stretching and blending to perfection is mesmerizing. My muscles burn. This is batch number three of five.

Sure, I have industrial mixers with the ability to do this for me. But if my grandma, who was no more than a hundred pounds—nothing but flesh and bones—could make this many, kneading each one with her frail, boney fingers, then I need to suck it up and push forward. I'm the third generation of Moores to make this recipe, and I refuse to deviate with modern conveniences.

As I finish placing the mixture into the container and seal it, before setting it in the fridge to chill, my ear is pinched and I'm dragged off down the hall.

"Seriously, Tilly, clip your nails." I swat at her hand but it's no use. She just squeezes tighter.

She doesn't stop until she's pulled me into the back office, hers not mine. Since she does the bookkeeping for both of us and my skills are best used in the kitchen, it seemed silly to take the space for myself. I let my unused office go to Jax. That way, he could work from the shop if needed.

"Sit," she orders as she shoves me into the nearby chair. She might be almost a foot shorter than me, but my sister can be scary when she's mad. Tilly takes a seat in her office chair, clasps her hands together, and sucks in a deep breath before pinning me with her intimidating stare.

Fuck, what did I do now?

"Well, tell me," she urges.

"Tell you what?" I glance around the room, looking for some hint of the conversation she thinks we're having, but come up short.

"Scarlett, what did she say when you brought her breakfast?"

Leaning back, I tilt my head up to the ceiling and let out a sigh. It's somewhere between being relieved and annoyed, leaning more towards the latter. I should have lied when she caught me sneaking out with my special delivery. Especially since it's not something I usually do. Hell, I'm still not even sure why I did it. There was just something unnerving about her absence. Probably because she comes in like clockwork and it's part of my daily routine.

"Thank you." I shrug.

"And what else?"

I sit up and see Tilly scarfing down one of the caramel tins of popcorn the city delivers to all the businesses this time of the year. I think for a moment. "She said *oh*."

"Oh?" Tilly frowns. "Like as in *oh my, how sweet of you? A* swoony *oh*?"

"No... it was more of a confused *oh* with a sprinkle of annoyance."

"Why would she be annoyed? Did you do something?"

"Yeah, I brought her breakfast." Clearly my little sister has lost her mind. "Now, if you'll excuse me, I have two more batches of Grandma's Christmas rings that need tending to."

"You did the thing, didn't you?"

Hand on the doorknob, I stop in my tracks and drop my head in defeat, because I know I'm not getting out of this room until my sister is damn well happy. "What thing?"

"That nervous, self-deprecating thing you do."

"I do not."

"You do." She shoves another handful of popcorn in her mouth. "I don't think you even realize it."

I collapse back into the chair and rub my temples, attempting to ease the headache I know is coming.

"Look, I know you were a late bloomer and all. But, I mean, if you weren't my brother, I'd find you attractive, I guess."

"Gee, thanks, Till Pickle."

She tosses a piece of her holiday snack with the precision of a professional athlete and gets me smack-dab in the forehead. I rub the spot and quickly regret it, as I realize my hands are still covered in butter. Grandma's mixture is extremely tacky, and it's the best way to keep the dough from sticking to everything.

"Dude."

"You know I hate when you call me that," she huffs.

"Well, I hate when my little sister kidnaps me and puts my dough at risk. You know how intensive this recipe is. If I don't get it righ—"

"Scott, this is important." She sits up straighter. "You barely have a week to make Scarlett fall in love with you."

I choke on my reply, because what the hell is she talking about?

"This is serious. You need to pull out all the stops, put all those years of watching romantic comedies to good use."

"Tilly, I love you, but I think those hormones of yours are really doing a number on you this time around." She frowns, and I hold up my hands in defense. "Jax and I, well, *Jax* was reading about this and it's one of those situations where he gave me a little too much information. But, the point is, it's perfectly natural."

"Don't you dare blame this on me being pregnant. *That* has nothing to do with what's going on with you." She's fuming now, and I know I have to tread lightly here, or risk having my obituary state something like: *died in a freak accident involving a popcorn tin to the head and one very pissed-off baby sister.*

"Think about it this way then. You pulled me into your office to talk about how to make your friend, who I'm not even dating, fall in love with me. Not to mention, I'm—"

"Don't you dare say it." An icy chill runs down my spine as she gives me an eerie *mom stare*. Those boys of hers aren't going to be able to get away with shit when they're older. "You're about to miss your moment, with a girl I think is perfect for you, for what? Some chick you chatted up online a few times, who failed to share very important information with you about her relationship status, all in hopes that she leaves her husband? And let's say she does, leave him that is. What's to say you two would ever work out? A woman doesn't leave a decade-long marriage with three kids and find her happily ever after with the first guy she meets online. This isn't hopelessly romantic; it's just hopeless."

"That's a bit harsh."

"You need to hear it. Let me ask you something. If Amanda called you today and said that she wanted to work on things with her husband, have a second go at it, would you stop her?"

"No, of course not..." I shock myself with the quick response. While I might not know her situation, if she loves her husband and wants to make things work, if that's what would make her happy and was best for her children, I would never want to dissuade her.

"Okay... so then, if Amanda heard that you might have the chance to find your perfect match, do you think she'd stop you?"

"But aren't you jumping the gun a little bit?"

"Says the guy who, after one date, announced his withdrawal from the dating pool to wait for a woman he hardly knows." *Shit, she has me there.* Tilly takes a deep breath and steadies herself. "Fine. Let me explain. Because I know this sounds impulsive, but it really isn't. I took time to think about it. We even did a pro-con list—"

"Please tell me *we* means you and Jax, and not the elders of Tral Lake or some shit."

"Of course not, that would be too biased, but seeing as this is a family matter, I did the only thing that made sense," she says as if I'm the ridiculous one. *And when did my relationship status become a family matter?* "We had an emergency meeting of the Moores, and we all decided you and Scarlett work."

"Goodbye, Tilly. I've got to get back to work. The food won't cook itself."

This has gotten way out of hand.

"Scott, don't you dare—"

I rush out of the room and shut the door on whatever else she has to say. I make it two steps down the hall before I run into her husband. "A pro-con list? Seriously?"

Jax shrugs without a hint of remorse. "There were some compelling pie charts too. Cassie and Tilly got really into it."

"All of you have lost it." I walk past the guy I used to think was my best friend and look for sanctuary in my kitchen. This is my place, where I'm in control. No one and nothing can take that away...

"Um, Scott," Gia says from the doorway to the main room. "There's a woman claiming she's your soon-to-be mother-in-law..."

Great. All of this craziness is going to spread through town quicker than how the bubonic plague hit Europe. My love life will be Tral Lake's flavor of choice before the dinner rush even starts. My family is one thing—while obnoxious, it was also inevitable—but it would've been nice to avoid the masses knowing and creating this awkward situation for the both of us when the holidays are over and we inevitably end up parting ways.

I wash up quickly and make myself halfway presentable, then rush out to the lobby. Scarlett's mother stands out like a sore thumb with her over-the-top, designer winter apparel.

"Mrs. Valentine." I extend a hand in greeting. I don't know the normal protocol in these situations but this seemed appropriate.

"Ginny, please," she corrects. "Relax. Have a seat," she directs me to one of the tables as if she owns the place. "I feel we have some important matters to discuss."

Taking a deep breath, I try to keep my cool as I follow her instructions. It's hardly been twenty-four-hours and it seems like I've already fucked up my fake engagement.

"Let me preface this by making one thing clear. I love my daughter."

"Okay." I tug at the collar of my shirt.

"That being said, she's a workaholic. Always has been and, unfortunately, always will be. Not that she'd ever admit it. But the Lord knows that girl never once listened to my warnings. You see, when you're involved with a man like Kasey, a man with a demanding schedule, you need to be flexible to his needs. You'd think she'd know that, growing up with me as a mother, that she'd watch me and learn how to be a good wife. But Rhea... sorry, *Scarlett* has always had a mind of her own. Which eventually doomed her and Kasey's relationship."

"Scarlett has done an amazing job with the inn," I'm quick to defend. "Her commitment to improving her guests' overall experience while maintaining your father's legacy, well, it's one of the things I admire most about your daughter."

Ginny waves me off. "Yes, that's good and all, but it's not realistic. A woman needs security, to be taken care of. *Children.* Which is why I need you to step up."

"Excuse me?" I lean back in my chair with my arms crossed over my chest.

"As I understand it, you're a workaholic too. At least that's the impression I get from my daughter, since all she can seem to tell me about you is that you work here and recently expanded your restaurant."

"Yes, but again, it's something we have in common."

Told you, Tilly's voice whispers in my mind.

"Although I don't get it, I can appreciate the fact that *Scarlett* and I have conflicting ideals when it comes to her future." Ginny looks down at her watch. "I'll get to the point. For all our differences, I know at the end of the day we want the same thing. A family." She glances over her large sunglasses at me. "Do you want children?"

There's that word again.

"Um..." I search around for something to drink, to relieve my dry throat, but come up empty. "Yes, I do... I mean, eventually."

Why is it so hot in here?

"Good." Ginny clasps her hands together. "Then it seems we have an understanding."

"We do?"

"Yes." She smiles and stands. "Now, if you'll excuse me, I have an appointment to get to. But I'll see you tonight."

"You will? I mean, yes. Tonight, when I come home."

"No." She chuckles. "For dinner." Then she straightens my collar. "I expect you to be cleaned-up and well-dressed by five sharp."

"I have—"

"Staff," she interrupts me, huffs, then rolls her eyes. "Scott, we discussed this. If you're going to get married, start a family, one of you needs to compromise when it comes to your schedules. Unfortunately, that will never be my daughter. At least not until she has a child of her own. While I don't know you well yet, from what I can see, you have the resources to ease your workload. Scarlett doesn't. So it's up to you to make this work." Her phone beeps. "Shoot, I have to go. I forgot what a number the winters here do on my hair. Hopefully the local salon is equipped enough to do a simple blowout," she grumbles to herself before focusing back on me. "But I *will* see you tonight."

Before I can object, Scarlett's mother saunters out the door. Leaving me—I chance a look behind me—and apparently my staff a little dumbfounded in her wake.

8

Scarlett

"Oh, Mr. Kelley in room eight likes—"

"His hot cocoa delivered at seven." Hannah sighs through the phone.

Initially, the inn was more of a bed and breakfast, but it only took me a few months to realize that feature was one of many reasons this place was hemorrhaging money. Most of the food was being put out and tossed daily. Tral Lake has so many wonderful places to eat, and we cannot compete with Moore Books and Coffee.

So I changed things up a bit, and instead of trying to serve food, I highlight our local specialties. That being said, we still keep supplies on hand to serve hot chocolate during the winter months. Mr. Kelley is a regular, who has a standing reservation with us each December while he visits his family for the holidays, and our hot cocoa is one of his favorite indulgences.

"Don't forget—"

"Two candy canes." Hannah sighs. "Scarlett, I got this."

I know she does. I mean, she started as a housekeeper when my grandpa was still around, then worked her way up to night manager. Sometimes I struggle to let go, though. It's just easier to do everything myself than to rely on others.

Not that Hannah's ever let me down. Unfortunately, it's just a side effect of my youth.

"I know. I'm sorry," I tell her.

"Don't apologize. I get it. But you have bigger things to worry about, like showing up to this dinner looking hot as fuck and giving that asshole a glimpse of exactly what he's missing."

I turn and look at my profile in the mirror. I suck in my gut, making my stomach flatter, to more closely resemble the beach body I used to have. When I exhale again, that illusion is shattered. "He's not missing much."

"Shut up," she scolds. "You're gorgeous. Now, did you decide what you're wearing?"

"Um..." I glance at what amounts to about half my closet lying across my bed. "I think my cashmere sweater with—"

"No," Hannah cuts me off.

I pick up the sweater in question and run my fingers across the material. "But it's soft and very—"

"No," she repeats. "Sweaters say I'm single and enjoy getting cozy with a blanket by the fire and masturbating to my favorite book. Oh, what about that strappy red dress?"

"Yeah, no. I'm not wearing that. For one, it's freezing out. And two, I bought it online when I was two bottles of wine deep and thought I could conquer the world. It's winter. The sweater is practical, and I can pair it with my skinny jeans and boots."

"You're a Minnesotan now. We don't let winter prevent us from showing the goods. Red dress, black tights, and your knee-high boots because they're fucking killer."

"Hannah..."

"Scarlett," she says in a mocking tone. "Trust me. You're a bombshell and that look will knock 'em dead. Especially Scott."

"*Shit...*"

"What?"

"I might have forgotten to invite Scott." I wince and wait for the reprimand I know is coming.

"You forgot to invite your fiancé to your big, fancy family dinner in the cities?"

"In my defense, he's not actually my fiancé." I reach for the outfit she suggested, hoping it'll distract her from the Scott issue. "It's fine. I'll just tell mom he had to work. I mean, it's not like it's a lie."

"I guess, but you're kind of making him look like an ass. His fiancée's mother is in town, and he can't spare a few hours to have dinner with her? Make a good impression and woo her like he did her daughter?"

"Fake," I remind her. "Besides, it's one dinner. I'll make sure to include him for the rest." I glance down at my legs that are far past *no-shave* November. "I'm wearing tights. Do you think I should—"

"Yes, for Christ's sake, woman, shave them. Last thing you want is to be halfway to Pound Town with Mr. Coffee, only to be forced to pause before he realizes the hedges haven't been trimmed."

"It's not that bad."

"If you have to ask, yes, it is."

"I knew I should've had them wax my legs when the girl was doing my Brazilian."

"Who gets their hoo-ha waxed and leaves their legs covered in fur?"

"Yeah, I'm sorry but my legs are one thing, especially since I've been waxing them so long the hair hardly grows anymore. But freezing tundra or not, I enjoy keeping things pristine in the vag area. Even if no one ever visits."

"Amen, sister! It's nice to hear you're more open to the idea of clearing out the cobwebs than I first thought."

"Well..." I turn on the bathroom sink, then gather up my razor and shaving cream. "If—and that's a strong *if*—Scott makes a move, I won't turn him down. I mean, he's doing me a huge favor, so it's the least I can do."

"I don't think you need to worry about the *if*. It's the *when*. And in that dress, I'd say by the end of tonight."

A bolt of lightning shoots down my spine, making my clit tingle at the thought. *It's been such a long time.*

"*Shit*." I'm so lost in my Scott Moore daydream my foot slips on the basin, and I almost slice my calf open. "Hannah, I love you. But this little fantasy of yours is already dead. Scott won't even be there. Now, unless I'm going for the no-skin look, I should let you get back to work."

"You never know. He is staying with you."

"You're impossible. You know that?"

Hannah chuckles. "Don't forget the red lipstick."

I end the call, set my cell on the shelf, and glance down at my progress. The first leg is done and the second is lathered up when there's a knock at the door. Knowing Hannah the way I do, I bet she came by to make sure that I'm dressed appropriately.

"Come in," I shout. The door opens and shuts before I add, "Are you here to check in on me? This is totally unnecessary, you know? Scott isn't coming and my mother, well, let's just say that no matter what, she'll find a flaw."

"There aren't any I can see," a deep, non-Hannah-like voice says from behind me.

I look up in the mirror. All the blood drains from my face when I notice a six-foot-plus hunk of man staring back at me, with his head cocked to the side and his eyes focused on my...

"Oh my god," I scream as I grab a nearby towel and attempt to cover myself up. At least Scott has the decency to look away and pretend that he didn't just get an eyeful. "What are you doing here?"

"I knocked," he replies, as if that explains the sudden intrusion. I guess it sort of does, but still...

"I thought you were Hannah. Besides, that doesn't answer my question. What are you doing here?" That's when I notice what he's wearing. Scott's dressed nicely, in a pair of black slacks and a hunter green sweater that I'm certain will make his eyes pop when he finally makes eye contact. "Why are you all dressed up?"

"Dinner."

"But I didn't tell you... *Oh no*."

"Yeah." He tucks his hands into his pockets as he relaxes, but he keeps his head tilted back and his eyes closed. "She stopped by the café today for a little chat."

I walk over to him, with the towel tucked firmly in place. "Shit, I'm sorry, Scott. I didn't think... well, that's a lie. The thought *had* crossed my mind. I suppose I was just hoping she wouldn't."

"It's fine. I mean, the whole town knows we're engaged now, but it's fine."

"No, it's not." I drop my head and let out a heavy sigh. "I didn't mean for this to get so out of hand. I understand if you want to set the record straight before things get too insane with the rumor mill."

His finger lifts my chin. I gaze up and, *yup,* those green hues have intensified tenfold. "It's fine," he repeats. "There's no turning back now."

"Why are you doing this? Helping me, I mean."

"Because we're friends."

"Friends help you move, not play your fake fiancé. It's too big of an ask."

"No, it's not." He brushes my hair back and tucks it behind my ear. "Besides, I already told you I needed a favor."

"And what's that?" My heart skips a beat as the realization that maybe Hannah was right sets in. I should be disappointed, but instead, the strong urge to drop my towel takes over. I mean, he's a guy. This is what he wants. It should be that simple, right?

"A date."

"A date?" I parrot. He nods, licking his lips while staring at mine like he's about to devour them. Or at least that's exactly what I want him to do.

"Yup."

"Do you have some ex you need to impress?" I can't imagine a reason Scott Moore would need help finding a date.

"Something like that." He chuckles. "We can talk about it later." Then his eyes rove over my body one more time before he adds, "Personally, I think you look amazing and should wear a towel all the time. That being said, I have a feeling your mom wouldn't approve of this whole *just stepped out of the shower* look."

Fuck. I completely forgot about my mom and her stupid family dinner. "Probably not," I huff and have to force myself to take a step back towards the bathroom. Because, right now, all I want to do is push Scott down on the couch and show him how grateful I am for his continued support. "If I'm being honest, I'm not even sure why I try. A full team of professional makeup artists could come in here and make me over, and that woman would still find a flaw."

"She might need to check the prescription on those designer glasses of hers, because you're beautiful," he tells me, and I almost believe him.

Which has me freezing to the spot, unsure how to respond. I mean, what do you say to that?

Scott senses my awkwardness and clears his throat as he glances around. "Um, I'll just wait... over here." He plops down on the couch. "I'm going to... read a book." He picks up a random title from the stack on the end table.

I eye his choice and chuckle to myself. "I never took you for a smut lover."

Scott glances at the cover before shrugging. "There's a lot you don't know about me."

I find myself breathless as the weight of his statement hits me. "I'm... going to finish getting dressed." I run to the bathroom and shut the door behind me, taking a moment to regain myself. The red dress hanging on the back of the door catches my eye, and a smile spreads across my face.

When, not if...

Hannah's words take up residence in my mind, so I decide there's nothing like living in the moment. With a new sense of confidence, I rush to finish shaving. The little mishap didn't leave me much time, but luckily I'm a pro at a quick updo. Then I slip into the dress and put on the final touches of my red lipstick.

I step out of the bathroom, and sure enough, Scott is reading the book. I mean, actually reading it, not just staring at the pages. I watch as he nibbles on his bottom lip. And, well, *damn*, has this man always been this hot? Especially with those black frames resting on the bridge of his nose.

"When did you start wearing those?" I ask, pulling Scott's attention from the book and up to me. And as though the glasses he's presently sporting are allowing him to see me for the very first time, his eyes slowly travel up the length of my body.

"Fuck me," he grumbles under his breath, and I send a silent thank you to Hannah.

9

Scott

As the radio in my pickup softly plays holiday music in the background, filling what for me feels like the most suffocating silence of my life, I've come to the conclusion that Scarlett Valentine blocks all common sense from entering my brain and forces me to do the complete opposite of what a sane person would do in any given situation.

For starters, take the whole cat and fiancé debacle that kicked off this mess. Then her mother shows up to my place of business and orders me around like her personal assistant. And now, I walk into her home and find her naked, a pair of perfect creamy thighs spread just enough to leave me wondering and not nearly enough to settle the lingering curiosity. Curiosity I shouldn't have when it comes to my baby sister's friend.

I'd be lying if I said I wasn't relieved that she thought I was Hannah. For a brief moment, this irrational, jealous part I wasn't aware I had within me took over. Instead of turning away, announcing my presence, leaving... I stayed, I watched, I lingered. And rather than redeeming myself, apologizing, setting things right... what did I do? I almost kissed her. *Again.*

Fuck, I wanted to do it so badly, and it might be wishful thinking, but I sensed that she wanted me too. *Maybe I should?* Maybe it would break this awkward tension between us. Then, once it's over, we would realize that there's nothing there and snuff out Tilly's little spark of hope that Scarlett and I could be something more.

Unless it does the exact opposite?

I shake the thought from my mind. I can't, well, shouldn't. This situation is confusing enough. And, clearly, Scarlett has a lot going on with her family while mine has lost their damn minds. It's better if we don't. Regardless of what the outcome might be, right now doesn't seem like the time to chance a major blowup.

Make it through Christmas, then maybe we can see? That's probably for the best.

Hopefully I'm right and she'll join me for New Year's. I still need a date and that seems like a better time to figure out *if* there is anything there and, more importantly, if it's mutual.

Though it doesn't help that she's wearing a dress designed by the devil himself. Or *herself*. Because as my eyes travel from top to bottom, I'm nearly convinced that the devil must be a woman looking to torture mankind. The material is fitted in all the right places, as if to show you everything you're missing beneath the shimmery fabric. And I swear the lipstick somehow makes Scarlett's already pouty lips plumper. Begging me to suck the tender flesh between my teeth. The image of that same mouth wrapped around my...

Pull yourself together, Scott...

Fucking Jax and Tilly are getting into my head. That's the problem. If it weren't for them, it would be so much easier to ignore this voice in my head that keeps whispering *just do it*. It wasn't all that long ago that the mere thought of Amanda and waiting for her was enough for me to swear off dating for the foreseeable future.

Now, it's starting to sound a bit ridiculous. I already knew, even if I didn't want to admit it out loud, that the chances were slim to none that she and I were going to work out. But even if the odds were stacked against me, the gamble seemed worth it, especially with no prospects of anything more than another atrocious waste of my time. And Scarlett, well, she seems like anything but a waste.

"So?" Scarlett asks.

My gaze flicks to the passenger seat, then back again. Even though she has her long black coat on, all I can see is that dress and what I shouldn't have but nonetheless learned exists beneath it. "Huh?"

She laughs and my cock perks up. Bastard is against me. "Glasses, I've never seen you wear them before," she repeats.

"Oh, yeah, these things." I push them up my nose, already annoyed by their existence. "I hate wearing them. They always get in the way. Especially in the kitchen. They fog up and never stay in place, so there's the whole food safety aspect of constantly touching my face, then having to wash my hands because of it. I can see well enough without them. But if I'm driving, especially at night, I need to have them on."

"Why not wear contacts?"

I shrug. "I tried but couldn't do it. The one and only day I wore them, it took me over an hour to get the fuckers in because I kept chickening out when putting my finger near my eye. It actually took Mom maneuvering the contact while Robbie held me down to even get them in. They felt a little weird at first, but it was like once it was done, it wasn't so bad. But then, one of the lenses fell out while I was baking. I couldn't find the damn thing and ended up having to toss a whole bowl of batter. So I vowed *never again*."

Scarlett chuckles, and now I'm half-hard. Thank god it's dark in the cab of my pickup and she hopefully doesn't notice. "Sorry... I shouldn't laugh but I can totally picture Robbie pinning you down."

"No worries. It's probably the least embarrassing thing about me."

"You're embarrassed about wearing glasses?"

I sigh. "Not exactly. It's just one of those insecurities left over from my youth."

"What do you mean?"

"Let's just say I wasn't exactly a stud in high school, and kids suck." I shrug, and Scarlett leans in to get a better look at me, as if she's trying to find my implied imperfection. "Trust me," I assure her. "We're talking not only glasses, but headgear, acne... and it took me a while to fill out. I was just this long string bean of a teenager."

"Oh." Scarlett sits there, staring straight ahead in obvious discomfort.

Damn it, is this that self-deprecating thing Tilly warned me about?

"But, hey." I turn and smile at her. "Their loss because, well, look at me now."

She giggles, but it lacks the enthusiasm from before. "Definitely their loss." Scarlett turns to look out the window. "I get it though. My mom..." She sighs. "She's that classic story. The one where the small-town girl runs off to LA with the hopes and dreams of being a star. What she got was a job waiting tables and some jackass who said that if she fucked him, he'd help her. And instead of a big break, my mom got knocked up. It turns out not only did he have zero pull to get her a gig, the only penny he had to his name was spent on the coffee he got at the diner she worked at. He had less than zero interest in being a father or giving her any support, and my mom's dreams got put on hold... because of me. Not just financially either. *Her figure was gone and no one in Hollywood wanted a flabby single mom in their movie.* Her words, not mine. As far back as I can remember, she began grooming me, preparing me for this life of stardom. Nonstop pageants, auditions, singing and dancing lessons... You name it, she tried it."

"I'm sorry." I know it isn't enough, but it's all I can think to say.

"Don't be. It's how she met my dad... I mean stepdad, but he's the only father I've ever known so the *step* title never really fit for me." Scarlett shakes her head and chuckles. "He was holding auditions for some sitcom. I wasn't right for that role, but it seemed we were exactly what he was looking for at home. He said it was love at first sight and Trisha, my stepsister, and I clicked right away. We were an instant blended family. While it wasn't exactly my mom's dream, the end result was the same. She had the big mansion, fame, money—and, well, I got the father I always wanted."

For the first time, I can see the lingering pain in Scarlett's eyes. Honestly, I think it's always been there and I just never made the effort to notice it.

And now I feel like a dick...

She pauses, looks off into the distance, then shakes her head as if she can shake the past away with it. "For a while, my mom was so happy that the pressure for me to be someone famous died down a little. Though I have a feeling that's because I'm five-one and no one was going to cast a girl that short anyway. Plus, dad knew all of it made me miserable so I'm sure he had something to do with my ability to finally step out of the limelight. It was my chance to live a normal life. I mean, as normal as one can have when their father is an in-demand director. But he made sure to keep Trisha and me out of the tabloids, as best he could at least. But my mom always insisted on perfection. *You never know where the paparazzi could be lurking*," Scarlett mimics in a haughty voice. "Then my senior year, when I was looking at colleges and careers, she went back to pressuring me to find my footing in Hollywood. If I wasn't destined to be on the screen, I could become a master behind it—like Dad. My compromise was taking theater as part of my studies."

"Out of curiosity, how many talents do you have?"

Scarlett laughs and counts on her fingers. "Ballet, piano... I can hold my own at karaoke. I love doing Shakespearean readings," she says in a dramatic tone. "Oh, and I make killer fish tacos."

"Fish tacos?"

"Don't judge. It might not be anything fancy, like your paella, but I promise my recipe will knock your socks off."

"I'd love to taste your taco." *Fuck, that sounded dirty.* "Your fish tacos, I mean." *Not that that sounds any better.*

"Your destination is on the right." The disembodied GPS lady interrupts this horribly awkward moment. "You have arrived."

"If you play your cards right, you just might." Scarlett winks at me before getting out of the car. Leaving me with a hard-on as I wonder what exactly she was suggesting I might get to taste.

Is it wrong that I kind of hope it's both?

10

Scarlett

I KEEP GLANCING AT Scott from the corner of my eye. He's been laser-focused on the menu since the moment they seated us. I'm starting to worry that the offer to *taste my taco* was a bit too much. Maybe I misread the situation?

"Whatcha thinking?" I lean over and whisper in his ear. His body tenses as my chest grazes his arm.

Scott swallows hard. "I'm torn." He clears his throat. "The ribeye with the truffle mash sounds amazing, but so does the twelve-hour braised short rib in the red wine reduction."

I chuckle. "Great minds."

"Huh?" His emerald eyes meet mine.

"I've been debating on the same two dishes as well. The reviews rave about the short rib—the biggest complaint I've seen is that they sell out of them nightly. But the truffle mash sounds just as amazing." An idea pops into my head, and before I know what I'm doing, I say, "Hey, what if..." Then quickly stop myself. "Sorry, never mind."

"What?" he asks earnestly.

"What if one of us orders the ribeye and the other gets the ribs, then we could share?" I wince at the question. Kasey used to get annoyed when I couldn't decide.

Whenever we went out to eat together, I would order several small plates and pick off each. My ex never had that problem, always knew exactly what he wanted when it came to *everything*. Which was basically the same three dishes no matter where it was we went. I understood a lot of the time he was on strict diets to keep screen-ready, but still, it just would've been nice to cut loose now and then.

"I love that idea." Scott smiles, his face filled with excitement. I know everyone says that the way to a man's heart is through his stomach. But with Scott Moore, it seems to be the *only* way. Not that I want to get to his heart...

At least I don't think I do.

No, the throbbing organ I'm interested in is located farther south. The guy might be a catch, but I've already learned the hard way that the only good boyfriend is fictional. Even if they're great at playing them on the screen, it never translates to real life.

"Yes, just water for me, but she'll have a Cabernet Sauvignon," Scott says to our server, who (based on all the closed and piled-up menus) must've been here long enough to take everyone else's orders. Scott then proceeds to tell her what we're having for dinner. "Sorry," he whispers as the server leaves the table. "I shouldn't have ordered for you without asking..."

I smile. "Thank you, but I don't mind. Especially since you got me exactly what I wanted."

"You two are just adorable," my mom coos from the other side of the table. "Okay, I'm dying to hear it."

"Hear what?" I turn to her, confused.

"The story," she says as if it should be obvious.

"Story?" Scott chokes out.

"Yes, I want to know everything about this blossoming love that my daughter has chosen to keep hidden from me until now."

"Oh, well..." Scott tugs at his collar. It's clear that acting isn't his forte.

I lace my fingers with his. "It's just one of those things. We've been hanging around each other for the last year. A glance here, a smile there."

My mom rests her face in her hands, enthralled by what little information I'm providing. Even Brittany appears to be listening intently, while my stepsister and ex seem extremely uncomfortable with the topic. They should be. Although my story might be made-up, at least it isn't as tainted as theirs.

I clear my throat before continuing. "There was a Halloween party at the bar in town. We were both there alone and quickly gravitated towards each other. At the end of the night, like the gentleman he is, Scott walked me home to make sure I got there safely. Then there was this moment at the door... You know the one where you're supposed to go but your legs can't seem to work, almost like there's this magnetic pull between you that you're hopeless to ignore. Before either of us knew what was happening, we were kissing and..." I remember that my niece is here, and that the PG-version of this story is necessary. "...as they say, the rest is history."

"And the engagement?" My mom doesn't let up.

"Oh, that was—"

"No, I want to hear it from Scott," my mom interrupts. We didn't craft this part of our tale, and given Scott's improv skills the other day, we're as dead as a Tuesday afternoon matinee at the local theatre. "I love a good proposal story. All the planning, the nerves, the anticipation..."

"There wasn't any," he says, and my mom quirks a brow. My ex and sister also seem more interested in this tale. "I mean, I had been thinking about it. But we'd only been officially dating for a month, so I kept telling myself it was too soon to even consider marriage. Terrified I'd scare her away by moving too fast. However, it was Thanksgiving, and one moment, we were enjoying this obnoxiously large dinner I prepared with my ever-expanding family; then, the next, my sister-in-law's water broke and we were rushing her to the hospital. I was sitting there, looking at my siblings, thinking about how crazy all their love stories were. I realized it wasn't important how their relationships started, because it got them all to where they were—*are*. Happy with their soul mates. It was in that instant that I knew it didn't matter if it was too fast, too crazy, or too unconventional, because all that mattered was that I loved this girl, and I didn't want to waste another second delaying the inevitable. So right there, in that waiting room, I dropped to one knee in front of Scarlett and proposed."

Mom fans herself. "Oh, that's so romantic."

"Would you mind if I pitched that to some of the guys I know?" Kasey asks as Trisha nudges him. "What? Your mother's right. Out of all the movies I've been in, that's still the most romantic thing I've ever heard." My stepsister shoots him a nasty glare. He ignores her and continues, "Heck, your entire town is the perfect place for this project my buddy has lined up. Think Hallmark: a small-town, Christmas love story. Tral Lake is exactly what he's been looking for."

"Honey," Trisha urges. "You know it's not polite to discuss business at the dinner table."

"Really?" Scott says, his excitement palpable as he talks over her. "That would be awesome. My sister's on the town's business and tourism committee. She could help pitch the idea and garner support. Oh, and my best friend—well, her husband and now my brother-in-law—he's an amazing photographer and knows the area like the back of his hand. He could take you around and capture some onsite shots for your presentation."

"He's the one who helped me with the new images of the inn," I add.

"No shit," Kasey says. "If he has time."

"Believe me." Scott chuckles. "For you, Jax'll make time."

I pat Scott on the shoulder. "Excuse my fiancé. He and his best friend happen to be your biggest fans."

"Is that so?" Kasey uses his million-dollar, Hollywood smile. One thing I'll give my ex credit for is how much he loves his fans. He never gets annoyed when someone asks for a photo or autograph. He's one of those few genuine stars, who does charity and public appearances because he wants to and not because his publicist tells him it's good for his image. "Well, in that case, I won't take no for an answer."

"Jax is going to die." Scott immediately texts Tilly's husband with the news. I can already hear the high-pitched squeal Jax is probably going to make when he reads it.

A few minutes later, our dinner is served. My mom clearly found the fanciest place she could in Southern Minnesota as they deliver each plate on a silver platter with a matching lid. It's effective, though, because when they lift the cover and reveal our dishes, the steamy aroma is mouthwatering.

Scott pulls out his phone and snaps photos of the table. "Sorry... I promise I'm not posting them on social media or anything. Just adding to my folder of food porn." Trisha frowns as Brittany giggles behind her napkin. "I mean... of food *inspiration*," Scott corrects himself.

My short rib is fork tender as I collect a bite. The juices explode on my tongue and a moan escapes my lips. "This is so good." I gather another bite and present it to Scott. "You have to try this."

His eyes lock with mine as he wraps his lips around the utensil, and my clit throbs as I imagine him savoring me the same way he is the meal. My thighs clench tightly as Scott's eyes roll to the back of his head.

"That's incredible," he moans. "Here." He grabs his spoon and scoops up a serving of the mashed potatoes. "What do you think?"

"Oh my god, they're so good and silky smooth. I could bathe in them."

"I know, right?" Scott takes another mouthful. "I'm going to have to figure out this recipe and add it to the menu."

Mom clears her throat, pulling my focus to her. Based on the awkwardness on the other side of the table, our enjoyment over the delicious food might have reached a pornographic level. Well, everyone but my niece seems to think so anyway. Brittany has the largest smile on her face as she devours her mac and cheese, oblivious to the adult content.

"I forgot how large the portions are in Minnesota," my mom says in that tone that implies she's trying to sound polite but is actually insulting. "Perhaps we should share my salad?"

I look between my delicious tender ribs and her boring, albeit more than likely very tasty, grilled chicken salad. Not that I don't like a good bed of greens—growing up in Cali, it was a staple meal. But right now, my body is craving red meat and those sinful mashed potatoes.

"As a bride-to-be, don't you think you should focus on fitting into your wedding gown?" Mom leans over the table to whisper. Which is pointless since everyone can hear her. "No reputable designer will do an expanded waistline."

"Oh... I mean..." I stutter. She's right. Even if I'm not getting married anytime soon, meals like this—and the daily muffin and sugar with a dash of coffee—haven't been the best for my figure. I'm about to concede and accept her plate when Scott scoops up another serving of potatoes and steak.

"Here, try them mixed together." He puts the food in my face and I'm too weak to resist. *God, it's so delicious.* "Oops," he says as he wipes the corner of my mouth with his thumb. Then Scott pins me with that intense stare of his as he sucks the digit clean. "It's perfect," he groans. "Just like you." He reaches over and pushes my mother's salad back. The entire time, he doesn't take his eyes off me. "She doesn't need to change her dinner." Unlike my mom, Scott doesn't pretend to lower his voice. "No matter what she decides to wear, I know Scarlett will be the most beautiful bride in the world."

Mom huffs out her displeasure but doesn't bring it up again. As dinner and conversation resume, mostly between my ex and fake fiancé, I sit here a bit dazed and confused. I know he's just playing his role and doing what I asked of him. But I wish he wasn't. Never has anyone ever treated me like this, not even *Mister Romance* sitting across from us at the table. Not that Kasey treated me poorly. It was just never... *this*.

I have to remind myself *this* is all fake, which is the only place men like Scott Moore (or rather this version of him) actually exist—in fiction. Still, for this one brief moment, I'd give anything for it to be real.

"More wine, miss?" a server asks me.

I pick up my glass and chug back the half that remains. "Yes, please," I reply with a forced smile. Because I have a feeling I'm going to need all the alcohol I can get.

11

Scott

"YOU'RE INCREDIBLE," SCARLETT SLURS as I help her make her way to the little cabin by the inn. Since it's down the path a bit, we can't park directly in front of the door. Thankfully the walkway's been shoveled, but I'm still afraid she'll break her neck trying to make it back on her own in these heeled boots. "Like super incredible."

The evening went well enough, but after the "salad incident" with her mom, my fake fiancée seemed to prefer a liquid dinner over a more solid one. Scarlett always appears so perfect and put together, never shy when it comes to showing off her curvy figure with fitted blouses and hip-hugging jeans that highlight her voluptuous ass. Until her mother showed up in town and somehow overshadowed all the confidence she typically exudes.

"Do you need a hand?" Kasey offers as they exit their rental car. His *real* fiancée frowns for the hundredth time tonight. At this point, I'm convinced that Trisha isn't capable of making an expression that doesn't resemble someone sucking on a sour lemon.

"He's all I need." Scarlett's finger traces over my chest as she continues her drunken rambling.

"No, thanks, but I've got her." I wave him off. As much as I appreciate the gesture, I have things under control. "Besides, it looks like someone needs your help more." I gesture to the little girl sleeping in the back seat.

Kasey laughs. "I swear that kid can sleep through anything." He proceeds to pick her up to demonstrate his point. Brittany doesn't stir in the slightest. "Goodnight, you two," he calls over his shoulder as he turns toward the main building.

"Take care, lovebirds," Scarlett's mom shouts in our direction, oblivious to the effect her comments have on her daughter. Or perhaps she knows and just doesn't care?

"Come on, Scar, let's get you home," I say, tugging her a little closer. Her body shivers against mine. "Are you cold?"

"No," she lies. But the streetlamp reveals her trembling bottom lip.

"Here." I take off my jacket and help her slide it on. "Better?"

She hums as she snuggles into the warmth. "It smells like you."

Chuckling, I shake my head and continue to escort her down the cleared path to her front door. I thought she was drunk on Halloween—clearly she was holding back. She's going to be wrecked tomorrow. We make it to the cabin and Scarlett leans on the doorframe as I reach into my jacket pockets, feeling around for the keys.

"You look really sexy with glasses." She grins and I try to ignore her comments. She's drunk, meaning I can't take any of what she says seriously. "Like Clark Kent... Then, when you take them off, you become Superman. But instead of shooting laser beams out of your eyes, your super power is making the gooiest muffins ever."

"Is that right?" *Where are those damn keys?*

"Yup," she pops the P. "Super Scott... making delicious food and coffee by day, saving damsels in distress by night."

"You're far from being a damsel in distress," I fire back. Our eyes lock and my hands pause in my pockets.

"It feels like for the past forty-eight hours all you've done is rescue me."

I brush back a loose strand of her golden hair that fell from the small pile on the top of her head. "Scarlett, you're one of the strongest people I've ever met. I promise you the last thing you need is rescuing."

"Scott," she whispers my name, and my first thought is that her super power must be liquifying whatever brain cells I have left. Because, once again, all common sense is thrown out the window as I lean down, drawn in by her pouty bottom lip. She's not in her right mind, and honestly, even though I haven't had a drop of alcohol, I'm not sure if I am either. She meets me halfway and closes her eyes.

Never in my life have I wanted to do anything more than kiss this woman. But as much as I want to, I know I can't. Not like this. Scarlett lets out a disappointed sigh as my mouth presses onto the top of her head.

"You'll thank me in the morning."

If she remembers, that is...

I find the keys and open the door. Scarlett stumbles inside without a word, a pair of shaky legs taking her straight to the bathroom, while I head to the couch where Bruce has staked claim to the middle cushion.

"Sorry, fluffy dude, that's not going to work for me," I say as I nudge him off.

"Meow," he scolds as he jumps onto the coffee table.

"Yeah, yeah... I'm sure your owner feels the same way."

I lie down as best I can. But no matter how I position myself, a limb hangs off an edge or my neck is crooked in the worst way possible. Closing my eyes doesn't help either. Because I'm left to wonder if Scarlett is okay. She's been in that bathroom for a bit now. I want to check in on her, but then again, I don't want to intrude.

I glance at the clock on my phone, realizing how much time has passed without her making a sound. Maybe I should knock? She might have blacked out on the floor or worse...

I sit up just as the bathroom door swings open. Scarlett steps out, her face clean of makeup and her hair piled high on her head. The dress is gone and in its place is an oversized t-shirt.

"Sorry... bathroom's free... if you need it," she says awkwardly.

"Are you feeling okay? I'm not sure what you have on hand, but if you need a surefire hangover cure, I can run home and grab some herbal tea. I have a blend that does wonders for me."

"No... thank you... I'm fine." She walks to the kitchenette, grabs a cup from the shelf, and fills it with water. Then she reaches into a jar, plucks two round white tablets from inside, and drops them into the cup. They fizz as they dissolve. "A little Alka-Seltzer and a good night's sleep, and I'll be right as rain in the morning."

"Okay." I can't help but smile as she sips the concoction, scrunching her nose each time she has to force it down. "Goodnight."

"Night," she says before disappearing behind the curtain that serves as the door to her makeshift bedroom.

I should pass out. I slept like crap last night and it's been one heck of a day. But all I can do is lie back and stare up at the ceiling. Despite the few hiccups, like Scarlett getting really drunk and her mother souring her mood, it was strangely the best date I've ever been on. Including that night with Amanda. Which is insane to admit, because they were both train wrecks in their own right. But going out with Scarlett was so... easy. Maybe it was because there was no pressure. This is all just pretend. Still, there's just something about her...

"Scott," Scarlett calls out from the other side of the curtain.

"Can I get you something?" I call back, already swinging my legs over the couch and onto the floor.

"Just..." She speaks so softly I can hardly hear her. Standing, I walk over, my hand pausing on her makeshift doorway. *Should I go in?* Maybe she passed out? Before I can make up my mind, she says, "Thank you."

"You don't need to thank me—"

"But I do. You have no idea how much this means to me. Not just the fake stuff, but the things you say and how you stand up for me when I feel like I can't stand up for myself. That might be fake too—"

"Scarlett," I cut her off before she can say more. As I open the curtain, she sits up, holding the blanket to her chest. While I have no right to invade her private space like this, I feel it's important she sees how serious I am. "I promise everything I've said to you is the truth. It's not for show. The only lies I've told are the ones needed to keep our story straight. The rest, well, that's just me."

She wipes away a stray tear and smiles.

"Now, get some rest," I tell her. "But if you need anything, just let me know—"

"Scott," she says as I'm about to walk away. "Would you...? I mean, why don't you come to bed? Here, with me?"

"I'm not sure that's a good idea—"

"Not like that... It's just like I said... you've been so great during this whole thing and the thought of you sleeping out there kills me." As if on cue, the muscle in my lower back pulls tight and I have to lean to the side to loosen it. Scarlett seems to notice the slight movement, her gaze focused on where my sweatpants hang low on my hips when she adds, "I've slept out there many times, and I'm a full foot shorter than you are. I can't imagine how awful it must be on your back. So, please, can you just sleep here, at least for tonight? Look." She pulls the blanket aside with a grin. "I even put a pillow wall between us."

I laugh. "Are you sure? You've had a lot to drink and—"

"I promise this isn't some drunken decision. I was planning on asking you earlier," she says and I glance back at the couch, where Bruce has made himself at home on the middle cushion again. "How about this? Z, X, Y... I mean Y, X. Okay, even sober I always fuck that up. Let's face it. The only people who can recite the alphabet backwards are alcoholics who practice so they can pass a sobriety test." She taps her chin. "Oh! Do you want me to jump on one foot and pat my head while rubbing circles on my belly?"

I laugh at the image. "That would be amusing." I pause to think on it for a second. "But no... I appreciate the offer and all. It just doesn't—"

"Please," she begs, her eyes wide and sparkling. "I'm not going to be able to get any rest thinking about you suffering out there."

"Okay," I reluctantly agree, climbing into bed while making sure to keep as close to the edge as possible without falling off.

Scarlett smiles. "Good night, Scott," she says, rolling onto her side, so that her back is to me.

"Good night, Scar," I whisper before doing the same.

12

Scarlett

My CELL SOFTLY BUZZING on the nightstand pulls me from the most amazing dream, where I was covered in whip cream and Scott Moore was just about to have me for dessert.

"Shh," I whisper as I press the button on the side to silence it. Hopefully I can fall back asleep and pick up where we left off. It buzzes again. "I'm too hungover for this," I huff.

More than likely it's Hannah begging for details about last night. I'm not ready to hear her analysis about the situation. A sliver of sunlight has managed to invade my space through a crack between the blackout curtains. Squeezing my eyes shut, I attempt to roll over but something heavy has me pinned in place.

"Brucey," I groan. "We're going on a diet at the start of the new year." My hand freezes as it meets a smooth, muscular arm and not the soft furry body I was expecting.

Whatever hopes I had of going back to sleep are obliterated as my eyes fling open to find our pillow barrier dismantled and Scott sound asleep, with one arm draped over my stomach and a leg hooked over my thigh. My fingers twitch with the sudden urge to reach out and brush back his messy hair.

How can one man look so incredibly sexy sleeping?

The corners of his mouth are turned up into the smallest of smiles, leaving me to wonder what it is he's dreaming about.

Is it wrong that I hope it's me? Or that I'm jealous at the thought that it probably isn't?

That fact alone should have me shoving Scott's arm aside and jumping out of bed, but it doesn't and I don't. Instead, I savor the moment. Because it wasn't until just now that I realized how much I miss waking up in someone's arms. So, eyes open and brain wide awake, I enjoy the fantasy that I'm his and he's mine. Imagining that the slight smirk spread across his handsome face is because he's thinking about me, *us*, while clinging to the idea that this is so comfortable because it's right rather than convenient.

No longer able to help myself, I comb my fingers through his messy hair to push it aside. A smart woman would stop there, but I never claimed to be smart. Especially when my hands seem to have a mind of their own as they continue to travel down his scruffy, chiseled cheek and proceed to dance across his shoulder. His arms flex under my touch.

Wow... I mean, I knew Scott was fit, but I never realized how large and sculpted he was until now. It's amazing what someone can hide beneath several layers of clothes and an apron, which leads me to wonder what other surprises he may be hiding under these covers. Based on the firm bulge snuggled against my thigh, it seems that *large* is a common theme with him.

Oh my god, Scarlett, that's going too far. I stop myself from sneaking a peek.

While I've regained some of my senses, clearly it's not enough because just as I'm about to trace back up his arm, Scott's emerald eyes open and lock on mine. We remain silent, staring at one another for a few seconds before his gaze drops to the arm he has wrapped around my waist and the leg he has flung over my thigh. He looks back at me and flashes a smile.

"My bad," he says softly as he pulls himself into an upright position. "Sorry about that." He scratches his head and looks around the room.

"It's okay." I shrug, slowly reaching out for the blanket to cover myself. "I didn't mind," I tell him, then quickly snap my mouth shut. *What the hell is wrong with you?* "I mean... there's no harm in some innocent snuggling. It does get a little chilly in here."

Scott chuckles. "Yeah, the wind was pretty intense last night. You should really put some plastic on the windows. You wouldn't think it, but it's great at keeping the cold out of the house."

"Oh, yeah, I've been meaning to do something about it. I just always seem to forget to stop by the hardware store." There's an awkward silence as we both sit there, each waiting for the other to make a move to stand. "You can use the bathroom first if you want?"

Scott looks down at his lap. "Um... no, you go ahead."

"Are you sure? I'll be longer and—"

"No, you go," he insists. "I need a minute to wake up."

"Oh, okay." Not wanting to make a big deal about it, I get up and rush out of bed.

As soon as I turn on the bathroom light, I regret it, but it's a necessary evil if I want to navigate the room without bumping into anything. Once I finish taking care of business, I go to wash up in the sink and unfortunately catch a glimpse of my reflection in the mirror. I didn't wash my face as well as I thought I did last night.

Oh my god, no wonder Scott told me to go first.

I look like hell warmed over. Remnants of my mascara streak down my cheeks while my lips appear like something straight out of Rodeo Clown Chic Magazine. I rush to grab my makeup-removing wipes. My face is red by the time I'm done scrubbing myself clean. Hopefully my moisturizer will help even things out and cool me down so I don't look like a cherry tomato.

I lift my arm and gag at the scent. *God, I'm disgusting.*

I grab my spray deodorant and coat myself with a heavy layer. I'd love to take a shower, but I'll have to wait until Scott leaves. There might be a curtain, but it still feels like I'm bathing in the middle of my living room. Deodorized, hair and teeth brushed, and big comfy robe on, I finally exit the bathroom.

Scott is standing at the counter where my little coffee maker is running. "Sorry, I hope you don't mind. I found some pods in the cupboard and thought you might want a cup."

"I'll never say no to coffee." I grin lightheartedly as I take a seat at the tiny table barely suited for two. Scott brings over a mug and lowers himself onto the chair across from me. "None for you?" I ask him, noticing he's empty-handed.

"Oh, I'll just grab something at the shop."

"Too good for my insta-pods?" I tease.

"What can I say?" He shrugs.

"It might not be as good as the stuff you have at the café but it does the trick."

"No judgement, I promise." He laughs. "So, what's the plan for today?"

"Plan?"

"Yeah, yesterday, we were supposed to have a family dinner and it probably didn't look good that your mom was the one who had to tell me."

"I'm sorry about that..."

"No worries. It all worked out. But I'd like to make sure I'm here doing the *fiancé* things and what not. I have Gia and Logan to help at the shop. Just tell me where and when you need me."

"Well..." I pause to consider what I know my mom put on the itinerary. "Today we are supposed to go shopping around town, getting last-minute gifts. Then tomorrow, I'm going to have to do some serious prepping for a Christmas dinner I failed to properly plan out, before taking Brittany on a sleigh ride at the little Christmas Wonderland Eli set up at the orchard."

"Why do you need to plan a dinner?"

"I don't know. It's always been our tradition. Some fancy dinner on Christmas Eve and then presents and a buffet-style breakfast Christmas morning."

"No, I just mean we're getting married... or, well, that's what your family thinks. Right?"

"Yeah, I guess, technically. Why?"

"You should leave the cooking and prepping to me. It's what I do." He grins before dropping his voice an octave. "*It's what I live for*," he says, quoting the famous sea witch.

I shake my head and throw a palm to my face. "Really, Scott? *The Little Mermaid*?"

"Disney was a family favorite in our household." He shrugs as if that's all the explanation I need. "So, what do ya say?" he prompts.

"I don't know, Scott. It's one thing for me to invade your life. Which I already know sounds wrong, but to bring your whole family in on it? Yeah, that's asking way too much."

"What's a few more people?" Scott waves me off.

"Are you sure?"

"Positive," he says with a certainty I don't share. "Let's plan on everyone coming over Christmas Eve for the big dinner, then we can do the presents in the morning at the inn," Scott suggests, then frowns.

"What's wrong?"

"It's nothing," he insists, but for some reason, I want to know what is making this usually happy man so sad all of a sudden.

I cover his hand with mine. "It's okay. You can tell me."

He takes a deep breath and blows it out. "We've always done Christmas morning together, all the Moores, even last year after everything that happened." He doesn't say more and he doesn't have to. He means the car accident that took his parents' lives and left Tilly with a broken arm. "But now, all of them have their own families to wake up with in the morning, at their own homes. I guess it's just a strange feeling, realizing how different things are now, how I don't have anyone..."

"You have me," I tell him and I don't know why. It's not true. Not really. But it felt like the right thing to say. I *wanted* to say it. Scott turns his palm so that his fingers lock with mine. "So you won't be alone this year," I attempt to clarify.

My mistake is evident the second he lets go and pulls away. *God, Scar, does your foot just live in your mouth?*

"Look, I'm going to stop by my place and take a quick shower." He throws his legs over the side of the bed and stands. "Then pop into the café to make sure everything is running smoothly. Why don't you and your mom stop in for lunch and then I can join you both for shopping?"

"Really?" I raise a brow at his offer. Besides the fact I'm totally *Mood-killer Jane*, the fact remains... "You want to come shopping with me and my mother?"

"I want to go shopping with *you*. Your mom is just a bonus," he teases. "Besides, I need to get a few last-minute gifts myself."

"If it's not too much of an inconvenience—"

"None at all." As though whatever awkwardness there was from before has disappeared, Scott leans down and presses a kiss to the top of my head. Then he pulls back with a smile, grabs his jacket and keys, and crosses the room. "I'll see you later."

He slips out of the front door and I'm left stunned. *Was that real?* I know I was drunk last night and thought I imagined him doing the same thing. But now I'm more sure than ever that what I felt wasn't simply déjà vu.

13

Scott

"SO," LOGAN PROMPTS THE moment I enter the kitchen.

"Nope. Don't want to talk about it," I grunt as I set my stuff down on the counter and go to wash my hands.

"Come on, you're *engaged* to one of the hottest chicks in town." He pauses midthought as Gia enters the room and walks over to the shelf for some extra cups. "*Second* hottest chick in town." He winks at Gia.

She tosses a paper cup at his head and misses by a long shot. "In your dreams," she huffs as she stomps back up front, but adds an extra waggle to her step that even I notice.

"God, that ass. What I wouldn't give to..." Thankfully Logan stops himself short. "Sorry, now, where were we?"

"You were getting back to work. Proving to your boss that you deserve your paycheck this week."

"Oh yeah, I remember!" He misses the hint entirely. "Come on, spill already!"

"Logan, if and that's a big *if* anything were happening between Scarlett and me, you'd be the last person in this town I'd ever discuss it with."

He picks up a knife and pretends to stab at his own chest. "Ouch, you're killing me, chef."

"Fuck off, dude."

On any given day, I'd appreciate Logan's goofball attitude. He's been a refreshing addition to the team. But, today, he's more obnoxious than my little brother. Which says a lot.

"Still, what are we supposed to say? *Do*? I need instructions." He's practically bouncing on his heels and drooling from his mouth. I love my small town. I really do. There's something comforting about being part of the community of Tral Lake. Until I remember I'd never have to deal with this shit in the cities.

"What? You think you're going to be interrogated or some shit?" I cross my arms over my chest and shoot him a glare.

"Duh, I got a glimpse of Momzilla—the woman's scary. A total man-eater." Logan shivers at the thought.

"Well, then you better make sure you don't fuck up her lunch order." I pat him on the shoulder. "Otherwise, she'll come back here and gobble you up." I press my lips together and make a slurping sound for dramatic effect. I can't help myself. I like fucking with the kid.

"You think?" His eyes widen and he appears to hold his breath as he waits for my answer.

"Oh, for sure."

"Awesome." He grins, and now I'm fucking confused.

"Seriously? Is that supposed to be a good thing?"

"Um, yeah, dude. Her mom is scary hot and I'm always down for some cougar action." Logan makes a cat sound while lifting a hand to mimic the swipe of a paw.

"No wonder Gia won't give you the time of day," I taunt, knowing that since the guy was hired and first laid eyes on her, his main goal has been to get into her pants. Luckily, according to Gia at least, she's got enough common sense to not "shit where she eats."

"Yeah?" Logan pauses the spoon he's using to stir the pot of soup. "What's she said about me?"

"Honestly?"

"I don't want it any other way."

"That you're a pig." And that's me softening the blow. If I remember correctly, her exact words were *vile swine*.

Logan gives me another dopey grin. "She loves me."

"Whatever floats your boat, man. Now, are we going to discuss the menus for the rest of the week or continue to gossip like a bunch of schoolgirls?"

"Will there be hair braiding?" He looks up at me while batting his lashes, and I let out an exhausted sigh. "Just kidding." He turns the pot down to a simmer. "Here, let me show you what I've got going on."

"Got going on? I already made a menu." My temples twitch with the warning of an oncoming headache, one that I can't afford to have today.

"Can't I just show you?" he whines.

"Fine." I'm out of the kitchen for one day, and my employees have already gone rogue. I knew this was a mistake. The kid's not ready to be unsupervised yet.

Logan smiles and off he goes to retrieve his version of *my* revised menu. A few seconds later, he jogs back around the corner and comes to a quick stop in front of me. "Okay, look, your version was fine and all. I just wanted to try to elevate a few items and provide more complex alternatives. I didn't change the proteins, and we already have most of the ingredients on hand. I only had to order a few extra things but I kept it under our budget."

I look over the suggested changes, lifting a hand to scratch the back of my head. "Wow."

"Is that a good *wow* or a bad *wow*?"

"Good," I say, both shocked and a little impressed. I shouldn't be.

Logan has more culinary training than I've ever had. He actually attended school abroad and apprenticed under some world famous chefs. Besides the baking skills handed down by my mom, I'm self-taught, which means I go through a ton of trial and error. Not to mention, Logan came highly recommended by my friend Zach, who's earned two Michelin stars himself. So I knew the kid had talent. I guess he was just never given a chance to shine on his own here.

Maybe that's my fault? I admit I've been known to put some tight reins on my staff.

"Yes..." Logan whispers, clearly relieved by my reaction.

Zach warned me that the guy could be a bit of a hothead and that his smart mouth had gotten him banned from working in most of the reputable restaurants in Chicago—all while ensuring me he was a culinary genius, if he could just learn to shut up. Looks like my friend was right.

"Well, it seems you have everything under control. I guess you really don't need me?"

"Nah, chef. Take a few days off. Enjoy the holidays."

"Got any plans?" I ask, then a thought occurs to me. "I'm sure I can cover dinner service on the twenty-third if you wanted to take advantage of us being closed for the holidays. Go visit family back in Chicago."

"No." He shrugs. "I appreciate the offer, but I think I'm just going to chill at home, watch movies. You know, the usual stuff?"

I realize how little I've gotten to know Logan since he arrived on my doorstep looking for a job. For all I know, the kid doesn't have family in Chicago or, shit, anyone at all. "My family has a big party—"

"I appreciate the offer, but I don't need a pity invite from my boss." He drops his eyes to the pot of soup, pushing the contents around with a spoon as if he needs something to do with his hands.

"It wasn't pity," I assure him.

"Maybe not, but still... If I'm not working, I prefer being alone during the holidays."

I don't ask more. It's clear he doesn't want to talk about it. "Sure thing." I pat Logan on the back. "If you change your mind, the offer stands. I'm going to go check on Gia."

"I've got everything covered," Gia says as soon as I approach the front counter. She doesn't bother looking up from cleaning the espresso machine.

"Are you sure?" I tease.

Besides myself, she's been working here the longest. She started out as a dishwasher when she was fifteen. She quickly worked her way up and we eventually shared managerial responsibilities under my mom. It wasn't until last year, after my mother's unexpected death, that I officially became Gia's superior and declared her the assistant manager.

She glances up from her task and quirks a brow at me.

"Fine, but if you need anything—"

"Go away, Scott," she scolds before returning to her work.

It's weird. I've spent so much time here, at the café. Even before my parents' car accident, I always felt like this place would fall apart if I wasn't constantly onsite. Maybe I'm just one of those jackasses who likes to micromanage their staff?

"Scott," Tilly calls out from the bookstore, saving me from annoying my team more than I already have for the day.

Gia giggles when I roll my eyes. "Yes," I call back, already making my way over.

"I have something for you." Tilly reaches down, struggling as she tries to bend, and retrieves a small box from under the counter.

I inspect it carefully as she hands it to me. "What's this?"

"Open it, silly." Her tone is innocent enough, but there's a glimmer in her eye that raises my suspicions.

"If it jumps out and attacks me, I'm kicking Jax in the nuts," I warn her. For whatever reason, my family has decided I'm the easiest target when it comes to their pranks. I carefully open the box and am shocked by what I see staring back at me from inside. "Tilly?"

"Hear me out..." she tries, but I'm quick to stop her.

"No."

"She's your fiancée, Scott. She needs a ring." Tilly grins. I should have known she had something devious going on in that head of hers.

"For a few more days," I remind her. "Besides, we told her mom that it was being sized."

"Good, then this can be your grand Christmas surprise. You can say you got it back sooner than expected."

"It's Grandma's ring, Tilly. Mom left it to you."

"And I'm loaning it to my brother and friend." She shrugs. "All it does is sit in my drawer."

"Are you sure?" I glance down at the box again, then back up at my sister, whose eyes light up like it's Christmas morning already. "Guessing that was a dumb question." I sigh.

"When are you going to give it to her? Oh, will you drop to a knee?" Tilly jumps up and down while clapping her hands.

"I'll figure it out," I say as I tuck the ring into my pocket. My next thought is *perfect timing* as the bell chimes over the door and I watch Scarlett and her mom walk into the bookstore.

"Welcome!" Tilly announces.

"Hey, Tilly," Scarlett greets my sister with a smile. "This is my mother—"

"Ginny," Tilly fills in, as if they're old friends.

"I still cannot get over how radiant you look." Mrs. Valentine tugs my sister into a hug while air kissing each of her cheeks. "See, Scarlett? Pregnancy has many positives. Even with every top-of-the-line skin product currently at my disposal, my skin has never been nicer than when I was carrying you."

"Oh, I forgot you stopped in here yesterday," Scarlett says through clenched teeth and a fake smile. "Without me."

"A good thing too. Otherwise your fiancé wouldn't have known about our dinner," Ginny scolds, before turning back around to greet me the same way she had my sister. "Scott," she hums.

"Good morning, Mrs. Valentine."

"Oh, call me *Mom*. We'll be family soon enough."

I struggle to maintain my smile. It's not that I have a problem with Scarlett's family. They're not perfect but we all have our own issues. It's more the fact that I've only ever called one other woman *Mom*, and she's not around to hear it anymore. It almost feels sacrilegious. Besides, I know I agreed to this, but the fakeness is starting to get to me. I really hate lying to people.

"I appreciate the offer of lunch and shopping," Ginny prattles on, clearly unaware of my discomfort. "I was beginning to worry I'd hardly get a chance to see you while we're here."

"It's been two days, and you've seen him twice." Scarlett's jaw is clenched so tight I'm worried she may crack a tooth.

"Oh, Scar," Tilly interrupts. "We got a new shipment in this morning. Some of those covers are..." My sister trails off, and if I didn't know any better, I'd think she might be drooling. She regains her composure with a smile. "Trust me, you should check them out."

Scarlett mouths, "Thank god," before walking over to the display.

"I'm going to see if our lunch is ready." I try to use this moment as an excuse to escape and get my bearings.

"Oh, Scott, before you go... would you mind helping me put these books out?" Tilly motions to the stack piled up next to her on the counter. "Jax is with the twins, and I don't want to risk lifting—"

"Where do you want them?" I cut her off and reach for the books.

Tilly smiles. "Oh, over there, on the new release display. Jax must have missed a few."

"Sure thing, sis." I take the stack and walk to where Scarlett is standing. She's reading the back of a book. I lean forward to inspect the cover. It has some big blue muscular guy and a woman on the front. "Looks interesting."

Scarlett shrugs her shoulders, but I also notice how her cheeks have turned an adorable shade of pink. *Is she blushing?*

"You know—" I start to say.

"Oh, hey," Tilly calls out. "Look at that."

Scarlett and I both turn to glance over our shoulders at my ridiculous sister, who's pointing towards the ceiling. I follow her line of sight and sigh. *Why am I even surprised?*

"Mistletoe!" Ginny announces, just as excitedly as Tilly appears to be. "You have to kiss. It's tradition!" I look down at Scarlett, her eyes wide with panic. "Come on, lovebirds," her mother urges.

"We don't have to," I whisper so that only Scarlett can hear me.

She gnaws on her bottom lip as her mom cheers us on from the sidelines. "No, we have to," she says as though she's being forced to do this. Which I guess she kind of is. "We're adults. It's just a kiss."

"Yup, no big deal," I tell her.

"A peck on the lips," Scarlett continues to pump herself up.

"What's taking you guys so long?" Tilly says. "It's like you've never kissed before."

I hate my sister.

Taking a deep breath, I decide it's better to just rip off the Band-Aid. So I lean down, brush my lips across Scarlett's for hardly a second, and quickly pull back again.

"Boo," my sister says unhelpfully. "That's not a mistletoe kiss."

"Yeah, that was pathetic," Ginny joins in.

"Let's just get this over with," Scarlett tells me, her jaw set tight in annoyance. "They aren't going to stop until we do."

Fuck it. If they want a mistletoe kiss, I'll give them one.

Scarlett jumps when she feels me thread my fingers through her hair and pull her face to mine. She's tense at first, but when I turn my head to get a better angle and lick her bottom lip, she melts into me, grabs my belt loop, and pulls me closer. The world spins and fades away around us as we continue to devour each other. I forget everything. Where we are, what led us to this point... None of it matters. All I care about is kissing this woman and the fact that nothing in my life has ever felt as right as this present moment.

When I pull back, Scarlett's eyes are closed as she attempts to even out her breathing. "Wow," she whispers.

"I think I need a cigarette," her mom says, fanning herself. "I'll be outside."

The interruption breaks whatever spell Scarlett was under and she quickly comes to. "Oh... um..." She adjusts her clothing and hair. "That was..."

"Hot," a voice answers for her, and I frown at my dipshit little brother, who I hadn't realized was even here.

"Fuck off, Jake."

"I just might," the horny little bastard replies. "I didn't know you were doing live shows."

"Don't you have a video store to manage?" I remind him.

"I can't believe that worked." He high-fives his twin as he saunters back over to his side of the business.

Tilly smiles, seemingly proud of herself. I'm about to say something when her phone rings and cuts me off. "Moore Books and Coffee," she sings in her best customer service voice.

"Come on." I drape an arm over Scarlett's shoulder and guide her in the direction of the restaurant. "Let's get some lunch." When she doesn't immediately answer, I glance down and see her fingers hovering above her kiss-swollen lips.

"Yeah, lunch..." she finally mumbles in reply.

14

Scarlett

It was just a kiss... Two adults sharing a simple yet somewhat intimate embrace...

Who the fuck am I kidding? It was two individuals becoming one as their lips locked together and their tongues danced to the rhythm of their souls, to an unspoken beat shared between them. Sounds dramatic but that was exactly how it felt. There was nothing sweet or innocent about that kiss. Hours later, my mouth still tingles, still tastes like him. I can't look at Scott without thinking about it, wondering when we'll do it again and if he wants to...

Oh my god, was I bad? Is that why he hasn't tried anything since?

Get it together, Scarlett...

First off, it's not like you're alone. No, you're walking around with your mom in tow. Not exactly the ideal conditions for another PG-13 make-out session. Still, we need to talk.

Don't we?

"Oh, Scarlett," my mother calls out from the dress rack behind me, while Scott's off towards the front of the boutique scoping out a present for his sister. "Look at this dress."

I plaster on my best smile and saunter over to the rack she's been combing through. She holds up a shimmery gold dress. "Wow," I say, impressed that she's actually picked out something I'd like for once. Not that she doesn't have a great sense of style, but this screams *me* and that isn't usually something my mother likes.

"Come on, try it on," she insists.

"When am I ever going to wear it?" Where she's from, dresses like this are perfect for the various red-carpet events she's known to attend. Here, in Tral Lake, not so much.

"There is always an occasion, Scarlett. Haven't I taught you that?"

"Yes, but you also used to say that special events aren't meant for what's hidden in your closet and always require something new."

Mom smiles, knowing I'm right. God forbid we ever wore the same dress twice. Nope, every outfit saw the light of day once, if it was lucky, then it was donated. Which, I admit, was a good feeling. I liked knowing that someone else would get use out of my things even if I couldn't.

"Amuse your mother." When I don't budge, she adds a dramatic, "Pleeeeease."

"Fine." I snatch the hanger from her hands and stomp towards the back of the store.

"Thank you," she calls after me, as if I had a choice.

I enter the first available dressing room and strip down. The bra I'm wearing is all wrong for the swooped cowl that extends almost down to my navel. This is the kind of gown you don't wear anything underneath, at the risk of something showing through. But for trying it on, undergarments are a necessary evil. It takes a lot of arranging and sucking in, but I'm finally able to pull the tight fabric over all my curves.

I glance in the mirror and am shocked. "Things sure have come a long way," I say aloud as I take a better look at myself.

There's not much give to the material but it does have built-in shapewear, which is perfect for me, as the lining was custom designed to snatch your waist without advertising its existence. Plus, the first layer is sewn in, to avoid rolling, and there's even a bottom flap, so you don't have to strip naked in a stall every time you have to use the restroom.

As much as I hate to admit it, mostly because this was my mother's choice, I love this dress on me. Still, though, when am I ever going to wear it?

"Scarlett, let me see," my mom orders from the other side of the door.

Taking a deep breath and hopefully standing an inch taller, I walk out to where she's waiting for me. Her eyes flick up and down before she steps forward to perform a proper inspection. My mom spins me around to get a better look at each angle.

"You look beautiful," she says after a moment of quiet contemplation. And I'm immediately taken aback. I don't think I've ever heard a direct compliment from this woman. Especially not when it comes to my appearance.

"Really?"

"Yes." She nods, and I smile as my chest fills with an odd warmth.

Is this what they call *motherly love*?

"Thank god designers have expanded their sizes." *And there it is.* The mother I know has returned with an all-too-familiar vengeance. "Scott," she calls out. "What do you think?"

"Mom, no, please." I don't want him to see how stupid I must look. I mean, it's a proven fact that dressing room mirrors are angled to make you appear thinner. Like a fucked-up funhouse, where the real horrors are the price tags.

Mom waves me off. "Where is that boy? Scott!"

The man himself magically appears as if he's been summoned. "Sorry, I was—" His jaw goes slack as he drinks me in. "Fuck." He scrambles to find words, and I can't be certain, but I think he wipes away some drool from his chin. "I mean, you look amazing."

"That'll be all." Mom shoos him away.

Scott looks at me confused, and I shrug, unsure what just happened myself. As if he doesn't know what else to do, he wanders over to a random clothing rack.

"For the most part, men are helpless when it comes to fashion. But the one thing you can count on is their blind reaction. And that, my dear, was a resounding yes," Mom tells me once Scott is out of earshot.

"How's everything going? Do you need me to grab something similar or perhaps a different size?" The clerk steps up to check on us, interrupting my train of thought. I'm still trying to wrap my head around the whirlwind of emotions that have hit me over the last few minutes.

"No, this one is perfect," Mom says as she inspects me from top to bottom for a second time, then looks back to the woman. "What do you have for accessories?"

The clerk's eyes light up with invisible dollar signs. "You're in luck. I have just the pieces set aside—they'll complement that design perfectly."

"Good. We'll take one of everything," she says to the woman before turning to me. "You're still a size seven in heels?"

I glance down at the price tag hanging just under my arm, and all the blood drains from my face. "Mom," I whisper harshly. "No."

As usual, she dismisses my concern with another wave of her manicured hand. "Pull a seven and a seven and a half."

"Yes, ma'am." The clerk scurries off, probably in search of something else she can tack on to the bill in hopes of cushioning her commission. Not that I blame her. I'd do the same if I were in her shoes, and it isn't like my mother doesn't have the money to spend. But still...

"Mom, this is too much and I'll never have an occasion to wear any of it."

"Hush. I've come to realize that you don't always have to shop with a particular event in mind. Sometimes, you just need to buy the dress and the right occasion to wear it finds you." Mom frowns for only a second before plastering on a smile. "Besides, it's Christmas. If there was ever a reason for me to splurge on my daughter, this is it."

It feels like it's been forever since I've had the urge to show my mother any sort of affection. But right now, I find myself wrapping my arms around her shoulders and hugging her. It's obvious the gesture is foreign to her as well, as it takes her a moment to reciprocate. But when she does, she squeezes me tightly.

15

Scott

My day with Scarlett has been a roller coaster of emotions, and I'm not sure if we've gotten off the ride yet. One moment, we're kissing, the next having lunch and pretending it didn't happen, then we're shopping. I'm not sure what happened in that dress store when I slipped away to find Tilly a last-minute Christmas gift. But her mood has shifted ever since we stepped back out onto the sidewalk to make our way down Main Street.

She's quieter, her prior enthusiasm about the upcoming holidays somehow soured. I'm guessing it has to do with her mother, but honestly I can't say for sure. I'm starting to realize there's a lot I don't know about Scarlett Valentine. More than that, there's a lot I want to know...

"What's the plan for the rest of the night?" I ask, hoping to break the awkward silence.

Maybe it's me? Maybe I've upset her somehow?

"Oh..." Scarlett says, then appears to consider her options for a second. "Nothing. We get to relax. Or, I mean, if you have stuff to do..."

"Today's Wednesday, right?"

She glances at her phone. "Yup, why?"

I smile as an idea takes shape in my head. "Are you up for going out?"

"Out?" She scrunches her brows together. "With my family?"

"No, just us." This finally has her smiling again.

Okay, maybe it's not me.

"What do you have in mind?" she asks.

"It's a surprise," I tell her. I'm not sure what's wrong, but I know one thing that helps me whenever I'm having a less-than-fantastic day.

"Really?" Scarlett questions as she looks up at the glowing sign looming above us like an oasis in the desert. Clearly she doesn't see it the same way I do.

"What? You don't like bowling?" I ask, honestly shocked by the idea.

"I wouldn't know. I've never... *bowled.*"

"Even better. Come on." I exit the vehicle, walk around the front of the truck, and let her out on the passenger side. She places her hand in mine as I help her down. "I promise you're going to have fun."

"Okay," she agrees but I can tell she doesn't exactly mean it.

The moment we enter the old alley, we're greeted by the sound of clacking pins, arcade music, and endless chatter. This place is packed, but lucky for me, it's Wednesday night, which means...

I glance around the open space until my eyes land on our usual spot, and sure enough, the guys are there. "Come on." I tug Scarlett along to the front desk to get shoes. Then go to the lockers to grab my own footwear and ball.

"You really like bowling," she says, as if it was some long-kept secret.

"Yeah, and trust me, after you try it, you'll understand."

"It's really busy in here."

"It usually is," I tell her. There isn't much to do around town, especially this time of year in the evenings, since most shops are closed. But not Tral Lake Lanes. It's the best hangout spot for us locals. "Lucky for us, we have a standing reservation."

"Us?" Just as she asks the question, a set of pins crashes in the distance and my little brother's celebratory hollering can be heard from across the room. Scarlett's gaze flicks to Jake before bouncing between a few other familiar faces. "Scott, I'm not sure about this. I don't want to intrude..."

"Scarlett, you've basically attended every family function and at least half of our Sunday lunches. Pretty sure they consider you an honorary Moore by now. Besides, Jake's always looking for a reason to show off in front of an audience—God knows he needs the ego boost." I roll my eyes and see a small smile start to form on her face.

Scarlett bites her lip, seemingly unsure, before she finally says, "Okay. But don't expect me to be any good."

"Trust me, you'll be fine." I grab her hand again and tug her over to our little group. "Mack's been bowling for years and still throws a gutter ball every other time."

"Hey!" Mack says, catching my off-handed comment. "I've gotten better." He smiles. "It's more like every third time now."

Everyone laughs at his expense, but Mack's always the first one to make fun of himself. He really is a good sport, win or lose. Unlike some of my other siblings...

"Why, Scarlett..." Jake beams in her direction. "I guess Scott's finally decided to introduce you to his inner circle."

Mack looks confused. "What do you mean *finally*?"

Robbie elbows Jake, his way of telling our baby brother to keep his mouth shut. And I send him a silent *thank you*. If Mack's out of the loop or just oblivious to the town gossip, it's better to keep him that way. It'll make it less awkward when this charade is all over and everything needs to go back to the way it was between Scarlett and me.

Something about that last thought tugs at my chest. Before I can figure out what, Letty pulls Scarlett in for a hug. "Oh, yay, another female. Now we can do teams and kick these boys' asses."

"I mean, I'm game if you wanna rough me up a bit," Jake says as he drapes an arm across Letty's shoulders. "But, babe, there's just a small problem with your plan here. There are two girls and four boys. I love you, but there's no way you're going to win."

"Want to bet?" Letty doesn't shy away from the challenge even if the odds appear to be against her.

"Um, I've never bowled before," Scarlett is quick to confess. "So please don't bet on me."

Jake's smile widens. "Whatcha thinking?"

"If I win..." Letty leans up and whispers in my brother's ear. Based on his expression and how he adjusts himself in his pants, I know she said something dirty. Letty pulls back with a smile. "And if you win, you can do whatever you want."

"Anything?" Jake attempts to clarify. "Even..."

"*Anything*," Letty repeats, sealing her promise with a handshake. Scarlett's expression is panicked throughout their entire exchange. "But you're right, Jakey-Poo. Things are a little uneven, so which one of you fellas wants to channel your feminine side for the night?" She looks at Robbie but shakes her head until her gaze lands on Mack. "You."

"Really?" Mack isn't the only one who's shocked. It doesn't make sense for Letty to pick the worst player on our team.

"Yup." She nods as if she knows something we don't. But that's Letty for you. She'll fake it until she makes it every time.

"Letty..." Scarlett cautions.

"Don't worry." She smiles. "Win or lose, I still *come...* out on top. Now, let's get a couple of pitchers and some balls rolling. It's time to show these boys what we're made of!"

"Oh my god!" Scarlett screams as she jumps up and down, clearly excited about her second strike in a row.

"I'm starting to think she played us," Jake leans in to whisper in my direction, but he's not quiet enough.

Letty frowns at him. "Don't be jealous, Jakey-Poo. Scar here just has God-given talent." She looks him up and down. "Something you're clearly lacking," Letty adds with a smirk.

"Your pussy begs to differ," my brother murmurs into his beer as he chugs it back.

Letty blows him a kiss, while Robbie quickly claps his hands together to get our attention. "All right, Scott, you're up."

As I pass Scarlett on my way to the ball return, I give her a high-five. "You're amazing."

She blushes. "Really? I've never done this before—I swear."

"I believe you," I assure her. "More importantly, though, are you having fun?"

She nods her head, her smile wide when she says, "I don't think I've ever had this much fun before. I can't believe I haven't stopped in here sooner. The nachos alone are worth it."

"You should try their burgers. They're the best in town," I say loud enough that, even at a distance, Letty can overhear me.

"I heard that!" Letty scolds from her seat, not taking too kindly to my dig at Harper's.

"Come on, Scott!" Jake hollers. "Flirt on your own time."

"Sorry. Good luck." I'm stunned as Scarlett presses a kiss to my cheek. The group collectively *aws* like a bunch of immature teens during lunch period.

I grab my ball, but instead of focusing on my lineup, I keep thinking about Scarlett, her lips, that kiss, how hypnotizing her breasts are when she jumps for joy...

"Dude!" Jake whines.

"Oh, leave him alone," Letty chimes in.

I ignore their bickering, and not because I'm trying to concentrate on my roll. No, because I honestly don't care. Closing my eyes, I take a deep breath, allowing muscle memory to kick in, and just like I have done hundreds of times before, I launch the ball down the lane.

Except, at the last minute, I hear the beautiful music of Scarlett's giggle, aim too far to the right, and roll a straight gutter ball. Jake and Robbie groan their disappointment.

"I guess it's true," Letty snickers. "Scotty doesn't know... how to bowl." She practically falls over laughing at her own lame joke. I hate that stupid movie. Not that it isn't funny. But ever since it came out, people take whatever opportunity they have to sing out the lyrics like it's the first time I've ever heard them.

Still, I'm not mad at Letty or bummed about my gutter ball. No, I'm all smiles as Scarlett's face is the brightest I've ever had the privilege of seeing it. We have a lot to do, and a long week ahead of us. But this brief reprieve, seeing how visibly happy she is... it's beyond worth it.

16

Scott

Great, even on my day off, I find myself waking up at three in the morning. At least, I assume it's that early. My eyes flick over to the window, where not even a stream of sunlight is peeking out. Then I reach over and grab my phone. Yup, three-fucking-fifteen on the dot.

I guess it's not in vain, seeing as I need to stop by the orchard and load up the apples Eli keeps in his cooler for me. I could store them at the café but it's better this way, ensures they don't get bruised or anything in my tiny fridge. I need to prepare the apple filling for the coffee rings so I can start assembly tomorrow.

Resigned to the fact that I have too much to do to lie around and stare at the ceiling in hopes I fall back asleep, I sit up and glance over at Scarlett, who is fortunate enough to be knocked out cold. Then, careful not to wake her, I slide off the bed and make my way across the room. My hand clutches the curtain, about to tug it back and head to the bathroom, when I'm suddenly rooted to the spot at the sound of Scarlett... *moaning?*

No, there's no way—

"Please... don't stop..." she whispers in her sleep.

Common sense decides to speak up for the first time since this whole fake relationship started. It tells me to leave. As desperate as I am to hear her moan again, it's wrong... *so very wrong*.

"Scott," she calls out, and I freeze, assuming I've been caught being the perverted bastard I've apparently become. "I want to come... I've been such a good girl."

Fuck, fuck, fuck...

I'm fucked. Because common sense only made a brief appearance before it decided to leave the building. And now everything inside me is telling me to stay, watch. Because, holy fuck, Scarlett Valentine is having one hell of an intense dream—and it's about me.

I've been standing in the dark long enough that my eyes have adjusted, allowing me to see that she has the blanket pushed down to her waist. I watch as one of her hands slinks across her stomach and, yup, I've just secured my seat in hell because when she slips her fingers beneath the waistband of her sleep pants, instead of giving her privacy, I take a step closer to get a better look.

Her back arches off the bed slightly as I assume she found her own sweet spot. What I wouldn't give to be able to see where that is. I mean, if I'm already damned, might as well get the full picture. As stupid as I am for intruding on this moment, at least I have retained enough sensibility not to attempt to join in. That's what I tell myself anyway.

My feet remain cemented to the floor as she continues to pleasure herself, grinding her hips and moaning my name. It takes every ounce of restraint I possess to keep from taking care of the painful morning wood presently tenting my pants. Although doing so would solve one of my problems, the truth is... good intentions aren't what's holding me back—no, it's the fact I don't want to miss a single fucking moment of what's going on in front of me.

"*Oh, Scott... I'm going to...*" Scarlett cries out her release, and I no longer care about earning myself a permanent spot on Santa's naughty list, because it was the most magnificent thing I've ever heard, *seen too*. The only thing that could have made it better was if I had been the one to do it for her. But I guess knowing the dream version of me was along for the ride will have to be good enough.

Before I make a bad situation worse, I leave. But not to the bathroom. No, I go home because one more second in that cabin and I'll be beyond fucked.

Do you know what I love about peeling apples? Getting lost in the repetition of the action, how you get into this groove, which then allows your mind to open. I've come up with some of my best recipes while in the zone like this. Today, though, it's a fucking curse. Because my thoughts can't help but drift back to Scarlett. My imagination is running wild, conjuring up images of her fingers thrusting in and out of her—

"What are you doing?"

I jump at Logan's question, like some teenager whose mom walked in on him watching porn. "Nothing," I say a little too forcefully as guilt has my heart racing in my chest. "I wasn't doing anything."

Logan crosses his arms over his chest and studies me. "Really?" He lifts a pierced brow as shame boils over and drips down my forehead. "Because it looks like you're in here cooking when you're supposed to be on vacation."

I let out a giant sigh of relief. "Oh, yeah... this is personal, not work."

He remains silent, clearly not satisfied with my answer.

"It's for the Christmas coffee rings. My family makes a bunch and gives them out each year. My kitchen can't exactly handle the volume, so I do all my prepping and cooking at work." It's not a lie. My grandma could hardly handle the few dozen she'd make in her home kitchen. Mom added to that list when she included one for all the business owners in town, in addition to close friends, so now it's double that.

"Makes sense." Logan continues to eye me with suspicion. "So then, why do you look so guilty?"

"I'm not guilty," I say, once again a little too high-pitched. I clear my throat. "I'm not. It's my business. I can use the kitchen as I wish."

Logan leans in, searching for the lie hidden between the truth. Bastard is like a bloodhound for self-condemnation. Pulling back, he smiles. "Need help?"

"Help?" I parrot, and he nods to the large bushel of apples. "Oh, yeah, help... if you have time."

"Well, since it looks like you already pulled today's bread to rise, have muffins in the oven, and the doughnuts iced—yeah, I have some time."

I shrug. Old habits die hard. "Here, you peel and core, and I'll get started on the filling."

I take the already prepped apples, slice them up, and add them to my giant commercial kettle. When I was little, my grandma had this big twelve-quart kettle that hardly fit on her stovetop with the overhead range. She'd pack that bad boy to the brim with apples, and it would make enough filling for about six to eight rings. She'd have to repeat the process several times, in batches. But now, thanks to technology, I only need to do it once. While there are a few things I won't ever change about how her rings are made, that is one convenience I'm thankful for.

Logan takes a slice of apple and plops it into his mouth. He hums his satisfaction. "What kind are these?"

"Jonathan," I inform him.

"Really? I didn't think people grew those anymore." He grabs another slice. "My grandma used to bake with them all the time."

"Mine too," I say. He's right. Jonathan apples don't bode well in high volumes and have become increasingly hard to find. Fortunately for me, I have a guy. "Eli still grows 'em. He likes them for his cider blend. Besides him, there are a few others who are adamant about using them in their classic recipes."

"I take it you're one of those few."

I shrug. "What can I say? I've tried other varieties, but none of them come close to the real thing. These little guys are perfectly tart and balance out the sweetness."

"I get it." Logan nods. "There are just some things you don't change."

"Exactly," I tell him as our hands stay on task. The hour flies by as we talk about different foods and recipes. It's impressive, hearing about how this kid's mind processes flavors and comes up with new combinations.

"Oh, Scott," Gia interrupts with a mocking tone, and I have the sudden feeling that she's about to ruin what was turning out to be a good morning. "You have a customer."

Great, I'm guessing my not-so-soon-to-be mother-in-law has come to share some new words of wisdom with me.

"I'll only be a minute," I tell Logan. I notice he's almost done with the peeling and coring. "But if I'm not back in time, here's the recipe." I grab the folded piece of paper from the locked cupboard. Before handing it to him, I pull my hand back, hoping he understands my seriousness. "Do not deviate whatsoever."

"Sure thing, chef."

He tries to snatch the paper from my fingers, but I continue to hold it just out of reach. "And this is top secret." He rolls his eyes, so I add, "No joke."

"Fine, I won't change it or steal it... I promise." He holds up a pinky.

I ignore the gesture and give him the card. Taking a calming breath, I wash up and prepare myself for whatever new hell is waiting for me at the front of the store. When I finally walk out to greet her, I'm pleasantly surprised to find that I was only half-right. There is a Valentine woman standing by the front counter, but she also happens to be the one I've been aching to see.

"Hey." I step closer, lean forward, and rest an arm between us. "You look amazing."

Scarlett blushes as she glances down at the drink she's holding. "Thank you," she says, but doesn't sound so sure about that. "I'm sorry to bother you. I just—"

"You're not bothering me." I smile. "What's up?"

"Oh... um... you weren't there when I woke up. So I wanted to check in, wasn't sure if something came up."

"Sorry about that. Force of habit. It seems I can't sleep in, so I figured I'd stop by the shop and get a head start on making Christmas rings for everyone."

"That makes sense," she says, her tone a bit reserved. "I'm taking my niece to the Christmas Village at the orchard tonight. Are you... are you still coming?"

My mind flashes to the scene from this morning. Scarlett's head tossed back, her spine perfectly arched like she was offering herself up to me, as I learned exactly what *coming* for her looked like.

Stop it. As far as you're concerned, that never happened.

When Scarlett's pouty lips form a frown, I realize I haven't answered her. "Yes, tonight. I wouldn't miss it for anything."

"Are you sure? I mean, you don't have to—"

"Scarlett." I lock gazes with her. "I promise I'm looking forward to it."

She smiles, but it doesn't quite reach her eyes. "Okay," she says, sounding unconvinced.

Once again, this woman has me losing all sense. Because I do something I really have no right doing while every fiber of my being tells me *she needs this.* I walk around the counter and stand in front of her. Scarlett's breath hitches in her throat as I thread my fingers through her hair and pull her mouth to mine. Although this kiss doesn't last as long as the one from yesterday, the sensation is just as intense—if not more so.

God, this was a terrible idea.

Because now I'm half-hard and have to go back into the kitchen and deal with Logan. Hopefully his presence alone will be enough to help kill the obvious bulge in my pants. But then, when Scarlett rewards me with a satisfied grin and I see that whatever doubt had plagued her before is gone, I realize (a little too late) that jerking off is going to be the key to my survival this holiday season.

"I'll see you tonight," I tell her, while reminding myself to keep an extra bottle of lotion handy.

"Okay." Her fingers touch her lips as she turns towards the exit.

"Scar," I call out. She spins around with a confused expression on her face. I hold up her to-go bag. "Forget something?"

She reaches out for her muffin. A bolt of electricity passes through me as her fingers brush mine, and her cheeks are flushed as she clutches her food close to her chest. "Thank you," she says awkwardly before scurrying off, appearing a little shell-shocked

Me too, babe. Me too.

17

Scarlett

IF I THOUGHT I was confused after what I've deemed *the mistletoe incident* yesterday, well, now I'm downright flabbergasted. I was able to rationalize that first kiss. No matter how incredible it may have felt, how his taste lingered on my lips all day, the fact remained that it was forced. Orchestrated by Tilly, while Scott had no choice but to perform as the diligent fiancé.

Acting Lesson 101: Kisses shared on stage are not real... even if they feel really, really good.

Because you put yourself into those roles, pretend to be other people, so whatever you feel in the moment is cultivated from that. Nine times out of ten, a real-life repeat doesn't have the same effect and you both quickly realize it was all part of the show, the show of playing the part.

But the kiss at the café was different. There was no one sitting in the audience, no outside influences looking to force his hand—or should I say his mouth? This morning it was just Scott. So, it has to be real, right? Or is he just one of those method actors who never turns it off until the performance is wrapped up for good?

I need help!

I pull out my cell and check to see if Hannah has read my text yet. She hasn't. As her boss, it makes me happy to know she isn't spending her shift with her eyes glued to her screen. But as her friend, I'm pissed off. She got me into this mess and now she needs to get me out of it.

Me: HELP!
Me: SOS!

The little circles still haven't turned blue, which means she's not looking. *Damn it.*

"I did it!" Brittany cheers as she gives Scott a high-five.

My eyes flick over to where they're standing at a little dart-throwing game. He looks genuinely happy to be at the orchard with me and Brittany. I know he said he wanted to be here but saying it and meaning it are two different things.

"Are you sure you haven't done this before?" he asks her.

She giggles. "No, Mommy would never let me play with sharp stuff."

He looks around the room. Then he leans in and whispers, "This will be our little secret."

"Here you go, hun." The attendant grabs an obscenely large stuffed moose and hands it to my niece.

"Look, Auntie Rea-Rea. It's so big and fluffy!" she squeals.

"It sure is," I say with a chuckle. Good thing I know my mom travels on a private jet, otherwise I'm not sure how they'd fit the stuffed toy in their luggage. "Okay, what's next?" I ask, my eyes scanning the various booths for options. I feel like we've done almost everything Eli has to offer. We met Santa, took a sleigh ride, ate too many donuts, watched apple carving, and played several carnival games.

"Hmm..." Brittany taps her chin. "Oh, I know." She grabs Scott's hand and tugs him away. "Come on, Auntie Rea-Rea."

I jog after them. "Where are we going?"

Scott shrugs. "I don't have a clue," he says with a big grin on his face.

"Come on," Brittany continues to urge—it's clear she's growing impatient with our adult legs; they can't keep up with the whims of an overeager seven-year-old. She doesn't stop until we all arrive at a little photo booth. "I want to do pictures."

"Right on. Do you want me to hold your moose while you go in?" Scott offers.

"No, silly, all of us." She shoves Scott into the tiny compartment, then grabs for my hand. "Come on!"

"Coming!" I huff out a breath as I attempt to squeeze into the booth alongside them. The seat is barely big enough for Scott and me to share, so I snuggle in close to him. Brittany hops up on our laps, a leg thrown over my left thigh and Scott's right, and holds her new stuffed animal.

"All right, Brittany, important question for you," Scott says in a serious tone. "Do we start with happy faces or silly ones?"

"Oh, happy for sure."

"You got it, kid. Here." He hands her a ten-dollar bill to insert into the machine.

I mentally add it to the growing total I owe him. He didn't let us pay for lunch yesterday. I get that he owns the place, but still, I don't do handouts. We all have businesses to run and can't go around giving freebies to everyone we know. Especially in a small town.

Then he bought my mom a tin of chocolates from Patty's when we were out shopping, followed by a new pair of gloves for me because I lost mine—not to mention, he wouldn't let me pay anything for bowling. Which brings us to now. So far tonight, he's paid for our dinner at the diner, for us to get into the Christmas Village, and pretty much everything else since we stepped foot on the orchard. I've tried to pay, believe me, but Scott Moore is sneaky.

Brittany calls out the expression at the start of each countdown, while Scott and I have no choice but to appease the giggling tyrant. "Happy face... sad face... oh, now goofy ones... kissy faces!"

I freeze on that last one, no better than a deer in headlights, as Scott grips my chin and pulls my mouth to his. Our lips lock and the camera flashes. Like twice before, my mouth tingles and every inch of my skin is desperate to find out if the sensation will be as effective on other parts of my body.

"Are you okay?" Scott asks, and I realize the photos are done and my niece is already out of the booth waiting for the prints.

"Um... yeah... just tired," I reply, trying to play off the fact that I lose all my senses the second he touches me.

"It's all that sugar. I warned you you'd crash."

"But those donuts were so yummy." I wipe my mouth, paranoid that I'm drooling at the mere thought. Scott leans forward and kisses the top of my head.

Yup, there's that tingle.

"Come on," he says, reaching down to grab my hand. "I think we're all about ready to call it a night. I bet you five bucks she passes out on the drive back."

I glance in Brittany's direction, watching as her mouth opens into a big yawn. "Heck, she'll probably conk out before we reach the gates and you'll have to carry her to the car."

As nice as it's been, being stuck in this little booth with Scott's thighs pressed up against mine, I force my legs to move. Scott follows behind me.

"What do you think?" Brittany shoves the pictures into Scott's hand before the largest smile I've ever seen spreads across his face.

"These are amazing. What do you think?"

It takes me a moment to find the words because... "They're perfect," I whisper.

"Right?" He's quick to agree. *Clearly, I didn't say it quietly enough.* "Can I print extras?" Scott inspects the machine until he finds the correct option and pays for two more sets. "All right, ladies, are you ready to go home?"

Brittany and I glance at each other, our aunt-niece telepathic link strong. Then we turn back to Scott and yell, "No!" In unison. I take her hand as we make a mad dash to the mini-donut and apple cider stand.

"You're both going to have stomachaches," Scott calls out. I don't have to look behind me to know he's amused by our antics. I can hear the laughter in his tone as he chases after us.

18

Scott

"I CAN CARRY HER," Scarlett offers as I tuck her niece tighter to my chest.

"It's fine. She's light as a feather," I say.

Scarlett was right. After their last serving of mini-donuts and cider, Brittany was too exhausted to walk back to the car and quickly passed out in my arms. She didn't even stir when we buckled her into her seat or when we took her out again once we arrived at the inn.

"Okay." Scarlett wrings her hands together as we walk down the path to her sister's room. Fortunately, the inn itself consists of a long strip of rooms with a covered exterior walkway. So it isn't much of a trek from the car to get her here. Granted, the kid is so light I could probably navigate the entire town with her on my back and forget she's even there.

We stop outside the third door and Scarlett knocks. It only takes a moment for her stepsister to answer. Trisha takes one look at her daughter and frowns. "How much sugar did you give her?"

"Oh, this." Scarlett points to her niece. "I didn't give her sugar."

"Oh, really?" Trisha questions. It's clear she's not buying that story one bit.

"She's a total lightweight. Three shots of tequila." Scarlett claps her hands. "And out like a light."

For the first time since I've met her, Trisha smiles. "God, you're a terrible influence."

"Let me guess, too much sugar?" Kasey comes up behind her, placing a hand on his fiancée's shoulder.

"Just feed her one of those awful green smoothies you drink every morning. It'll balance everything out," Scarlett tells him.

"Here, I'll take her." Kasey reaches out and scoops Brittany into his arms.

"Thank you again," Trisha says when he leaves to tuck the little girl into bed. "It feels like forever since we've been able to have a night alone together."

"Can't Mom watch her for you?" Scarlett asks.

"You know her... If it's anything more than an hour or two, she gets all flakey. But even when we do get time alone, we're never really *alone*. We're always off to attend these big award ceremonies or have people stopping him on the street for a selfie. I love that he's so humble and kind to his fans, but sometimes I just wish..."

"You could have a moment alone," Scarlett finishes for her.

"Yeah." The two women share a strange look, before Trisha says, "Anyway, it's getting late."

"Um... yeah, we should get to bed. Big day prepping tomorrow," Scarlett replies.

"Don't forget we've got a spa day with Mom," Trisha adds with a forced smile.

"Shit," Scarlett mumbles. "I totally forgot."

"Sorry, but a sudden bout of willful amnesia isn't going to get you out of this one. If you force me to spend the entire day listening to Mom complain you aren't there, I'm going to die a slow and painfully annoying death, then come back as a ghost and switch every coffee you order from here on out to *decaf*."

"You wouldn't." Scarlett presses a palm to her chest and gasps. Trisha crosses her arms. Her only reply is a pointed stare that screams she's not joking in the least bit. "Fine," Scarlett groans. "I'll move a couple of things around."

Trisha flashes her a satisfied grin in response.

"You and me..." Kasey reappears, gesturing a hand between us. "We have business to discuss tomorrow."

"Business?" I parrot back. *Did I forget something?*

"You, me, and your best friend. I talked to Jax when we were out visiting the shops earlier today. He said he'd take us around to do some location scouting tomorrow."

Okay, at least I didn't actually forget something, seeing as this is the first time I'm hearing about concrete plans. I'm sure I have a million squealing texts from Jax. I've just been so caught up in spending time with Scarlett and Brittany I never thought to check my phone.

"Sounds like a plan," I tell Kasey with a curt nod.

We all say our goodnights, leaving just Scarlett and me alone for the first time since my *Peeping Tom* incident this morning. My heart races as we continue back down the path in silence. The sound of our boots crunching in the snow is almost deafening. And before I know it, we're standing under Scarlett's little porch light, the only thought in my head...

We got here way too fast.

She opens the front door and waits on the threshold. "Are you coming in?" she asks me.

"No," I tell her, shocking not only Scarlett but myself too.

"No?" she repeats with a frown. Then her shoulders sag. "It's fine. I get it. I know I've been asking a lot, and tonight... well, it was incredible. But I can't keep asking you to pretend. Don't worry about this whole thing." She waves a hand between us. "I'll come up with something—"

Before I can think better of it, I pull her into my arms and crash my mouth onto hers, silencing whatever she was about to say. Scarlett doesn't hesitate to tug me closer, but I stop us from stepping inside.

"Scarlett," I say against her lips. She hums her acknowledgment. "I can't go in there."

That knocks her out of whatever daze she seemed to be in. "What? Why?"

I sigh. "Today... yesterday... no, more like every second we spend together is amazing. Honestly, these past few days have been the best ones of my life. But that kiss, then this morning..."

"What happened this morning?" She cocks her head to the side and studies me.

Although this is one dirty secret I would love to take to my grave, nothing more can happen between us until I'm completely honest with her. I know how that sounds. It's a weird hill to die on with your *fake* fiancée. But it's starting not to feel all that fake anymore.

"This morning." I swallow hard. "You were dreaming." Her face goes pale as realization appears to set in. "I should've left, but you were so gorgeous and those little noises you were making..." I rub at the back of my neck, where there's a sudden accumulation of sweat despite the chill in the air. "So I stayed and watched you—"

"You..." Her cheeks turn a deep shade of red as all the pieces click together.

"And now, after spending this incredible evening together... Fuck... I just can't go into that small little cabin and pretend that I don't want you. That I don't know how beautiful you sound when you come. I can't lie and say that I'm going to sleep, when what I'm really gonna do is stay up all night hoping like hell you do it again."

"You want me?"

I chuckle at the absurd question, because out of everything I said—*admitted*—that's what stuck. Not to mention, who the fuck wouldn't want her?

"Sorry... *want* is an understatement. I *need* to touch you, taste you, fuck you. I'm starving for you, and I—"

This time, Scarlett is the one to cut me off with another searing kiss. "I want you too," she tells me. "You're all I can think about. That kiss... dreaming about what your lips could do to the rest of me..."

The thread of self-restraint that's been keeping me from crossing that line thins by the second. "Are you sure? I know we've been treading dangerous waters the past couple of days, but if we do this, there's no changing—"

"I know..." Scarlett grabs me by the belt loop, and I don't resist as she tugs me through the door. "And I don't care." As soon as it shuts behind us, there's no holding back.

I crash my mouth onto hers and my first thought is that her lips are sweet. They taste like sugar and apples. I savor the foreign flavors until I find the one that is uniquely *her* beneath it all. "You taste incredible," I groan as my hands reach down, grip her ass, and lift her up.

Scarlett wraps her legs around my waist and we continue to devour each other as we make our way to her bed. She's at the perfect position to rock against my firm cock. As soon as my legs tap the metal frame, I lay Scarlett back and cover her body with mine. My lips travel down her jaw, until she grips my head and leads me to the places she wants me to go. When I reach the collar of her sweater, I sit up enough so that I can clutch the hem and rip it over her head. Scarlett smiles, her soft curls a mess as she looks up at me.

"You're fucking breathtaking," I tell her and I mean it. I've never seen something more perfect than the woman in front of me. She turns away from me at the compliment. But I refuse to let her fold in on herself, not this time, so I grip her chin and pull her focus back to me. My eyes lock with hers.

"Do you have any idea how drop-dead-fucking-gorgeous you are, Scarlett Valentine?"

"Scott..." She tries to pull away again, but I hold strong. "Please..." she says while chewing on her bottom lip.

It's clear this isn't a habit I can break in a single evening. Not that I wouldn't love to try, but based on the few encounters I've had with Scarlett's mother, I gather there is a lot of baggage there—baggage that includes a huge pile of self-doubt.

"Fine." Instead of continuing to argue, I decide to distract her with another searing kiss. "But this conversation isn't over," I vow against her lips. "I'm going to remind you every day, replace every negative word you've ever heard and have locked up in that head of yours, until you can look me in the eye when I call you beautiful. Then, do you know what will happen?" I pull away and gaze down at her swollen lips. She still appears a little dazed.

"What?" she asks on an exhale, almost as if she forgot to breathe for a moment.

I flash her a half-cocked smile. "Well..." I trace a finger down the smooth buttons of the blouse she had hidden under her sweater, undoing each one as I go. "You're just going to have to be a good girl and find out." When my hand lands on the hem, her top falls open. "Absolute perfection." I gaze down at her large breasts, testing the strength of the fabric holding them in place, her nipples like little diamonds threatening to poke a hole through the lace bra.

Burying my face into her neck, I proceed to taste her as I knead one of her voluptuous breasts. Scarlett's legs spread below me, and my cock rubs her through the several layers of fabric still separating us—begging to be let out to play.

My lips continue to work their way down, licking and sucking each inch of flawless skin as it's revealed. Even though I'm trying to take my time, savor her, it's not long before my mouth lands on the center of her stomach just above the waistband of her jeans. Scarlett's breath hitches as

I take the first button between my teeth. It pops open with a snap. I repeat the action until she can raise her hips and I can tug her legs free, pressing kisses from her inner thigh down her calf as I go.

With one layer of clothing successfully tossed aside, I allow my tongue to travel along the path my lips laid out before it. I glance up when I reach the junction of her thighs. Scarlett's eyes are on me as she sucks her bottom lip between her teeth. Without breaking eye contact, my mouth latches on to her mound, and I lick her through the lace of her thong, getting my first real taste of the meal I plan to feast on.

Scarlett lies there, head thrown back and chest heaving, as I remove the last barrier separating me from what I crave the most. My thumbs run up her smooth lips before parting them. I take a modest sample, a quick lick of her clit. Her body jolts as her flavor coats my tongue.

"God, your pussy is so fucking delicious. Best part...? It's all mine," is the last thing I say before I delve deeper and devour her. My fingers and tongue work in perfect synchrony as I play with her clit and thrust in and out of her center. "I could eat this pussy forever," I say against her slick flesh.

Scarlett's legs tense as her orgasm approaches, and her thighs clench around my head, muffling her beautiful cries as she comes apart. Her juices explode on my tongue as I lap up every drop. She's still breathless as I come face to face with her.

"Wow," she pants, jolting back when my fingers find her clit again. "Wait... I don't think I—"

"You're so fucking gorgeous," I tell her. "But as much as I love tasting you when you come, I want to watch your face this time."

"But I can't—" Her statement is cut off as her eyes roll back and she squirms below me. It doesn't take long before her legs go straight, and she traps my hand within the clutches of her thighs.

"That's it, Angel. Come for me," I urge her. "Let me see how pretty you are as you cream on my fingers." It's not long before she rewards me with the most beautiful sight I've ever had the privilege of seeing. I brush her damp hair back from her face. "That was perfect." I don't give her a chance to look away as I capture her mouth with mine.

Scarlett reaches for the hem of my sweater, making her intentions clear. I strip it off for her, along with my undershirt, and toss them both to the floor. Her eyes go wide as her nails trace along the pattern tattooed on my left pec. "Wow," she says in obvious amazement. "I didn't realize how far the design went." She glances down at my abdomen with an arched brow.

I chuckle. "Sorry, Angel, nothing's hidden down there."

"Angel?"

"Yup." I smile. "Your pussy is soft." I run my fingers through her slick mess, gathering up some of her juices. "Creamy... and tastes like strawberries." I suck the digits clean. "It's just like eating angel food cake."

Scarlett pulls me in, sampling her flavor on my lips as she undoes my pants and begins to push them down. She gasps as soon as my cock is freed from the confines of my boxers and lands hard on her leg.

"I thought you said you weren't hiding anything down there?" I glance down, confused by the accusation, until she says, "You have an anaconda in your pants."

I laugh against her lips as I position myself between her legs. "You can take me," I assure her. But before I let myself get too carried away, I reach into my wallet to grab a condom—grateful I always keep one on hand just in case. Especially with the way my family likes to reproduce. I toss my pants onto the rest of the clothes we started to pile on the floor. "Tell me," I say as I rub my tip between her folds. "How do you want me to fuck you?"

She hums, as if she needs a moment to consider her options. She seems nervous before she finally answers, gnawing on her lip in the most adorable way. "From behind."

I let her up so that she can get onto her hands and knees, and I'm beyond thankful for the new view of her glistening center. I can't resist the temptation and get another fix, my tongue delving between her folds and savoring her from this new angle.

"I'm never going to get enough of this pussy," I say as I slide on the protective layer of latex, quickly line myself up, and am immediately met by resistance. All that foreplay, she's practically dripping for me, and yet it still feels like it's her first time. "You're so fucking tight," I tell Scarlett as I slowly work my way inside. She cries out and her face drops to the bed as I fill her to the brim. I pull out to the halfway mark, then thrust back inside again. I continue at this languid rhythm as Scarlett mews beneath me. "It's like you were made to take my cock."

"Harder," she moans.

I pick up my pace, mesmerized by the image of my cock disappearing inside her, watching her ass cheeks jiggle with each thrust. "I love this ass," I tell her, tapping a heavy palm against one cheek for good measure. Scarlett moans and clenches, clearly enjoying a little rough play, so I do it again, but a little harder this time.

"Fuck," she groans into the bedsheets. "More..."

I do as she asks, increasing my tempo and spanking her ass until the flesh turns a healthy shade of red. She drops closer to the mattress as her orgasm approaches. "Stay on your knees," I tell her.

"I can't... I need to come..."

I grasp her hips and roll us over so that we're both vertical and she's riding my lap. My free hand then wraps around her throat to clutch her jaw. I turn her face so I can admire her profile. "That's it, Angel. Now you can come."

As she continues to fuck herself on my cock, my fingers slide off her hip to rub her clit. "*Fuck, fuck, fuck...*" she cries out as her pussy clamps me tightly. The pressure sends me over the edge. My lips slam against hers, and I swallow down the rest of her cries and feed her my own as we come together. "That was..." she pants when she can finally speak again, slumping over to lie beside me.

"Incredible," I finish for her.

"I forgot how good sex could be. Then again, for me, I don't think it was ever like that." She shakes her head. "Just... *wow*."

I turn to face her, my head propped up with one hand as the other traces patterns on her soft stomach. "I take it it's been a while." I'll probably regret broaching the subject, but she brought it up first, so the timing seemed appropriate.

"Define *a while*." She chuckles. "According to Hannah, I've reached the point of revirginization."

"How long does that take?"

Scarlett shrugs. "She says twelve months."

Fuck, that *is* a long time. But then I remember she moved to town *over* a year ago, and now I have a sudden urge to find out the guy's name and kick his ass.

Who the fuck am I? I'm starting to sound a lot like my brothers and I'm not sure that's a good thing...

I'm so lost in my head, wondering who was in this bed before I was, that I don't realize Scarlett's still talking until she answers my lingering question without me even having to ask it.

"But since it's been double that, I'm not sure if it makes me an ultra-virgin or something. Honestly, I don't know..." she rambles on. "Hannah says the craziest shit sometimes." She laughs.

Two years? I find myself grinning as a strange sense of satisfaction settles in my chest.

"So," she draws out the word. "Since we're on the subject, what about you? How long has it been since your last... you know?"

"Not twelve months," I tell her.

"What? Like three weeks?"

Ah, that's what she really wants to know.

I decide to stop evading the subject and ease her worry. "No, more like four months."

"Four months?"

I see the unspoken part of the question on her face. But, no, we aren't taking this conversation to that level. She really doesn't need to hear the details about how I had a brief, sex-driven summer fling with Kat, a girl who was helping wait tables at Harper's during her break from college. The relationship was nothing but a bunch of heatwave-induced lust, and it was over the second the record-scorching temps broke. I won't lie, though. It's nice to see I'm not the only one with green eyes tonight.

"Yup, but it doesn't matter."

"It doesn't?"

"Nope." I cup her breast in my open palm. "I'm far more interested in this moment," I say, then suck her nipple between my teeth. "Nothing else matters."

She combs her fingers through my hair and pulls me tighter against her chest. "I like that," she mumbles, and I suck harder while she arches her back.

I release her tit with a pop. "But if we're gonna go another round, we're gonna need some supplies."

"Supplies?"

"Yup." As much as I hate to do it, I push up from the bed, remove the used condom, and pull on my pants. "Food... and more condoms."

"I might have one of those things covered." Scarlett bites her lip as her eyes dart to her nightstand. I follow her line of sight, pull out the top drawer, and sure enough there's a brand-new value pack nestled next to an intimidating army of vibrators. I arch a brow, and she chuckles. "What? A girl has needs."

Surplus in hand, I jump back into bed and pull Scarlett on top of my waist. Her hair curtains her face as she smiles down at me. I brush it back to get a better view. "Don't worry, I'll make sure that pussy of yours is well taken care of."

"They... they don't bother you?"

I can only assume she means the vibrators. I shake my head. "No. Maybe one day soon your battery-powered boyfriends can join us. But right now..." I kiss the column of her neck. "I want you all to myself."

"We still need food," she reminds me.

I tug her face back to mine. "You'd be surprised what I can whip up with a few pantry staples," I say, then seal my words with another kiss.

19

Scarlett

MY HEAD RESTS ON Scott's chest. This morning the roles have reversed and it's my arm and leg draped over his. I've never been much of a cuddler. Didn't matter if I was the big or little spoon, I always felt trapped and had to escape within five minutes. But now, waking up tangled in Scott's arms, I dread having to move. But unfortunately, my bladder demands it.

As gently as I can, I crawl out of bed. If I'm lucky, I can take care of business fast and be back under the covers before he knows I'm gone. I stand from the bed and stretch my limbs. Every inch of my body hurts in the most delicious way possible. Muscles I haven't used in what feels like forever are now beyond exhausted. I put on Scott's discarded shirt and, out of habit, grab my phone from the nightstand as I sneak away to the bathroom. My legs still wobbly from our sexcapades.

When I open my lock screen, it's no surprise that there are a hundred texts from Hannah.

> **Hannah: Sorry. I'm here. The newlyweds clogged the toilet and things got a little messy.**

Hannah: But don't worry, everything is all cleaned up and operational. Told them condoms belong in the trash can. You'd think every adult would know that by now.
Hannah: What's going on?
Hannah: Babe? Are you okay?
Hannah: Who do I need to kill?
Hannah: I knew it! The sweet, quiet ones are always the crazy axe murderers.
Hannah: Okay, Scar, real funny. What's going on?
Hannah: Scarlett?
Hannah: Okay, I just saw you and Scott drop off the kiddo and walk back to your place. So I know you're alive. Still not cool. Answer me!
Hannah: The only acceptable reason to be ignoring me right now is because Scott is balls-deep in your vag. If not, our friendship is over.

I glance at the time and see it's still early enough that she should be here. Sheila is known for being late for shift change. I'd fire her if I wasn't desperate for staff as it is.

As much as I want to get dressed and talk to Hannah in person, I also want to crawl back into bed and pray Scott doesn't regret what we did and, if I'm lucky, wants to do it again.

Me: Busy?
Hannah: You're a cunt!
Me: Sorry...
Hannah: Just tell me that this radio silence is because your hands were full... playing with his dick.
Me: We did it.

My phone vibrates immediately with an incoming call. "Hello," I whisper.

"You did it?" she screams. "As in had sex, not played Parcheesi?"

"Yes, we had sex. If you can even call it that."

"Did he insert his dick into you? Because if he did, then, yes, I'd call that sex."

"Yes, he did. Several times." I smile just thinking about it. "It's just... I've had sex before and that... *that* was something else. Oh my god, he's so big I can hardly close my legs right now."

"Knew it," Hannah mumbles to herself. "It's always the ones you'd least suspect who end up being hung like a horse."

"You have no idea." My core throbs at the memory. "He lit up my body like a Christmas tree. There wasn't an inch of me he didn't lick, suck, caress. I've just never felt anything like it before. And the things he said—"

"Babe, calm down." Hannah chuckles. "It's been a long time since you've had something that wasn't battery-operated between your legs, so of course it felt incredible."

"Hannah, trust me. This wasn't because I've been deprived for so long. This was *all* him, and I think he really likes me. I've never felt like this. Not even with Kasey. That's crazy, right?"

Hannah sighs. "I don't know, Scar. This is uncharted territory for us both. I just... I don't want you to get hurt. Remember, you guys are playing house. I mean, you know me and I'm in total support of you getting as much Grade-A dick as you can during this whole charade. Just don't forget that's what it is. Besides, not that I think Scott's the type, but still... you're kind of a celebrity." She sighs into the phone. "Do me a favor? Please keep your heart out of this, or he's going to break it."

I promise everything I've said to you is the truth. It's not for show. The only lies I've told are the ones needed to keep our story straight. The rest, well, that's just me.

Scott's words whisper in my ear, sending a shiver down my spine. I know Hannah is just looking out for me. But she hasn't been here, seen us. If she had been, she'd see it too. At the same time, I respect my friend's opinion so I take what she has to say and tuck it into the back of my mind to consider at a later date.

"Okay," I agree. "You're right. Last night was just really great."

Hannah chuckles. "He must have dicked you real good."

"You have no idea."

"Well, what the hell are you doing talking to me? You're off the clock, boss. Go get your fill. Enjoy. You deserve it."

"I will."

"Just remember," she says, and I can hear her grin through the phone. "Think of me when you're riding him."

"Fuck off." I giggle and hang up.

I quickly brush my teeth, put on some tinted moisturizer, run a brush through my hair, and dab some gloss across my lips. Not too much, just enough to *not* look like a hot mess. Then I pop a couple of Tylenol, because I have a feeling my body is going to need it—especially if this morning goes the way I hope it will.

Fortunately, Scott's still asleep when I walk back through the living room, past the curtain, and into my bedroom. As though I never moved, I slip his shirt off my shoulders, let it drop to the floor, and crawl into bed, repositioning myself on his chest. Scott stirs beneath me, so I close my eyes and pretend I'm asleep before he notices. He presses a soft kiss to the top of my head as he brushes my hair back. I feign waking up and snuggle into him.

"Morning," I yawn.

"Morning, gorgeous," he replies, and my heart flutters at the compliment. "How are you feeling?"

"Sore." I laugh, then clarify, "But in a good way." He lets out a relieved sigh. I guess he had the same morning-after concerns I did. "And you?" I ask him. He seems to be in good spirits but part of me needs to know if he regrets this. Whatever *this* is.

He quirks a brow and lifts the comforter, revealing that he's already hard and ready to go for round... Honestly, I've lost count. "Awake," he tells me with a grin.

I reach down and grip his erection, giving it a few gentle strokes. "We have a lot to do today," I remind him.

He kisses me. "Yup, cooking... prepping... you've got the spa with your—"

"Don't say her name..." I give his cock a firm squeeze. "Still... we should get up and—"

Scott rolls me onto my back and pins me to the mattress. "We have plenty of time," he says as he trails kisses down the valley between my breasts, giving them each a small suck before continuing lower, to my thighs. He hooks one leg over his shoulder. "Besides..." He smiles, reaching out a hand to repeat the action with my other leg. "Breakfast is the most important meal of the day, and I intend to have my fill."

That's the only warning I get before he latches on to my still-swollen clit. "*Fuck,*" I moan as I buck below him. But Scott doesn't let me move an inch as his strong arms hold me wide open for him.

"This fucking pussy..." His deep voice travels through my body in waves, adding to the pleasure of his tongue. "It's so delicious I could eat you all day."

"Don't stop," I moan. He sucks my clit between his teeth and tugs on it gently. "Keep talking to me."

"You like that?" he says with his face buried between my thighs.

"Yes..." I whimper. "It's like a vibrator."

"Whisk together flour, sugar, dark cocoa powder ..."

"*Holy shit.*" As he continues to recite some recipe he appears to know by heart, I convulse beneath him.

"Baking soda, dark chocolate chunks."

I grip his head. "Is that the list of ingredients for my muffin?"

He laughs, and I can't take it anymore. My legs go straight, clenching his head in place as I hold on to him for dear life. Afraid that if I let him go, I'll float away into a sea of bliss.

"*Fuck, fuck, fuck...*" I cry out my release as sugar plums dance across the ceiling and stars explode behind my eyes.

As the world around us comes back into focus, I realize that Scott is hovering over my body, his face glistening as he smiles at me. "Look at you," he coos. "I love how you blush after you come. You're so gorgeous." Once again, my heart flutters and the instinct to look away takes over, but Scott doesn't let me. Instead, he grips my chin and forces my gaze to his. "Feel what you do to me." He rubs his firm cock against my tender slit. "Only you can make me so hard, so desperate to sink back into the sweet pussy of yours that it hurts."

"Then..." A spark of confidence lights up inside me. "What are you waiting for? Fuck me."

Scott grins. "Happily." I let out a small yelp as I'm suddenly flipped and spread across his lap. "But first, I want something from you," he says as his hand caresses my ass.

"W-what's that?"

"Tell me something you like about yourself."

"Scott—" I try to sit up, but a sharp smack stops me in my tracks.

"Let's try that again. All I want is one thing, one tiny little thing you like about yourself, then I'll fuck you any way you want." He rubs my tender skin, waiting for me to respond. When I remain tight-lipped, his hand comes down on the other cheek. "Fine. I'll start. Your eyes, I could get lost in them. The orange ring in the center reminds me of the hot spring I saw in Yellowstone as a kid. I thought that was the most beautiful thing I'd ever seen... until you."

My heart races. Growing up, Mom used to make me wear contacts to hide the defect. I've always been so self-conscious about it.

Smack.

"Ouch," I grumble as the slight sting pulls me out of my crappy past and into my sexy future.

"I love your pouty lips. When you wear that red lipstick you have..." His cock twitches below me. "I imagine what they'd look like wrapped around my dick. Now, come on, Angel, be a good girl and tell me one thing... anything... as long as it's positive."

"Um..."

Smack.

"I love your ass. It's smooth and curved like a juicy peach I just can't wait to bite into. I love the way it shakes when I fuck you from behind," he tells me, and a new wave of warmth floods to my center as I recall how amazing that felt. "And right now, I love the pretty shades of pink it turns after I smack it. Though I'm curious how red I'm going to make it before we're through here. Unless you have something nice to say...?" He raises his hand, preparing to land another strike.

"My tits!" I shout, and Scott pauses. "I love having big tits. I like to show off my cleavage, use it to distract from the areas I hate."

Smack!

"Hey," I grumble. "I said something positive."

Scott blows a cool breath of air across my heated skin to help soothe the burn. "Yeah, but it was followed by a negative. It's a start, though." He runs a fingertip along my spine, before dipping it between my leg with a thrust of his hips and a groan. "Because hearing how much you love your tits was the hottest thing I've ever heard. Now..." Then he pushes to his feet, and I feel weightless with how easy he maneuvers me so that he's lying on his back and I'm straddling his waist. "Show me how pretty those tits bounce while you ride my cock."

As I reach into the nightstand to retrieve a rubber, my breast rubs against Scott's face. He latches on to it, sucking hard on the nipple. I rock against his pelvis as I enjoy the sharp sensation, followed by the soft licking meant to soothe the sting. He releases me with a pop.

I scoot back to his thighs and grip him firmly. "Shit," he groans. "I love how you handle my cock."

My chest fills with pride as I admire how he squirms at my touch. I enjoy stroking him up and down before I finally rip open the foil packet and roll the latex down his impressive length. Taking a deep breath, I hover over him and prepare myself to be filled. You'd think you'd get used to it after doing this a few times. But so far, that hasn't been the case.

As the head of his cock breaches my entrance, I cry out. The pain more than worth the pleasure it brings. If I'm being honest, I love the sensation of my body stretching around him. Scott grips my hips and helps guide me down. Once he's fully sheathed inside me, I take a moment to adjust.

"Ready?" I ask him with a grin.

Scott rests his hands behind his head while shooting me a satisfied smile. "Show me what you got, babe."

"All right," I caution. "But, remember, you asked for it."

He doesn't appear concerned in the slightest, but he's about to learn what years of yoga and belly dancing can do for your core. With my back straight, I partially lift off his cock and go back down. I rinse and repeat until I find my perfect rhythm. As soon as I do, I twist my hips in a figure eight motion.

"Holy fuck." Scott's biceps flex as he fights the urge to reach out and grab me. I pick up my pace, enjoying the way his eyes roll back into his head as I ride him. "Don't stop," he urges. I place my hands on his chest to brace myself, then proceed to circle my hips around and clench my muscles as hard as I can, before I continue to bounce. "Yes," he hisses and grabs my head. "Just like that, Angel," he encourages as my nipples rub against his chest. "God, I love the way your tits jiggle while you fuck me."

"Oh god," I moan, because at this angle, he's hitting a spot that has my rhythm faltering.

"Don't worry, Angel, I got you." Scott grips my waist and takes over as he fucks me from below. The sound of our bodies clapping fills the small space. I drop my head into the crook of his neck, panting through each thrust of his hips. "That's it. Be a good girl and let me hear how pretty you cry out my name when you come."

"I don't think I can—" My body is coiled so tight but I can't seem to find my release.

The world spins as I'm now on my back, with my ankles by my ears and Scott's body still between my legs, fucking me to the hilt as he slams himself inside me. His pelvic bone hits my clit and—

"Oh, fuck, fuck, fuck." I let out a deafening cry before everything goes black.

I blink until the room comes back into focus. "Shit," I groan. Scott's dressed and I'm tucked into bed. "How long was I out?"

Did he seriously make me black out from coming so hard?

He presses a kiss to the top of my head. "Not long."

"Why do you have clothes on, then?"

"Okay," he concedes. "Maybe for a little while. But you looked so beautiful passed out I didn't want to bother you. But it's noon, and I have to meet—"

"Noon?" I bolt up in bed. I've never slept this late before, not even as a teenager. I grab my phone and see a gazillion missed messages from Hannah, plus a couple from my mom and Trisha, probably reminding me of our appointment this afternoon. "Fuck." I scramble to get dressed.

"Sorry, if I heard—"

I press my lips to his and silence his unnecessary apology. "It was on silent. Besides, if it was really bad, she would've come knocking."

He lets out a relieved sigh. "Okay, as much as I hate to go, it looks like you have work to do—"

"Yeah, and so do you, Mr. Puts-Tral-Lake-On-The-Map."

He presses a kiss to my lips with a chuckle. "We'll see. In the meantime, don't work too hard." I quirk my brow, and he adds, "I'm going to want dessert before bed."

20

Scott

WHAT DOES IT SAY if I'm out with one of my all-time favorite actors, touring my little town, pitching it for a movie his friend wants to make—a huge potential boost for tourism, my business, the whole town's income—and all I want to do is rush back to Scarlett's little cottage and drown myself in her?

If it weren't for the fact she *had* to go and take care of stuff for the inn, I would have played hooky, called in *getting laid.* I know Scarlett wouldn't have batted an eye if I suggested skipping her spa day with her mom. Besides, let's face it, Jax is the one with the eye and I've just been pretty much tagging along for the ride.

"This is beyond incredible," Kasey says as we stand at the top of Make-Out Point.

I wonder if Scarlett would let me drive her up here and fool around in the back of my pickup like a couple of teens?

I never got to experience that growing up, and now I'm grateful for it, because no crush of mine from back then can even begin to hold a candle to Scarlett Valentine.

"I mean, it legitimately looks like a postcard up here." Kasey grins as he takes in the view.

"I actually had postcards made up with shots I took last year. I have a whole pile of 'em back at the store," Jax says. He's become the town's official photographer and the primary source for producing picturesque advertising images.

"Did you ever watch *Yours for Christmas*?" Kasey asks.

"Only a hundred times," Jax fanboys, and Kasey chuckles.

"All the equipment in the world at our fingertips, the ability to digitally enhance every shot with picture-perfect blankets of snow, and none of it can begin to compare to this view right here."

"If you film during January, I can promise digital enhancement won't be needed. By then, we usually have a decent buildup of natural snow. It's too cold to melt, and almost every day or two, an extra half-inch is added on top," I chime in.

"That's exactly what Fletcher needs. He wants somewhere genuine, raw... He's tired of these spruced-up sets that have been regurgitated countless times."

"Well, if he's seriously interested, I can help put the pitch together. I know several members of the committee are highly motivated to find new ways to improve our economy and boost tourism, so the interest is there. But from experience, I also know that they usually want the cons upfront. If we lay it out straight for them, I'm sure they'll go for it. Especially since any minor inconveniences caused by the influx of people and equipment while filming will occur during our quiet season," Jax says.

Kasey smiles and shakes his hand. "You've got a deal. This is perfect." He gazes back out onto the horizon. "I should bring Trisha up here. She would love it."

"Really?" I ask, shocked. Not that the woman's said much to me, but based on how many layers of clothing she seems to wear every time I've seen her, I assumed winter wasn't her thing.

"Yeah, I know it doesn't seem like it, but she loves the snow. Her dad used to rent a cabin in the mountains for skiing, and while she was never the athletic type, Trish always appreciated the backdrop. She and Rhea—sorry, I mean Scarlett. She and Scarlett would always hang out in the lobby, sipping cocoa and reading whatever books they packed for the trip." Kasey must notice the confused expression on my face, because that sure as hell doesn't sound anything like their relationship now. "I know... Things didn't used to be this tough between them. There was a time when the girls were inseparable." He sighs. "I know they miss each other, but they're just both too stubborn to admit it."

I consider pressing for more details, even asking what happened, but decide to bite my tongue. Not that I don't want to know. I'd just rather hear it directly from Scarlett. It feels like the sort of thing she should tell me, when she's ready.

Kasey's watch beeps. "Speaking of, the girls are done at the spa. I should probably head back and rescue Trisha from Ginny."

I glance at the time. I can't believe how long we've been driving around.

"Brittany has been going on and on about that Christmas Village in town, so we're going to take her again tonight. Plus, I wanted to talk to the owner about the venue. I swiped up a few brochures showcasing some of the weddings they've hosted there."

"You're thinking of getting married *here*?" I ask. With all the money and resources at Kasey Dawson's disposal, I'm honestly surprised he'd consider getting married in our little town.

"Thinking about it," he says. "At least for our real wedding. I want something quiet and private so that I don't have to worry about paparazzi crashing in on us. Then we'll do a more public reception later. Plus, if we have it here, Scarlett can't get out of attending." He smiles, pauses, then sighs. "Look, I know I have no right to ask, but do you think you could talk to her? I really think if Scarlett and Trish could sit and talk, even for five minutes, they could start to put this all behind them."

I chew on my response. I know something big must have happened to cause the divide between the sisters, but at the same time, I don't get the sense that there's a lot of animosity coming from Scarlett's side. Though it's clear that—whatever history these three have—it bothers her. I consider my options for a moment before deciding that, at the end of the day, as much as Kasey Dawson happens to be one of my all-time favorite actors, the fact remains that Scarlett Valentine is my friend.

If we can even call what we are that anymore?

No matter what we call it, my answer remains the same. "Kasey, I'm sure you have everyone's best interests at heart but—"

"Enough said, man." He gives me a friendly pat on the shoulder. "Honestly, I'm an idiot for even asking. I'm glad she found you. Rhe—*Scarlett* deserves to be happy. I've known her since we were kids, and you... I've just never seen her this happy before."

"Thanks," is the only reply I can muster up. I'm too stunned to communicate how relieved *and* confused this makes me.

"Are you going back to the inn?" Kasey asks me.

"Actually, I'm going to head over to my family's house. I need to prep a few things for tomorrow."

Jax looks surprised by my answer. Probably because I delegated the majority of the prep work to Logan, so that all I had left to do was cook on the day of.

"Sounds good." Kasey nods. "Do you need a ride there? Or I can..."

"No, it's on the way home for me," Jax interjects.

"See you guys tomorrow," Kasey says, then turns around and makes his way back to his vehicle.

"See ya," Jax and I say at the same time.

Jax turns back to me as soon as Kasey is out of earshot. "What happened?"

"Nothing—"

"Dude, don't even try lying to me. I'll drag your ass straight to Tilly, and good luck trying to pull that shit on your sister," he threatens.

"I hooked up with Scarlett." I sigh and rake a hand through my hair.

"Okay," Jax draws out, appearing confused. "I don't see the problem."

"I think that's exactly it."

"Now you've lost me."

"I don't think I can pretend with her anymore... I don't want it to be fake."

"So, you like her? Like really, really like her?"

"What are we? Twelve?" I roll my eyes. "Of course I fucking like her. I think I might even—" I stop myself from saying that heavy, four-letter word. "I think if we gave this a real go, she might be the one. I'm not sure I can keep pretending when what I'm feeling is very real."

Jax scratches the top of his head. "Maybe you should talk to Scarlett? What if she's feeling the same way?"

I consider his very valid point before shaking my head. "It's just a few more days, then I can tell her."

"Why not tell her now? If she's having the same doubts or worries as you—"

"What if she's not?" I admit my greatest fear. "What if this is all one-sided?" I take a deep breath and regain my composure. "If it is, I don't want to make this holiday harder on her than it has to be. She needs my help. That's all that matters right now. When Christmas is over and her family is gone, we can talk."

"And until then?" Jax asks, clearly displeased by my answer.

"I'll enjoy what little time I have left with her and hope that this is the very rom-com-esque version of our beginning..."

21

Scarlett

USUALLY, GETTING A NIGHT off work to read a book is my dream. This particular title has been on my TBR for months, waiting for this exact moment...

Except I've been reading the first chapter for an hour and couldn't tell you a fucking thing about it. The words are nothing but jumbled letters on the page because I've lost my ability to concentrate. Something—no, *someone* else is on my mind and he's clouding my abilities to do anything but think about him.

When Scott texted and said he was doing some preparations for tomorrow and not to wait up, I should've been happy for the relaxing time alone. The ability to prepare *myself* for the big family party that will be our hardest test to date. Not only does it rely on us looking like a couple, but we have to ensure his siblings play along too. So his message was like a lead balloon in my stomach. Because last I heard, he told me his staff was doing all the actual pre-day prep.

So what's changed? Did Kasey say or do something? Or worse? Did that girl Amanda reach out, tell him she's free, and now he's regretting whatever it is we're doing here?

What are you? Five?

Sure, I could sit here and let my mind run wild with all the worst-case scenarios, or I could get my ass up and go straight to the source, demand answers. Decision made, I set my Kindle on the coffee table, bundle up, and drive across town.

Before I realize what I'm doing, it's too late. Because I'm already standing outside Scott's childhood home, knocking on the front door. No one answers. The lights are on, so I assume he's still here or at least someone is. I knock a little harder this time.

"It's open," I hear Scott yell out from somewhere inside.

Sure enough, I try the doorknob and it's unlocked. I walk back towards the kitchen, relieved when I find him elbow-deep in baking supplies. *At least he wasn't lying to me.* Not that we're out of the woods yet, but I'm looking for all the positives I can at this point.

"Hey," I say, leaning against the entryway.

Scott looks up from the bowl he's whisking with a surprised expression on his face—an expression that quickly morphs into a smile, which helps ease away more of my fear and leaves me feeling just a little stupid. Of course, he's here. He's a workaholic, a trait we both have in common. It may just be a family dinner but it doesn't change the fact that Scott can't let go of the reins, not completely at least.

"Hey," he says while continuing to mix his ingredients. "What's up?"

"I was..." I pause. Telling him I was worried sounds silly, especially now. "...just curious if you needed any help."

"You bake?" he asks, knowing full well I don't.

"No, but maybe you could teach me," I say with a sly smile.

"You've got perfect timing." He nods to the fridge. "Grab the bowl of chopped up butter." I do as directed and set it on the counter next to him. "The key to a good pie crust is keeping everything cold—you want it chilled until you're ready to use it."

"Is that why you're cooking at your parents' house?" I ask as a shiver runs down my spine. I thought my little cabin was cold, but Scott's younger brother keeps this place like an icebox.

Scott chuckles. "That's one reason, but also, it's the kitchen I'm most familiar with. I can find everything I need in here with my eyes closed."

"Now I'm torn between wanting you to teach me how to bake and putting that *blind baking* to the test," I tease.

Scott stands so that I'm stuck between him and the counter. "Why not both?" he fires back with a cocky grin.

"You're pretty confident in those culinary skills of yours, aren't you?" Then again, I know for a fact he's not just a talented chef, because the man sure as hell knows how to make magic happen outside of the kitchen as well.

Combined, though? I'm already wet and he hasn't touched me.

"You have no idea." Scott presses his chest to mine as he leans forward. His nose brushes against my cheek as his lips graze along my jawline. I'm thinking he's about to do a lot more than teach me to bake when he pulls back, having grabbed a white cloth from the countertop behind me. He folds it into a rectangle, then ties it around his head, covering his eyes.

"Are you seriously going to trust me to do this while you're blindfolded? I suck at cooking. Like, I can actually burn water," I say nervously. I really don't want to ruin his recipe.

"What about those award-winning fish tacos you teased me with?"

"Okay, sure, I can cook some things... but this? I'll ruin it."

"Do you trust me?" he asks.

"Yes," I answer without a second thought.

"Yes, chef," he corrects in a more commanding tone.

"*Yes, chef,*" I purr.

"Good girl." He grips my hips firmly and turns me to face the counter. "Do as I say, and it'll be perfect."

Did someone turn up the heat in the house? Because I went from freezing to needing to fan myself in seconds.

"Okay." I nod and he smacks my ass. "I mean *yes, chef*."

"That's my angel," he whispers in my ear. "I've already whisked together the dry ingredients. Now, you need to cut in the butter."

"Cut in the butter?" I repeat on a chuckle. The concept sounds ridiculous.

"That's fancy baking lingo for mixing it in. Since the butter's cold, it needs a little more muscle to combine it with the flour. You could do it with a food processor but I much prefer to do things by hand. Crust is too delicate, in my opinion, to entrust to machines. I like being in control."

A shiver runs down my spine. Clearly Scott's need for control extends far past the kitchen.

"Pour the chopped butter into the bowl of flour," he tells me, and I do as instructed. "Grab the pastry knife."

My eyes flick around the counter but come up short. Without having to look, Scott reaches across and grabs this weird curved tool with a handle and places it into my open palm.

"Push it down into the butter and rock it forward," Scott says. Then, like he's a master puppeteer, he maintains control of my hand and demonstrates. "Do this... while rotating the bowl."

"Like this?" I ask as I follow his instructions.

"Perfect," he says into my neck. "Keep going. You want to mix until the dough is reduced to pea-sized clumps."

"No wonder you have such strong arms," I mumble. Mine are already exhausted. "Is this good?"

Scott reaches into the dish and touches the dough. "A little more," he tells me, and I complete a few more rotations. "That's good," he declares a few seconds later without even having to check. "Wait here." Scott hardly uses his hands to help guide himself to the freezer, where he retrieves a bottle of vodka before resuming his position beside me at the counter.

"Impressive," I say with a low whistle.

"This is just the start, Angel. I can show you much more fun things to do with a blindfold. It's amazing what happens to your other senses when one is deprived."

I suddenly lose all interest in baking, and as if sensing my change of heart, Scott returns my focus to the task at hand.

"If you're a good girl and do as I say, maybe I'll show you."

"Yes, chef."

He clears his throat. "But first, we need to finish this crust. Otherwise, we'll have no pies for tomorrow. And believe me, you don't want to see what sort of temper tantrums Jake can throw if he doesn't get his Christmas pies."

"Fine," I huff, and Scott swats my butt again. "Yes, chef." I roll my eyes because, let's face it, seeing Jake have a meltdown would be hilarious.

"Now, you need to put a quarter cup of ice-cold water into the measuring cup. Use the strainer to prevent ice chunks from getting in." He hands me the utensil in question.

I bend over to get eye level with the cup, purposely rubbing my ass against his crotch. "Like this, chef?" I tease.

Scott grips my hips, holding me firmly against his erection. "Yes, now..." His voice is deeper, and I can sense his waning control. "Add a quarter cup of vodka. You should have a half cup total." I pop open the bottle and add the liquid to the water. "Stir it..." He massages my ass as I try to keep my hand steady. "And add the water to the mixture." I grab the measuring cup. "No," he barks out to stop me, and I freeze to the spot. "Add a tablespoon at a time. The last thing you wanna do is add too much liquid and ruin the mixture."

"Maybe you should do this." My nerves prick up and goose bumps travel across my skin.

"You've got this, Angel," he tells me.

I take a deep breath. "Yes, chef."

"Each time you add a tablespoon of liquid, use the spatula to mix it all together. Stop adding when the dough starts forming large clumps."

Cautiously, I add a tablespoon of water and mix until the measuring cup is empty. "Um, Scott, I ran out of water and it's still not that clumpy."

"Don't worry, that happens sometimes. Baking is a form of chemistry while recipes are just baselines, giving you an idea of what you should do. But things like humidity, heat, even the blend of the flour can affect your overall result. It's another reason why I do all my doughs by hand, because sometimes you need less than what's called for." Scott grabs the measuring cup, places the strainer on top, and pours in a little more water, followed by an impressively equal amount of vodka. Then he pours himself a small shot. "Sometimes you need more. It's always easier to add liquid than it is to remove it," he explains before tossing back his drink.

I add another tablespoon and I think it's clumping up the way he wants. "Is this good?"

He grabs the spatula and stirs. "You're a natural," he hums, and I grin at the praise. "Okay, now move the bowl and sprinkle flour down on the counter. Not too much, just a light dusting." I do as he says and wait for his next instruction. "Pour the dough on top. Cover your hands in flour." He puts some on both of our hands. "This is the fun part. We're going to fold the dough. Really mix the flour into the fat." He demonstrates what he means. "Keep doing this until it's completely mixed." Scott lightly holds on to me, stroking up and down my forearms, which allows him to see what I'm doing by feeling my movements.

"Some of it keeps crumbling off?"

"Dip your fingers in the ice water. The moisture will work into the dough and help get those last few pieces."

It's not long before the small clumps form a solid mass. "I think it's mixed."

Scott inspects my handiwork by feeling the giant lump of dough on the counter. "It's perfect. Now you just need to roll it into a ball. Then cut it in half."

"Okay, done."

"Next, use the rolling pin to flatten each ball into a disk that's about an inch thick."

"Is this good?"

He inspects my little pucks of dough. "Perfect. Now we have to wrap them up and set them in the fridge." Once again, Scott navigates the kitchen effortlessly as he grabs the plastic wrap and returns to secure the balls of dough himself. Then he places the trays in the fridge.

"Now what?" I ask him.

"We wait."

"How long?"

"Overnight," he tells me.

"Oh, so we're done?" I'm not sure why but I'm a little sad it's over.

Scott crowds my space, my body pressed against the counter and his pressed against me. "You sound disappointed?"

"No... I guess I just thought there was more."

"Nope." He grins. "Crust works better when it sits overnight. This is the part of the evening where I'd usually clean up and pass out so I can wake up early and make the pies."

"I can help—"

"I don't want to clean up right now."

"No?"

He shakes his head and removes his blindfold. His emerald eyes burn with lust as he gazes down at me. Scott presses his lips to mine, and the kiss quickly escalates to full-blown making out. I'm breathless when he finally pulls away again.

"Turn around," he tells me. I do as he says and place my hands on the counter. Scott brings the cloth around so that it covers my eyes this time. "Do you trust me?" he asks for the second time tonight.

"Yes, chef..."

22

Scott

"Good girl," I growl into Scarlett's ear before fastening the makeshift blindfold over her eyes. I didn't think it possible, but somehow she's even hotter here in my kitchen, covered in flour, her hands spread wide. "You're incredible, you know that?" My palm hovers over her ass as I take an extra second to appreciate just how gorgeous it looks right now, bent over, begging for me to spank it, and how pretty it's going to look in a few minutes.

"I guess." Her tone tells me that our little lesson from earlier has already worn off. That's fine. I'm more than happy to give her another.

"*Tsk, tsk, tsk*," I scold as I pull down her leggings and reveal her bare cheeks. "What's this?"

"What?" Scarlett wiggles her ass. "I was a little sore earlier. Commando was the more comfortable choice."

"Was I too rough?" I inspect her flesh but don't see any marks.

"No, it was amazing. It was just a little tender at first. I feel fine now."

"Are you sure?"

"Yes, chef." The title drips from her tongue like honey.

"Good, because it sounds like you haven't learned your lesson." I reach into the drawer, and Scarlett jumps at the sound. I retrieve a spatula. "Now, Angel." I trace the rubber tip around the curve of her rear. "Do you have something nice to say about yourself?"

When she shakes her head, I strike her twice. "Oh," she moans as she bends forward.

"You like that?" In the light of the kitchen, I'm immediately gratified by the pinkening of her skin.

"Yes..." she says, and I swat her twice more. "Yes, chef."

"Good girl. Now, tell me what I want to hear," I urge her. Once again, she refuses and earns herself another quick reprimand. I reach between her legs, and my fingers find her slick to the touch. "Hmm, it seems like you like this too much," I hum, and she widens her stance as I find her clit. "Perhaps we need to change tack." Scarlett rocks into me as I continue to rub her little nub. "New rules." I lean in to whisper in her ear. "You don't get to come until you tell me what I want to hear."

"Scott," she groans and is immediately rewarded with a strike. "Chef, please..."

"You know what you have to do." I continue to work her over, and just as I feel the telltale signs of her tensing up, I back off and spank, then resume the process all over again. "It drives me wild when you bite your lip. All I want to do is suck it between my teeth and taste how sweet you are." Scarlett's head drops to the counter. "Come on, Angel, tell me one thing."

"I... can't..." she pants, so very close to capturing her release. Until I stop and she huffs out her irritation.

"I think it's sexy that you're so passionate about your business, that you put so much of your heart into turning the place around. That while you've worked to keep the inn as close to the original as you can, there are sprinkles of you all over it."

"Please," she begs and pounds a fist on the counter.

"Gimme one thing. That's all I want." I keep my pressure on her clit light. Barely there.

"I'm... I'm brave..." she gasps, and I encourage her by picking up my pace. "I was terrified to move here, start over... but I did it."

"That's it, Angel." I drop to my knees and bury my tongue in her pussy as I continue to work her clit. "Come for me. Let me taste what a good girl you are."

"Fuck," she cries out as I hold her steady and savor each drop. Once she's finished, I push to my feet, tug her leggings the rest of the way down, and lower my pants. I palm my cock and groan. "W-what's wrong?" she asks in a breathy tone.

"Unfortunately, I'm gonna have to ask for a rain check."

"Why?"

"Our supplies are back at the cottage, and as desperate as I am to sink into this dripping pussy of yours, I really don't wanna be forced to scavenge through my brother's room."

"It's fine," she says, and I hesitate, unsure what she means. "I'm on birth control, and..." Scarlett turns to look at me, even though she can't see me through the blindfold. "I trust you."

"Are you sure, Angel, because we can—"

"Yes, chef," she tells me, and I almost come on the spot.

"You're so fucking amazing," I remind her as I trail kisses down her spine. Once I reach her perfect ass, I give the plump flesh a small nibble, grip her ankle, and bring it with me as I stand. Scarlett leans up as I rest her leg on the counter, spreading her wide for me. I grip the edge to keep her steady as my free hand guides the tip of my cock into her entrance.

"Oh my..." she cries out as I enter her.

"Fuck, Angel, this pussy is so fucking hot and wet." I savor the sensation of having no barriers between us by pulling in and out of her slowly. Picking up my pace, I struggle to hold on as she mews beneath me. As much as I want to come, mark her as mine, I don't want this moment to end. "I love how good you are at taking my cock."

"I'm so close," she cautions as her body coils tight. Her thigh muscles flex against my forearm.

I fuck her faster and push her over the edge. I hold on by a thread as she comes, because I'm nowhere near finished with her yet. I help her lower her leg and turn her to face me. Her cheeks and sweater are covered in flour as I crash my mouth to hers and guide her to the floor, so that she's on top of me.

Scarlett takes the lead as she slams down on my cock. "Fuck," I groan, and she shoots me a cocky grin before she rides me. "Good girl... Faster." I encourage her with a slap on the ass.

She rips her sweater over her head. The blindfold comes off in the motion, and I'm grateful because it allows me to watch her beautiful face as she comes. Scarlett braces herself on my shoulders as she maneuvers her hips. Her tits slip out of the tank top she's wearing. I lean up and suck her nipple in my mouth. Scarlett digs her nails into me as her movements become more erratic.

"I love how wild you are when you come." I hold on to her hips to guide her as we both reach our respective climaxes. She collapses on top of me, spent, and I press a kiss to the top of her head as I stroke her hair back. "You're incredible," I tell her.

She smiles at the compliment instead of shying away. "Um, Scott... I should've asked this sooner, but when do you expect Letty and Jake to get home?" Scarlett asks as the realization that we're mostly naked on the kitchen floor of someone else's house finally dawns on her.

I chuckle. "Jake said he was on shift, so not until the morning. I'm not sure about Letty, but I think he said she was closing tonight."

"Oh, that's good." Scarlett relaxes in my hold and sighs. "Tell me something."

"Something," I tease.

"No." She playfully hits my chest as she gazes down at me. "I want you to tell me something about you, something that no one else knows."

"Something that no one else knows?" I lift my arms and slip them behind my head as I try to think of something to tell her. The linoleum is killer on my back but I have no intention of moving right now. Not with a view this good...

"Yup," Scarlett prompts as she traces a finger across my pecs.

"Okay, but you can't share this with anyone. Not a soul. No one, not even my family, knows about this."

Scarlett perks up a bit. "Oh, now, this is juicy."

I give her a pointed glare, and she zips her lips shut. Taking a deep breath, I hesitate, until I realize I actually want to tell her. "I hate coffee."

"What?" she sputters.

"Yup, it's fucking disgusting. I love the aromatics of it, but I can't stand the taste. No matter how much cream or sugar I pour in, it still tastes like ass."

"You, *Mr. Makes the best coffee I've ever had in my life*, hate coffee? How do you make it then? It isn't like you just brew a good cup. You have specialty drinks."

"Mom... she was the coffee connoisseur. She established all the blends, and I've never messed with them. As for the lattes and stuff, I know flavors and quality. Also, Gia helps. She's been working there almost as long as I have and practically lives with a caffeine IV pumping in her veins."

"So no one knows? Seriously?" Scarlett asks in disbelief.

"I think Mom suspected, and maybe Gia too, but neither ever called me out on it."

"How do you function? I mean, I can't tie my shoes without a hefty dose of caffeine."

I chuckle. "I still get caffeine." She waits for me to elaborate. "Tea," I explain.

"Tea?"

"Yup, tastes a thousand times better, and it has other properties that can provide a similar stimulation without the overdose of caffeine."

"So, you're saying less is more?"

"For me, yes. When I drink coffee, I always get jittery—and like I said, I can't stand the taste. But with tea, I enjoy the flavor, the variety, the different homeopathic applications. I feel there isn't anything a good cup of tea can't cure... That and soup."

"Wow." Scarlett lies down next to me, using the crook of my arm as a pillow. "This paints you in a whole new light."

I lean up on my arm. "And?"

"Strangely, I think it makes you sexier? How is that even possible?"

"What can I say? I'm like an onion—"

"Are you really going to quote *Shrek* to me?"

"What? It's true." We both laugh but the room quickly falls silent. "Okay, my turn to ask you something."

"Uh-oh." She cringes.

I feel guilty, because I know I'm about to ruin what's been another perfect moment between us. But I need to know, and I hope that she'll feel comfortable enough to open up to me. "Kasey," I say his name, and she frowns before I even finish the question. "What happened with you two?"

"Does it matter?" Scarlett sits up and puts some distance between us.

"No, but he mentioned something today—"

"Were you talking about me with him?" She pushes to her feet, frantically looking around the room for her clothes.

"No... not exactly." I follow after her, but she's an expert at avoiding me.

"I can't believe this." She finds and pulls on her leggings as I tug on my pants.

"Wait." I grip her shoulders and force her to look at me. I need her to know that I'm not lying. "All he said was that you and your sister used to be close. He didn't tell me what happened, and I didn't ask. I'll be honest. He did mention wanting me to talk to you, to encourage you to speak with her. Settle whatever—"

"Of course he did," Scarlett scoffs.

"I told him no," I say, and she freezes. "It's not my place to tell you what to do or how to manage your family. I'm only asking because I want you to know you can talk to me, without judgment." Scarlett stands there, looking at me, as she silently processes my statement. When she doesn't respond, I drop my hands and let her go. Clearly I misread our connection. "I'm sorry. I shouldn't have asked—"

"I loved Kasey." She sighs. "We've known each other since we were kids. Dad loved to travel around with us, made sure all the kids had tutors and on-set classrooms. It was a requirement of his, for the children actors. The three of us were always close. Trisha, Kasey, and me. Until we turned sixteen, and Kasey started to look at me differently. It was obvious he didn't look at my stepsister the same way, and I knew it hurt her. But we were fine, *seemed* fine, especially when she found her own boyfriend... well, *boyfriends*. One loser after another, all looking to get an *in* with our dad. It's how she ended up pregnant with Brittany. Some asshole knocked her up, thinking it was his lucky day, then bailed when Dad refused to give him work in front of a camera. But Trisha wasn't our problem. She never was. The problem was me."

A tear rolls down Scarlett's cheek, and I fight my need to wipe it away. I'm not sure she wants to be touched right now, and I don't want her to stop talking. Because something tells me she needs to get this off her chest.

"The more famous Kasey became, the more of a toll it took on our relationship. I never wanted the spotlight. Not ever. Sure, in the beginning, I thought if I wasn't the one they were looking at, it would be okay. But when I started reading the articles, judging me, questioning how someone like him could be with someone who looked like me.

Comments about how I wasn't tall enough, skinny enough, pretty enough." She wipes away a tear. "There was one asshole who would literally follow us around and purposely take the most unflattering pictures of me. Then he'd post them all over the internet for everyone to have a good laugh at. Of course, Mom was no help. She just insisted that I needed to diet. Get a nip here, a tuck there, and then they wouldn't have anything to write about."

My fists clench at the thought of all those comments destroying Scarlett's confidence, then her mother sealing that negativity in stone.

"So we agreed to stop doing public appearances together. Then Dad died, and the vultures came looking for another photo op, images of the grieving family. It eventually died down again, until Kasey became this big star, and it was impossible for us to manage his fame. He was always gone. We hardly ever saw each other. People were constantly asking him why he was flying solo on the red carpet, speculating as to why I wasn't there. But I think his proposal was the final tipping point. He was in the fast lane to stardom, and all I wanted to do was live a simple, quiet life—it's still all I want to do. So when he dropped down on one knee and asked me to give up my dreams of normalcy for good, I started to wonder if love was enough."

Scarlett swallows hard.

"We argued constantly. Mostly because I wouldn't give him an answer. I loved him, that much was unquestionable, but I wouldn't just be saying yes to him. I would be marrying a lifestyle I hated and knew he had no plans of giving up. Eventually, I told him I needed some time... apart. You know, to really think things over. That's when my grandpa died, and since Mom had no intention of returning home or handling his affairs, I used the opportunity to escape for a little bit and get to know the man I never had the privilege of meeting in life. While I was here, in Minnesota, discovering that my grandfather shared a passion for hospitality, that he had this beautiful inn, and that strangely enough he left it all to me... while meeting all of you and hearing your stories about him and learning more about my mother's roots... Kasey was home with Trisha, discovering that they were each what the other was looking for."

"You mean?"

"Yup, I came home to find that my almost fiancé was fucking my stepsister. You'd think I'd hate him, right? Funny enough, I don't. We loved each other but also brought out the worst in one another. I knew we were done and that I was leaving before I saw them together. But Trisha... I just couldn't forgive her. She was my sister, my best friend, and the second I was out of the picture, she took what she had her eye on since we were teens."

I can't believe that was what Kasey wanted Scarlett to talk about and what...? Get over? I love my brothers, but I'm not sure I'd be able to forgive them for something like that. At least not right away.

"I was back in Cali long enough to grab my stuff and go. This is actually the first time I've spoken to Trisha since."

"Do you think you'll ever forgive her?" I'm not sure it's my place to ask, but I can't help myself. The question was just bouncing around in my head because... *why should she?* What has Trisha done to earn that forgiveness?

"Honestly? I don't know. Every time I try, I remember coming home, finding them—"

"Oh no..."

Scarlett doesn't need to paint the picture. I see it clear as day now. How she's playing nice, I don't know. Because I'm not sure I can go in tomorrow and play happy fiancé, knowing how much they've hurt her.

"Yup." She tries to laugh it off, but I can tell it still hurts.

"I'm sorry." I wrap my arms around her. I'm relieved when she does the same.

"You have nothing to be sorry for. It's not like you fucked my sister... unless there's something you're not telling me."

"No. Nope, never gonna happen." I make sure to slam that door shut before it can fully open. "Still, I can't imagine how much that must have hurt you and then for them to show up unexpectedly."

"After everything that happened, I told myself I didn't need anyone. That happily-ever-afters only exist in fiction. That no matter what, they end in heartache in the real world."

"And now?" I risk asking. I hold my breath, waiting for her reply.

Scarlett pulls back and looks up at me. "And now." She smiles. "I'm not so sure."

My heart pounds, telling me that this is it. Now is the time to tell her what I'm feeling. But the sound of the front door opening and closing interrupts our tender moment. Scarlett squeezes her eyes shut as the steps grow closer. I swear it's like a scene out of a horror movie, and we're the horny teenagers just waiting to be murdered. I pull Scarlett behind me, using my body to shield hers. Not that she's nude, but it's clear she's embarrassed.

Letty walks into the kitchen. She doesn't look at us as she opens the fridge. "It smells like sex and pie in here." Shutting the door with a beer in hand, she pops the top off, leans against the counter, takes a swig of her drink, and eyes the scene in front of her. An apology is on the tip of my tongue, but it dies there when she smiles. "Jakey-Poo owes me big time. I'm going upstairs and turning on the TV, so you guys enjoy." With that, Letty exits the room, and Scarlett and I break into laughter.

"Oh my god, I can't believe that just happened." Scarlett's face is beyond flushed.

"We should get going." I grip her ponytail and angle her head back. "I mean, we can stay if you want." I lick her jaw. "But there were a few more tricks with a blindfold I wanted to show you, and I thought you might prefer the privacy of your home."

"Is that right?" She smiles. "You aren't tired?"
"Of you? Never..."

23

Scott

As consciousness seeps in, the haze of sleep clears from my view, and I notice Scarlett at the end of the bed. "What's this?" I ask as I sit up, grab her around the waist, and pull her back into bed. She lets out a surprised scream, and I roll over so that she's beneath me. "Good morning."

"Good morning," she repeats with a matching smile. I press a kiss to her lips, but her hand goes to my chest to stop me. I pull back and quirk a brow at her. "I have to go."

"Go?"

Scarlett sighs. "Yeah, Sheila called out this morning. I need to relieve Hannah so she can get some sleep."

I let her up. As much as I would love to crawl back into this bed with her and fuck the day away, I understand she has a business to run. "What about tonight?"

Her smile grows wider. "Don't worry, I'll be there. This is one of the rare times I'm happy the inn has vacancies. My honeymooners check out today, and from my brief conversation with the other two tenants, I understand they're going to their own family events. I've already communicated that the front desk will be closed tonight and tomorrow for the holiday, but that I'd have the phone on me in the event of an emergency."

"So..." I reach out a hand and trace the line of buttons on her blouse. "Tonight, you're mine?"

"Barring an emergency, yes," she says before taking my extended finger and sucking it into her mouth.

"You're cruel," I tease.

"Perhaps, but you're the one who pulled me back into the bed I struggled to get out of in the first place."

"Touché." I grin, push to my feet, and offer a palm to help her up. "Now, you go to work and do amazing things."

"What about you?"

"Well... I guess I should probably go finish making those pies. I was going to make them last night, but *someone* decided to distract me."

"Hey! You said the crust needed to sit overnight."

"Maybe." I shrug. "Or perhaps I just said that because some temptress appeared in my kitchen under the guise of wanting baking lessons."

"Jerk," she says teasingly as she pushes me back down onto the bed.

I grip her hips and rest my forehead against the junction between her thighs, when what I really want is hidden behind layers of fabric I want to tear off. "You should go," I caution her.

Scarlett tilts my face up and kisses me. I squeeze her ass tightly, fighting all my instincts to pull her back. She breaks our kiss and smiles.

"See ya." As if our embrace left me weightless, she somehow gathers the strength to push on my forehead and send me backwards. "That was mean," I shout, while staring up at the ceiling.

"Maybe you can teach me a lesson later tonight," she taunts as she exits the cabin.

I'm fucked. I know it. Funny part is... I don't even care.

The wind howls outside and a cool breeze passes through the cabin. The pies can wait. Right now there's something more important I need to do.

The door to the hardware store sticks, making it a chore to pull open. Thinking back, I can't remember when it ever worked the first time. Which is funny, since they clearly have everything they need to fix it at their immediate disposal.

"Welcome," a feminine voice shouts from somewhere in the shop as I finally make my way inside. I glance around, but Leroy has this place packed tight with shelves. It's like a maze, easy to get lost in while trying to navigate the various aisles. "I'll be right with you."

"No worries, Toni. I know what I'm looking for," I say as I turn a corner. While the place is a little chaotic, at least they don't move things around. Once you find something, you always know where to find it again.

"Oh, okay." I hear the sound of metal and plastic hitting the floor, followed by a string of expletives. "I'm okay," Toni announces.

There's stomping coming from the far stairs that lead up to the second-floor apartment. "What's all the racket?" Leroy calls out.

"Sorry, Dad," Toni says. "Just a little slip. Nothing for you to worry about."

"Are you sure?" he asks. "I can help—"

"Dad," she scolds. "You should be resting. Get on upstairs now."

"Do you have kids?" Leroy asks me, knowing full well that I don't.

"Not yet," I say, hopeful that one day my answer will be different.

"Word of advice," he says, leaning in to whisper. "Don't have daughters. They can be overprotective pains in the you know where."

"What did I say, old man?" Toni pops up out of nowhere like one of those rodents in a Whac-A-Mole game. "Back upstairs, before you scare away the only customer we've had all day."

"See?" Leroy says before doing as he's told.

"Oh, Scott, hi," Toni greets me. "What brings you in today?"

I hold up the roll of plastic and a thing of double-sided tape. "Just some drafty windows."

Toni frowns. "Weren't you in here last month to stock up?" Her face morphs from friendly to panicked. "Was it faulty? It was a new brand. We couldn't get the 3M in stock—"

"Oh, no, this stuff works great. It's not for me. It's for my..." The word *fiancée* almost slips off my tongue. "...friend. She has a very drafty cabin."

"A lady friend." Toni wiggles her eyebrows up and down. "Might this be the town's mysterious blonde bombshell?"

I shake my head, laughing as I hand her my stuff to ring up. "So, I guess word's spread?"

"Like wildfire." Toni grins. "What is it with you Moores? It's like you lot are all people can ever gossip about."

"It's a blessing and a curse," I tell her.

"Well, anyway, congratulations on your engagement," she says. "While sudden, it honestly wasn't very surprising."

"Really?" My brows knit together in confusion.

Toni shrugs. "I don't know. I guess I kind of predicted it. Well, that she'd settle down with one of your lot, since y'all seemed to have adopted her. And out of the three of ya, you seemed the most compatible."

"You need a hobby." I shake my head.

Actually, now that I think about it, this whole town does.

"Why would I want to do anything else when the gossip at Patty's is about as delicious as her fudge? That'll be $15.78, please."

"Oh, by the way..." I say, suddenly recalling the announcement I read in the town's paper on Sunday. "I guess congratulations are in order for you as well. You and Josh finally tying the knot?"

"Yup," she says, with a bit of hesitance and not with the level of excitement I'd expect from someone newly betrothed. "It seems like time to finally settle down, start a family."

Toni is a few years younger than me. Besides knowing her because her dad runs the only hardware store in town, she used to date one of my good friends, Zach. But that's been over for nearly a decade now. I'm glad that she's moved on. Not every story is lucky enough to end like Jax and Tilly's. And, well, Zach... I know he's never coming back here.

"Yeah, I think we've all reached that age," I tell her, because I know it's all I've been able to think about since last year. "Well, I've got some windows to seal."

"Good luck," she says. "Oh, and, Scott?"

"Yeah?" I pause with my hand on the door.

"Merry Christmas."

24

Scarlett

FUCK, FUCK, FUCK... CAN today get any worse?

I shouldn't ask that. Because, yes, I'm sure it can.

I dig through the desk to find my grandfather's old Rolodex. I know it's in here somewhere. "There you are," I say when I find it, then flip through in search of Malcom's number. Not the main one to his service—that's closed for the holidays by now. No, his direct line that he only gives out to his special customers, an exclusive group my grandfather used to be part of. "Come on," I groan as the phone rings. "Answer—"

"Hello?" a man says.

"Malcom?" I question.

"Yes, how'd you get this—"

"My grandpa, Edgar Peterson," I tell him.

"Oh, you're the grandbaby he used to go on about? How are you, dear? Though, I assume if you're calling me, the answer is *not good*?"

Malcolm's statement catches me off guard. Obviously, I knew my grandpa had some level of knowledge of my existence, especially since he mentioned me in his will. But the idea that he talked about me a lot is surprising. He barely knew me...

But I'll have to dwell on that later. I have bigger problems right now. "Yes, sorry, I know it's the holidays but one of my vacant rooms decided it's the perfect time to have a pipe burst. I turned off the water in the unit to stop the flooding, but I'm not sure what happened or if other rooms are at risk."

"The number one culprit this time of year is a frozen pipe," he verifies my worst fear.

"I make sure to keep the vacant rooms' thermostats up to sixty-five, just in case." I was lucky that I decided to do a random room check, otherwise I might not have noticed until the damage was far worse.

"With the winds we've been having this year, you aren't the first call we've gotten like this. Unfortunately, dear, I've retired." *Great.* My hope deflates until he adds, "One sec... Junior? Think you can make a house call?"

"On Christmas Eve?" I hear a male voice grumble in reply.

"Family friend."

There's some more muffled conversation before *Junior* says, "Sure, Pops."

"Okay. Junior will be there in about twenty. He'll assess the damage and see if any other pipes are at risk of doing a repeat."

"Oh my god, thank you so much." I'm not sure what I would do if they couldn't come out today.

"No worries, dear. Your grandpa helped me more times than I can count. It's the least I can do for his granddaughter."

"Still, thank you, and Merry Christmas."

"What in the holy hell happened here?" Hannah asks as she splashes through the puddles that accumulated in the now-flooded unit.

"Pipe burst," I say as I continue to wet-vac the standing water. "Wait. What are you doing here?"

"Figured I'd stop by on my way to the obligatory family dinner, hoping there was some sort of emergency that required my immediate assistance and sudden inability to attend, much to my dismay of course. And, look, it's a Christmas miracle! Despite what I tell the boys, I must've been a very good girl this year."

"Sorry to disappoint, but I've got things under control here."

"Babe, did you forget that you have your family in town at your *fiancé's* house, a bunch a people they hardly know?" *Shit, I totally did.* "That's what I thought." Hannah removes her jacket and sets it on the chair. "What do you need me to do?"

"Nothing. I've already called the plumber and started the insurance claim online. I took a bunch of photos of the damage, and now I'm just waiting for the professionals to show up and verify that no more pipes are going to explode and put my inn underwater."

"Scarlett, let me handle this—"

"No, this is my business. Everyone will understand why I'm late. I already texted my mom and warned her."

Hannah waves me off as she throws her voluptuous curls up into a quick messy bun. "What do you need me to do?"

I sigh, knowing there's no talking her out of this. "Keep wet-vacing. I'll grab another bucket and mop."

"Knock, knock," a man calls out, then sighs from the doorway of the room as he takes in the scene in front of him. By the tone, I can tell this is the last thing he wants to deal with right now. Not that I blame him. "My grandfather said something about..." His frown quickly morphs into a smile as his eyes land on Hannah. "...some pipes needing to be looked at," he says with the hint of innuendo as he continues to eye-fuck my friend.

Based on the way she's biting her lip, it seems Hannah's holiday just got a thousand times better.

"Yeah, one burst in this unit. But I have eight other vacant rooms that I want to make sure aren't at risk of doing the same."

The guy finally notices that I exist and clears his throat. "Okay, if you can show me which rooms—"

"I can," Hannah volunteers like an overeager student on the first day of class.

"Are you sure?" I ask teasingly, aware she's more than willing to follow the handsome plumber around for the evening.

Hannah looks him up and down before replying with a grin, "More than sure. Besides, there are a few drains around here that could use a good unclogging... if you have time, that is?"

"Suddenly, my calendar is wide open," he says, obviously playing along with her flirting.

"See?" Hannah shoves my jacket in my arms. "Don't forget you have that fiancé of yours waiting for you. Go, be merry, get laid." She leans in so that only I can hear. "And I'm going to do the same."

I shake my head and chuckle. "Are you sure?"

"Yup, me and..." she prompts.

"Malcom," the guy says. "But everyone calls me Junior."

"Junior and I got things covered. So, go have fun, and I'll keep you posted."

"Okay," I hesitate. While I trust Hannah to do what's necessary, I still hate the idea of leaving all this on her shoulders. "If there's an emergency..."

"I'll call. Now, go." She practically pushes me out of the room.

I glance down at my soaked outfit and groan. "Guess I need to change," I say to myself.

I rush to the cabin and frantically pull different options out from my dresser and closet. Nothing says *Christmas*

Eve. It all says *I run an inn and desperately need to update my wardrobe.* Then my eyes land on a fitted red sweater that still has tags on it, hanging at the far end of my closet. I bought it last Black Friday because the sale was too good to pass up, but regretted it as soon as I got home and saw how unforgiving the material was. My shoulders sag until I hear Scott's voice in the back of my mind, telling me how beautiful and perfect I am.

"Fuck it," I say as I tear off the tags. Deep down, I know Scott is going to die once he sees me, and that's all the motivation I need to step out of my comfort zone.

25

Scott

I GLANCE AT THE clock for the hundredth time. Everyone is here and Scarlett is still a no-show. I check my phone. No new messages and mine are left unread.

"What's up, lover boy?" my annoying-ass little brother asks while draping an arm over my shoulder. "Heard you were here making some *cream pies* last night."

I shrug him off and sigh. "Scarlett's late."

Jake glances around as if he's just realizing she's not here. I don't blame him. Our smallish family has practically tripled over the last year—add in Scarlett's bunch and we're packed in like sardines. "I'll call in, see if dispatch has been sent out to the inn or seen her car. She still has that older two-door green Wrangler, right?"

Fuck!

I hadn't even thought of that. It's windy and the roads are covered with thick layers of black ice. What if she's stuck in a ditch somewhere? Meanwhile, I'm sitting here pouting like some selfish asshole, instead of growing a pair and going out there to look for her. I know I've fucked up when Jake is the reasonable one between the two of us.

"What's going on?" Derek, my brother's best friend and one of the local cops, perks up at the mention of dispatch.

"Scarlett's missing," Jake tells him, and now I'm rushing out the door.

A few people ask me where I'm going, but I don't respond. Hopefully Jake and Derek have enough sense to not scare her family until we know something for sure. I'm so stuck in my head, going over every worst-case scenario, that I don't look up until I run into a tiny figure in the driveway.

"Ouch," Scarlett says and stumbles back a step.

"Thank god!" I reach out to steady her and quickly tug her into my arms.

"Oh, hey, what's going on?" she asks me, her eyebrows knit with confusion.

"You're late. I didn't have a message from you, and you weren't reading mine. I thought..." I stop, realizing how quickly I jumped the gun and let my brother's off-handed comments send me into a panic. Sometimes I forget he's a firefighter and that's just the way he thinks. I guess the fact that we lost our parents in a car accident last year doesn't help much either. "I was just worried," I tell her a little more calmly.

Scarlett grips my face between her hands and pulls me in for a kiss. "I'm sorry. I didn't think. A pipe burst and I was scrambling to deal with the aftermath. If I'm being entirely honest, I'm just so used to doing things on my own it didn't occur to me to reach out and let someone else know what was going on..."

"Is everything okay?"

"It will be," she says with a nod. "I have a plumber there now and Hannah is cleaning up the rest of the water. She was looking for an excuse to avoid her family. And then, when Junior dropped in, her eyes lit up like a kid on Christmas morning."

"Junior?"

"The plumber."

"Oh," I say as if I understand. I don't. But at least she's okay and so is the inn.

"Anyway, my cell died so I left it home to charge and just brought the emergency line with me, in case there are any more problems. I didn't mean to make you worry. I texted my mom so she knew to go ahead without me and I gave her the address. I thought she would've..." Scarlett shakes her head. "No, I should've messaged you. I'm sorry."

"All that matters is you're safe." I kiss the top of her head and try to ignore how much it stings to realize she didn't think to reach out to me when she needed help.

"Oh, and thank you," she says, and I look at her, confused by the sentiment. "For covering the windows. It's already ten degrees warmer in the cabin. It was nice getting dressed without shivering."

"Of course," I say with the makings of a grin.

"You didn't need to do that. Not that I'm not grateful, but I know you had a lot going on today—"

I stop her with a kiss. When I pull back, she's wobbly on her heels. "Don't you understand there isn't anything I wouldn't do for you?"

Scarlett looks at me as if the thought never even occurred to her. "I think I'm starting to."

I'm once again struck by that odd sensation in my chest, the one that urges me to tell Scarlett how I really feel. That I stopped pretending a while ago. But a strong gust of icy wind sends a chill down both of our spines, reminding us that we're outside and this has been one of the coldest Decembers on record.

"Come on." I drape my arm over her shoulder. "There are a couple of hot cups of peppermint cocoa inside with our names on them."

As soon as we walked through the front door and joined in on the festivities, whatever negativity I was feeling immediately dissipated. As much as I've enjoyed celebrating the various holidays and events at Jax and Tilly's place this year, especially considering their kitchen and common areas are much larger than the ones here, I love that we're doing Christmas at our family home. With the house full of people, the drinks flowing, kids laughing, and the aromas of the dinner—it's like our parents are here with us. Although no one's mentioned it out loud, as I look at my sibling's smiling faces, I know they feel it too.

"Come on, Alex, we've been practicing this," Scarlett says as she sits on the floor in front of one of the twins.

"Gavin, you can do it. Crawl to Mommy." Tilly is next to her, rooting for her other son. Both have been on the verge of crawling, and bets have been placed on which twin will do it first.

"Ignore them," Scarlett continues to coach little Alex. "He might be a whole two minutes older than you, but that just means you had longer to cook. You have those beefy little arms and legs, and your brother is just a noodle."

"Hey!" Jax interjects. "That's lean muscle. Ignore her, Gavin. She doesn't know what she's talking about."

"I don't know," Trisha speaks up, seeming oddly comfortable amongst the current crowd. "Scarlett is like the baby whisperer. Brittany was always a head of the curve when it came to development. I'd loved to say it was my good genes, but I know it had a lot to do with how much time Auntie Rea-Rea spent with her."

Scarlett smiles at the memory, and that hint of friendship these two used to have seems to spark to life. At least a little bit. Kasey has a pleased look on his face as he rubs his fiancé's shoulders.

"You got this, AJ," Jake cheers on, refocusing my attention on the baby race.

"I hate when you call him that," Jax grumbles.

"You're a Jacob, through and through. Show them what the will of a Jake can do."

"The will of a Jake?" Letty crosses her arms over her chest and turns her glare on him.

"Don't pretend that you don't know what I'm talking about." Jake pinches Letty's butt.

Though she bats his hand away, she's grinning from ear to ear. "Come on, Gavin, let's show Uncle Jakey-Poo who the superior twin is."

Jake leans in and whispers something in Letty's ear. I roll my eyes as she blushes. These two are unapologetic when it comes to their sexual escapades. Then again, it wasn't long after Scarlett arrived that I was already wondering how soon was *too soon* to sneak her away and have her to myself. So I guess I get it.

The front door opens and the Murphy brothers, the extended family we inherited when Cassie and Robbie got married, stumble inside. "Don't worry, everyone, I'm here. The party can officially start now," Killian announces as he holds two large bottles of alcohol, one in each hand.

"Fuck," Scarlett murmurs. "Cassie, come here."

"What?"

"Help Alex show them who's boss. I need to have a word with your brother."

"What? No, this is all you," Cassie says as she rocks her newborn in her arms.

"Don't pretend you don't have forty on Alex to crawl first."

"Forty?" Robbie says.

Cassie shrugs before handing my brother his baby. "Wish me luck." She kisses him on the cheek and quickly takes Scarlett's place.

"Killian," Scarlett scolds. "We need to talk."

He glances around the room before gesturing to his chest. "Who, me?"

"Yes, you." She pushes him into the study.

Curiosity pulls me away from the twin showdown as I follow them. I lean on the doorframe and watch the interaction from a distance. Just like the rest of the house, this room looks as though it hasn't been touched in over a year. So far, the only change I've noticed Jake make since having this place to himself is the pile of Letty's boxes stacked up in my old room. Otherwise, most of the square-footage appears untouched.

"I'm warning you now, Killian Murphy. My mom is off-limits." Scarlett jabs into his chest with her finger.

"What makes you think—" He pauses, peering around Scarlett's head and into the living room, until he catches sight of the cougar in question. "That's your mom? She's hot."

Scarlett hits him upside the back of the head. "No."

"But—"

She crosses her arms and taps her boot as she looks up at the man who not only has a foot of height on her but at least a hundred pounds of muscle. "Get your dick wet somewhere else."

Killian appears to consider his options for a moment before conceding. "Fine, maybe the firefighter will let me have a round with his girl. You know, spread the Christmas cheer and all."

"I don't care who you fuck, as long as it's not my mom... or sister. And I think it goes without saying, but my niece is also very much off-limits."

"You have a niece?"

"She's seven."

"Enough said." He shivers at the thought before eyeing Scarlett up and down. Killian puts his hand up on the wall and leans in a little closer. "Why, Scarlett, this is a mighty fine sweater you're wearing this evening," he says with a thick Irish accent, one he doesn't usually have unless he's putting on a show for his groupies. His fingers trace along the V-neck of the collar. "Care to see how it looks on the floor as I—"

"No," I interject and pull Scarlett to my side. "Back off. She's mine."

Killian frowns as he looks between us. "Really?"

Instead of responding, I show him by tipping Scarlett back and claiming her with my lips.

"Great, another one bites the dust." Killian shakes his head and walks away. But I don't stop as I turn and press Scarlett against that same wall.

"Scott," she whispers. She tilts her head to the side, giving me access to her neck as I trail kisses along the sensitive skin behind her ear. I suck hard on the tender flesh as my hand travels underneath her sweater and grips her breast. I release her with a pop and gaze at my handiwork. Marking Scarlett as mine gives me a new sense of satisfaction I've never experienced before.

"Did I tell you how sexy you are in this sweater?" I ask her.

"No." She chuckles. "But I can tell." She rocks herself against my hard-on. "Someone is going to see."

"Wait here," I tell her before walking to the door. I glance around, making sure that no one is paying us any mind, before I shut and lock it. Certain that we won't be interrupted, I return to Scarlett, who's still leaning against the wall where I left her. Her cheeks flushed and her lips pouty. "Now, where were we, Angel?" I stalk forward, and she quickly glances behind me. "It's locked."

"Still, what if someone hears us?" she asks me.

I lift her sweater over her head, revealing a lacy black bra. "Then I guess you'll just need to be a good girl and keep quiet."

26

Scarlett

Scott's an animal as he spins my body, then bends me over the desk. He's impatient as he strips down my jeans. He's always been a little rough, but right now, there's a new hunger that has me already dripping for him.

"Look at this," Scott says as he spreads my cheeks open. His tongue traces along my slit from front to back. "You're so fucking wet, Angel." I jump when his heavy palm lands on my ass with a quick swat. "Tell me who has you this wet?"

I turn to look at him over my shoulder with a smirk.

Smack!

I bite my lip to suppress my moan. Scott continues to deliver strikes to my ass, increasing their intensity as I avoid giving him the answer he should already know. My body jolts as the next whack is delivered to my pussy.

"Fuck," I cry out.

"Shh." He soothes the tender flesh by massaging it. "Fine, if you're not going to tell me, I'll just have to remind you who this pussy belongs to." Scott drops his pants and I brace myself as he slams inside me.

"Holy fuck—"

His hand covers my mouth and he shushes me again. I pant into his palm as he proceeds to fuck me from behind with a sudden sense of urgency. Grunting with each thrust. Just as I'm about to come, he pulls back.

"For fuck's sake..." I groan but am cut off as I'm turned and lifted to sit on top of the desk.

Scott gathers my hair into his fist, holding on as he plunges back inside me. "Eyes on me, Angel," he orders when my lashes flutter closed. "I want you to look at me as I make you come."

I do as he says—though the intimacy of the situation and change in angle have me struggling to not roll my eyes into the back of my head.

"That's it. You take my cock like such a good girl," he praises. I bite my lip in an effort to hold back my moans, but as my climax grows closer, it becomes impossible. "Come on, Angel, put me out of my misery. Tell me who—"

"You," I pant. "Fuck, I'm only... wet... for..."

Clearly satisfied with my answer and sensing my struggle, Scott pulls my mouth to his, and we swallow each other's cries as we come together. Then he rests his forehead against mine as he attempts to regain his composure.

"You're fucking incredible," he tells me.

"Do you feel better?" I chuckle.

Scott scratches his head. "Honestly." He smiles. "Yes. I don't know what got into me."

"I do." I kiss him. "And I liked it." As the commotion picks up outside, our little bubble is popped.

"We better get back out there." Scott sighs.

"Yeah, probably."

We both get dressed but share a smile as we exit the study. It's hard to walk and pretend he didn't fuck me six ways to Sunday just five minutes ago, his release still slick in my thong.

"I have to go serve up dinner," Scott says before kissing me on the cheek.

"Do you need help?"

He smiles. "No, I've got it. Go enjoy time with your family."

"Okay." I bite my lip as my eyes flick in their direction.

"You got this," he whispers. He kisses the side of my neck, and then takes off towards the kitchen.

It's weird how easily my mom and Trisha fit in. I was worried they'd look down on this intimate family affair, which is nothing like the lavish parties we used to host for the holidays. But my mom is conversing with Robbie—God only knows about what—with baby Nova in her arms. I'm guessing it's her way of savoring that *new baby* feeling. Mom and I have had our ups and downs over the years, but one thing I can say without a doubt is that she's a wonderful grandmother, even if she's not too keen on babysitting on her own.

Trisha is powwowing with Cassie and Tilly. If I had to guess, I'd say they're trading stories about motherhood. Even Kasey has found his place, chatting with Killian in the far corner. Granted, I wouldn't be shocked if they already knew each other. Kasey loves going to Vegas to watch the fights and usually ends up at the VIP after-parties.

I contemplate which group to join and quickly realize the little cluster of kids is the most appealing. As easy as it would be to play with Brittany and the twins, I know that's not where I *should* go. So I take a deep breath and make my way over to Trisha and the girls.

"Oh, hey, Scar," Tilly greets me. "I was wondering where you ran off to."

"Um..." I pull at the hem of my sweater and hope it's not as disheveled as it seems in my head. "Scott needed help in the kitchen."

Cassie eyes me up and down. Her smile says she's not buying it but she doesn't comment. "Well, you'll be happy to know we won."

"Alex crawled?"

"Yup," Tilly says with a grin. Even though I know she had her hopes set on Gavin being first, she's obviously proud either way.

"I'm sure Gavin will catch up any day now," I assure her.

She laughs. "He did, two seconds later." One of the boys starts crying, and Tilly waves an apologetic hand. "Mommy duty calls."

Seconds after the first one starts, the other one joins in, and Nova makes three. It seems the next generation of Moores is already on a synchronized feeding or diaper schedule. Cassie runs off to grab Nova, leaving me and my sister alone.

"Your friends are hilarious," Trisha says after a few moments of awkward silence. "I can see why you love it here."

"Yeah, the whole family, the town—it's something else really."

"When you left, I was mad," Trisha tells me out of nowhere.

"You were mad?" I hiss.

"Please... just give me a second."

I want to tell her no, that she doesn't deserve a second of my time, but when I notice the tears pooling in her eyes, I nod in agreement. We step off to the side of the party for a little privacy.

"I know what happened hurt you, and I'm sorry for that. It's a guilt I'm going to have to live with for the rest of my life. That being said, I won't apologize for loving Kasey or for being happy with him, because I'm not sorry for that. I hate how it happened and, more so, how you found out."

The flashback of seeing them together rears its ugly head in my mind, but I must have become desensitized to it, because it doesn't sting as much right now.

"I know it will take time... I just really hope that one day you'll be able to forgive me. You were my best friend—" I open my mouth to speak but she presses forward. "I know I fucked that up. Roles reversed, I'd hate me to—"

"I don't hate you," I finally admit not just to her, but to myself.

"No? Because not speaking to me for two years, ignoring my texts and calls, says differently."

"Fine, maybe I hated you a little at first," I confess. However, her quirked brow tells me she's not buying it. "Fine, *a lot*. I would curse your name every time the image of you fucking him decided it was time for me to have a good cry. But when all that anger faded away and the reality that I wasn't meant for that world—or *him* honestly—settled in, I just felt..." I take a deep breath. "...sad, embarrassed, stupid. I'm not sure what the right word is. I wanted to reach out, but I just couldn't."

"I know I have no right to say this, but seeing you here, your inn, your relationship with Scott... it truly seems like everything worked out for the best. I'm not saying that to justify my actions. It's just that I've known you almost our whole lives and I've never seen you as happy as you are here."

"Are you and Kasey...? Are you both happy?"

The biggest smile spreads across her face. "I've never been happier. I love him and so does Brittany. He adores and cares for her as if she were his own flesh and blood. He's already put in the paperwork to adopt her."

I glance out at the happy little girl and it warms my heart. I remember how special I felt when Trisha's dad, *my* dad, asked if he could adopt me. It was just a little piece of paper, but it meant the world to me. While my biological sperm donor wrote me off the day I was conceived, this man, who owed me nothing, chose me. I always feared Brittany wouldn't get to experience that. Despite everything that happened, I know Kasey is a good man, and I expect nothing less from him.

"I'm not anticipating that you'll just forgive and forget," Trisha says. "But maybe... we can start off slow? You know, talk again? At least more than once every two years? I know I'm asking a lot and it's selfish of me, but I miss having my sister."

"I'd like that," I tell her, and surprise myself with the admission. For as long as I could remember, Trisha was my confidant. As wonderful of a friend as Hannah is, she isn't my sister.

"Thank you." Trisha pulls me into a hug. "You have no idea how happy I am."

"Me too."

"With your next little niece or nephew on the way, I really didn't want them to miss out on getting to know their amazing Auntie *Scar*."

"You're pregnant?" I ask her, taken aback for a moment.

She nods with a genuine smile on her face. "I just found out the other day. I mean, I suspected it, but I just officially took the test."

"Does Kasey—"

"No, I'm waiting until tomorrow, as a Christmas surprise. You're the first person I wanted to tell."

"Congratulations." I squeeze her tightly again.

"We should get back to the party, before the boys worry about us." Trisha pulls back, her eyes land on my neck, and she laughs. "Here," she says, pulling my hair forward so it curls over my one shoulder. I give her a confused look, and she quickly clarifies, "Hickey."

"Oh, crap."

"Don't worry, I don't think anyone's noticed. Though, with the way you two seem to be going at it, who knows? Maybe you'll be joining me on this little pregnancy journey by the new year."

27

Scott

"Fuck," I groan as my eyes flutter open.

At first, I assume it's just a dream, *a very good dream.* But as her hot mouth wraps around my cock and her head begins to bob under the blankets, I quickly realize it's the best morning ever. I pull back the comforter. Her pouty lips are still wrapped around my length, her cheeks flushed and her hair a mess as she looks up at me.

Scarlett releases me with a pop and rewards me with a bright smile. "Merry Christmas."

"Merry *fucking* Christmas, indeed," I groan.

"I wasn't sure what to get you." She shrugs. "So I figured—"

I lean forward and capture her mouth with mine. "It's perfect," I tell her. "Just one small suggestion..."

"What's that?"

"Turn around so that I can feast on you."

"Deal." She pushes me down and hovers her ass above my face.

I take her round globes in both of my hands as I appreciate the gift I've been given. "Call me corny. I don't care. But all I want for Christmas is you."

Scarlet chuckles. "You're right. That *was* corny. Better eat up, because I'm willing to bet there's one eager little—"

Her statement is cut off as I ravage her pussy from behind. The room is filled with gargled moans as we pleasure each other simultaneously. As Scarlett gets close to climaxing, I tug her down onto my face, and she shamelessly rides my tongue.

"Right there," she moans as she reaches for her clit. It takes all my willpower not to come as she pleasures herself on my face. I pull her legs open wider, and her motions become frantic. The real treat comes when her release coats my tastebuds. She goes to finish me off but I stop her.

"No, Angel, just let me fuck you." I change positions so that I'm on top, nestled between her silky smooth thighs.

"You're a mess." She laughs as she gazes up at me.

"You're incredible." I lean down to kiss her, give her a taste of the treat she gave me, before I slide into her still-slick channel.

Unlike last night, I take things slow as I pump in and out of her at a steady pace. Scarlett wraps her legs around my hips, digs her nails into my back, and pulls me deeper. At this point, we're both so intertwined I can't tell where I stop and she begins. I don't want this to ever end, not just the sex... *this*.

But as much as I wish this could last forever, her body coils tight and her core clenches around my cock. It's a glorious feeling when she falls apart and brings me right along with her.

"That was—" Scarlett starts but stops and smiles instead. "Incredible."

"How did Santa find us?" Brittany squeals as she runs through the lobby and inspects the Christmas tree that was empty last night but is now filled with gifts.

"I already told you," Kasey says. "It's Santa magic."

"Brittany," Trisha scolds as the little girl is already digging into the presents.

"Please, Mom," she begs.

"We need to wait for Grandma."

"Fine," the little girl huffs out as she sits on the floor and continues to pout.

"Hey." I set down my morning cup of tea, lean up from my cozy chair next to the fireplace, and whisper, "Are you hungry?"

Brittany nods and her pout turns into a little smile, so I stand up, turn, and squat so she can crawl onto my back.

"Hop on," I tell her. She holds on to my neck and I lead her into the dining area, where I set her on a nearby table and pull out the spread.

"What's this?" Scarlett eyes the tray in my hands.

"It's a Christmas ring. My grandma used to make several every year and pass them out to all her friends and family. My mom took over the tradition when Nana passed, and I—"

Well, she knows. I don't need to explain about my parents and dampen the mood on Christmas.

"This looks amazing. What's in it?" Scarlett asks, and I appreciate her ability to steer the conversation into safer waters.

"Apples, cinnamon, lots of butter. I promise, once you take a bite, the holidays will never be the same without it."

"Sorry, sorry," Ginny apologizes, waving a dramatic hand as she enters the room. "That egg nogg was a bit stronger than I thought. What did I miss?"

"Nothing." Scarlett kisses her mom on the cheek. "Scott was just showing us the delicious spread he made while we waited for you to open presents."

"Well, let's start our first of many family holidays together," her mother says, and she begins dishing up plates.

The morning goes surprisingly well. Everyone is smiling, happy. Even I seem to fit in to this group as though we've done this several times before. Trisha and Scarlett have been talking and laughing with each other, which makes me believe something happened between them at the party—something cathartic. It only proves how amazing Scarlett is, because anyone else would hold that grudge until the day they died.

My eyes land on Scarlett's niece, who scarfs down her food without taking a breath. While everyone else's plate is still full, the seven-year-old declares breakfast over and runs from the table. "Brittany Marie Valentine," Trisha scolds. "Get your butt back here—"

"Trish." Kasey grips his fiancée's hand, and her mood immediately shifts. "It's Christmas morning and she's seven. Can you blame her?"

"I know, but Scott took all this time and made us a wonderful meal. She should show more respect."

"Don't worry about it. My brother is thirty and does the exact same thing," I assure her. "As long as you don't mind waiting to eat, the food will keep."

"Please, Mom," Brittany begs with a gift in her hands. "Here. This one is for you."

"Oh, fine," Trisha concedes.

We all relocate to the open area as gifts are passed around. To no one's surprise, most of them are for Scarlett's niece and very few are for us adults. Though I am shocked to find a few with my name on them, and not just from Scar. As the tree empties and the pile of wrapping paper forms, everyone shifts back to eating and conversing. Especially with Trisha's announcement that Brittany will become a big sister next year.

"Oh, Auntie Scar, it looks like you have one more," Brittany says when she finds the small box I tucked away on a tree limb. Since it hadn't been found, I thought about letting it go until later, but it seems fate had other plans.

"For me?" Scarlett looks down at the gift, her brows knit in confusion.

"Well, open it," her mom urges.

Scarlett looks for a name as to who it's from and doesn't find one. She shrugs before tearing open the decorative wrapping. But as soon as she opens the box and sees the jewelry case inside, she stalls, and I take that moment to drop to a knee in front of her.

Her mom and sister gasp while Scarlett looks at me with tears in her eyes. "Scott?"

"May I?" I ask her. Scarlett hands me the box. I open it and hold out the ring for her to see.

"What is this?"

"It came back from the jeweler's sooner than expected and I thought this would be the perfect Christmas present."

"You shouldn't have." Her hand hovers over the ring.

I take it and slide it onto her finger. "See? perfect fit," I tell her.

"Let me see." Ginny snatches her daughter's ring finger as Scarlett continues to stare at me. "That is incredible. Where did you get it? It looks vintage."

"It was my grandmother's—actually my great-great grandmother's—but my grandmother passed it down to my sister and, well, Tilly gave it to me."

Scarlett shakes her head as tears roll down her cheeks. At first, I assume... or maybe just hope that they're happy tears but when she excuses herself, I realize that I'm way off.

"Scarlett, honey," her mom calls out.

"I'll be right back," I say before chasing after my runaway bride into the snowy morning. "Scarlett, please."

"Your grandmother's ring!" she shouts. "Sorry... I mean, *your great-great grandmother's* ring. Scott, what are you doing?"

"I'm sorry... I thought—"

What the hell was I thinking?

"We told them it was being sized. We had it covered." Her words stab me in the chest. "This is too much. Here—" She tries to take it off, but I stop her.

"No, keep it," I say. She shakes her head, so I add, "At least until tomorrow."

"Sure..."

Best to keep up appearances.

The thought hits me like a semi-truck, and it takes me a moment to pull my head out of my ass. When I finally do, I find myself searching for the quickest escape. "Look, I should get going."

"Going?"

"Yeah, I want to stop by and wish my family a Merry Christmas."

"Oh, yeah, of course." Scarlett nods, her eyes focused on the snow piled up by her feet.

"I mean, if you want me to stay—"

"No." She swallows hard. "You should go. Be with your family. I should spend some time with mine before they fly out tomorrow."

"Okay." I take a step back and immediately tuck my hands into my pockets to keep myself from reaching out for her. "Are you still going to visit the café in the morning? I was hoping to give them a farewell breakfast."

"Are you not coming back tonight?"

"Yeah, I was just curious."

"Of course. We will be there tomorrow." She smiles, and I want to believe that there's hope there, but now I'm not so sure.

"Okay, I'll see ya." I fight my urge to kiss or hold her, and force one foot in front of the other as I make my way to my car.

28

Scarlett

WHY DO I FEEL like I've just been dumped? Maybe because I think I have.

God, Scarlett, why are you such a spaz?

Here Scott is, giving you this gorgeous ring that is a family heirloom and happens to conveniently fit you like a glove, and what do you do? Say thank you? No, because that's what a rational adult would do. Instead, you panic and kill whatever this is between you before it starts.

I walk around the inn, taking my aggression out on the wrapping paper that litters my entryway, shoving it with more force than necessary into the giant black bag.

It's all just for show...

I squeeze my eyes shut and try to ignore my toxic self-doubt. But I can't, because that finicky bitch is right. We had the ring situation covered, meaning the only reason to give me one was to put on a show for my family.

Or he was trying to tell you that this is real for him with some big romantic gesture... befitting of a guy who loves romantic comedies even more than you do? The rational part of my brain finally speaks up.

"Where were you an hour ago?" I grumble out loud to myself.

"Is everything okay?"

I jump at the question, press a hand to my chest, and drop my collection of garbage. *Scott? He came back?* I quickly turn around, only to be immediately disappointed by the sight of Kasey.

"You scared me," I tell him.

As he takes in my tear-stained face, he steps closer and rests a hand on my shoulder. "Rhea, what happened?"

"Nothing." I immediately wipe away the evidence that proves the contrary and shrug off his comfort.

"Scarlett," he tries again. "I know you better than that. What happened?"

"You happened!" I shock not only him but myself with the accusation. "Why did you have to come here? Everything was fine. You guys were over there, living your happy little lives and I was here... *existing* in mine."

"We came here to see you. I know what happened was wrong. I won't even try to justify our actions. But it doesn't change the fact that we missed you, all of us. I know it'll take time, but I really thought we made some good headway this week."

"Great." I resume forcing the evidence of what was a perfect Christmas morning into oblivion. I want to dispose of it. Just like all the other memories from this past week. "I'm glad you guys feel better. I was really worried about that. Now, if you'll excuse me, I have my life to pick up."

"Look, we deserve that and a lot worse for what happened. I won't ever try to convince you that we were somehow in the right, because we weren't. And whenever you feel like letting loose all that anger you've been holding on to these past couple of years, I'm here for it. Lay it all on me. But right now, whatever is pissing you off, it isn't me and Trisha. So, again, I ask, what happened?"

"You wouldn't understand..." I shake my head and focus on cleaning. Anything to distract me from the mess this day has become. It was supposed to be simple: eat, open presents, hang out, hopefully have a repeat of this morning later tonight...

Now, I don't know what I'm supposed to do.

"Try me," Kasey presses. At my silence, he adds, "Fine, let me tell you what I think, and you can just... fill in the blanks. You roped your friend in to pretending to be your fiancé and somehow, in the middle of it all, you caught feelings and you're now second-guessing everything."

My jaw drops at the way-too-accurate summary.

"Don't look so shocked, Rhea. For better or worse, we've known each other almost our whole lives. Besides..." Kasey leans into whisper. "...you may've always been a phenomenal actress, a natural, really. But I know you too well, Valentine. You might be able to fool others, but not me."

"Does my mom or Trisha know?" My shoulders sag as realization sets in. The jig is up...

"No, lucky for you, it takes a great actor to sniff out another one. You really should've pursued it."

"We both know I was never meant for the spotlight. I was always a behind-the-scenes kind of girl. So..." I cross my arms over my chest. "...did you know right off the bat, or did we slip up?"

"I had my suspicions. For starters, your *fiancé*," he says in air quotes, "is a terrible actor and wears his emotions on his sleeve, but some of it could be chalked up to nerves." *Valid point.* "But I knew for certain it was fake the second you both stopped pretending."

The tears I pushed down quickly emerge and threaten to break the surface. *Can today get any worse?* I find myself asking this question all over again.

I'm sure it could, and I really don't want it to. I want to rewind everything back to this morning when I fell apart around Scott's tongue. If I could, I'd live there forever.

"Now that we're both on the same page and you can drop this little act, I ask again. What happened?"

I collapse onto the nearby sofa. With my elbows resting on my knees, I hold my head and rub my temples as I think. "Nothing... everything... Honestly, I don't know. Things with Scott are so complicated. I want to believe this is real, more than anything. But... I just can't. What if this is all some bout of temporary insanity-induced lust?"

"And if it's not?"

"Here's the thing about Scott... He's been on this hunt, looking for his *one,* and before we even started this whole charade, he told me he found her. But she's still married or something, going through a separation?" Kasey looks as confused as I feel. "What if he's just killing time with me? Having fun playing house while he waits for her. Then, when she's free..."

"He dumps you? Like I did."

"Yeah." The tears fall freely now.

Kasey takes the seat next to me and drapes an arm over my shoulder. I lean into the familiar comfort. "First off, this is nothing like what happened between us. I loved you. I still do... but the love I feel for you isn't the same as what I feel for Trisha. It took us being apart for me to realize it. I'm not trying to justify how things happened—it was shitty of Trisha and me. But it doesn't make what we feel for each other any less true." Kasey wipes away the trail of tears from my cheek. "Secondly, what if spending this time with you has made Scott realize what he thought he felt for this other woman wasn't as true as he thought? What if everything he's been looking for... he found in you?"

"I don't think I have that kind of luck." I shake my head.

No, I get pipes bursting and rings I don't deserve.

"Really? Because I think if anyone is fate's lucky pick, it's you. A grandfather you didn't even know leaves his legacy to you in this picturesque little town, where the man of your dreams is desperately searching for you in all the wrong places, and he just so happens to find you when a cluster of happenstances puts you both in a situation you've been avoiding. Sorry, Rhea, this is my business, and you can't write that kind of manifest destiny."

"You really think so?" The light catches the diamond on the ring, and for the first time since this morning, it looks like it belongs there. That I deserve what this inanimate object symbolizes.

"I know so." Kasey smiles with a certainty I wish I felt. "How about this? Let's keep this little secret between us. We'll be out of your hair tomorrow and you two can sit down, have an honest conversation, find the reality in all the fiction, and then you can tell your mom."

"Do you think she'll be mad?" I wince. *If* Kasey is right and everything with Scott is real, and we do come clean, I don't want all the good of this last week to be tarnished by the lies.

Maybe you should have thought of that before asking someone to pretend to be your fiancé?

"Honestly?" Kasey chuckles. "I think she'll be proud that you put all your skills to good use and committed to preforming one heck of a show this week."

I laugh and wipe away the last of my tears. "You're probably right."

"Well." He pushes to his feet. "I should go check on the girls. They were in a sugar coma last I checked, and if they're going to function at all today, they're going to need some protein."

"Kasey," I call out, and he stops to look at me over his shoulder. "Thank you."

He smiles but doesn't say anything before leaving. I continue to clean up, but not out of stress, more as something to fill the time until Scott returns. While so much seems uncertain in the moment, one thing I know for sure is that I miss him, and I can't wait for tomorrow and the chance to finally make this all real.

29

Scott

I GAZE OUT THE still partially frosted windshield as I sit outside my family's home, looking for answers in the falling snow as to what I should do. On one hand, maybe Scarlett just needs some time to process things. Afterwards, I can explain that the ring might have been the wrong gesture but that the intention was the same. Not that I'm proposing, because that would be insane. Only that I can see a real future for us if we're willing to give it a genuine go.

Then again, maybe time and space are the worst things to give her? What if my window to salvage what's left of our relationship is closing as I sit here, while she's alone with her thoughts, convincing herself that this is all an act?

Knock, knock, knock.

I glance out my driver's side window and find my brother Robbie standing there.

"What are you doing?" he asks as I roll down the glass.

"Debating over the meaning of life," I admit.

My older brother chuckles as he shakes his head. "Seems like you're right on schedule. Why don't you come in? Everyone is waiting for you before opening presents."

That fact alleviates some of the looming negativity that seemed to settle around me. Honestly, I didn't expect anyone to wait for me now that they all have their own families. But there's still one problem. "Scarlett—"

"Come inside," Robbie urges. "Just trust me, okay?"

While you wouldn't think it, he's always had this weird sixth sense for this kind of stuff, and instinct tells me that he's right. My family put me in this mess; they can help take me out of it. With a renewed outlook on the situation, I get out of my truck and follow my big brother inside.

"Where's Scarlett?" My sister hounds me the second I step through her door.

"Hello, Tilly. Merry Christmas to you too."

She waves me off. "Yeah, yeah, where is Scar?" Clearly, I know where her priorities lie.

"She's back at the inn, with her family. What the heck?" I say as I almost step on a passed-out Killian Murphy. Though my first thought is *at least he's dressed*. Especially since the twins are using him as a backrest as they play with their blocks on the floor.

Tilly frowns. "She didn't want to come with you? I guess I can understand wanting to spend time with your family..."

"Scott's having some lady problems." Robbie hands me a beer. I don't normally drink at ten in the morning but *fuck it*. It's Christmas.

"Problems?" Tilly crosses her arms. "What did you do?"

"What did I do? Let's talk about what you did!" I fire back.

"Hey," Jax says and swoops in to run interference.

"I haven't done anything," Tilly says, and I give her a pointed glare. "Okay, maybe a few things, but still, this isn't my fault."

"No?" I question sarcastically before rising the pitch of my voice to mimic my sister's. "*Oh, Scott, give her this ring. It'll be so incredible.*"

Tilly winces. "I take it, it didn't go well?"

"She panicked and now... I'm terrified I've lost her." I collapse on the sofa as I say my greatest fear out loud.

"I'm sorry." Jax sighs as he takes a seat next to me. "Was it really that bad?"

"She ran outside and started to hyperventilate."

"Maybe she just needs time," Tilly attempts to reason with me, ever the optimistic. I used to be that way too until...

"Or *maybe* she was on the fence, and this scared her to the other side."

"Scarlett... she's complicated," my sister points out the obvious. "Give her some time, allow things to settle down."

"I hope you're right." I chug back the rest of my beer. "Otherwise, you owe me a date for New Year's."

"Deal." Tilly smiles. "And I'm only agreeing to spend the holiday away from my loving husband and my two sweet boys, because I know you aren't going to need me there. I promise, by tomorrow, everything will be better—no, it'll be perfect. You and Scarlett, it's meant to be."

"What's this?" Killian groans. "Scarlett's single?" he asks with that stupid glint in his eye. I kick the bastard in the side. He rolls over to clutch his stomach, and everyone laughs.

It's late by the time I make it back to the cottage. The lights are all off. As quietly as I can, I sneak inside. I feel like an ass for being gone all day, but the more I thought about it, the more I realized Tilly was right. Scarlett needed time to process things, and while I'm certain about my feelings, maybe she needed a moment to figure out hers?

Besides, despite all the bullshit, today was Christmas and her last day with her family. After tomorrow, we will have all the time we need to figure this out.

Since I have to be up early to open the café, I decide it might be best to sleep on the couch. I assumed I'd have a tubby furball to temporarily relocate. Instead, I find his owner curled up in a blanket with her discarded book on the floor. She must have passed out reading.

Was she waiting up for me? She didn't message me all day, so I assumed she was busy.

I pick up the book and carefully set it on the table so it doesn't get stepped on. Then I scoop her up in my arms, carry her to the bed, and tuck her in.

"Goodnight, Angel." I kiss the top of her head.

"Scott," she calls out, her voice groggy with sleep.

"Sorry, I didn't want to wake you."

"You came back." She sniffles.

Was she crying?

"Of course, I came back." I sit next to her on the edge of the bed. "Sorry, I lost track of time and I have to be up early tomorrow. I didn't want to disturb you."

"Don't go." She grips my arm. "Please."

"I'm not going anywhere, Angel." I crawl into bed behind her and pull her close to my chest. It's not long before her breaths even out and she's fast asleep. "I'll stay as long as you want. Forever would be my preference... but I'll take whatever you give me."

"Forever sounds nice," she says quietly.

"Then forever it is." I kiss her cheek. "Sweet dreams, Scarlett."

30

Scarlett

My disappointment at waking up alone, and not tangled up in Scott's arms, is quickly replaced by joy as I find his little note resting on top of my phone.

> *Good morning beautiful,*
> *I didn't want to wake you. You looked so peaceful sleeping. But I'm already counting down the minutes until I see you again.*
> *Love,*
> *Scott*

Grinning from ear to ear, I retrieve my phone and quickly shoot off a text message.

> **Me: I can't wait to see you too.**
> **Me: After my family leaves, we need to talk.**

Yesterday, I was on the fence. Especially since I hadn't heard from him all day. But after last night and now this morning, I have a new outlook on everything. Kasey is right.

We deserve to lay it out all on the line, without worrying about having an audience.

As I get dressed, I do so with ease. I don't second-guess my outfit or if it fits me right, because I can hear Scott telling me how gorgeous I look. Even my makeup is a breeze as I choose to simply wash my face and toss my hair up. Dressed and ready to go, I make my way to the lobby and am shocked to find Hannah already at the desk.

"What are you doing here?" I ask her.

She eyes me from over the counter. "This is new. I like the natural beauty look." I wait for her to explain her reason for being here, so she adds, "What? I knew your family was going home today and you might need some help."

I cross my arms and tap my foot. "This doesn't have anything to do with a handsome young plumber stopping by today?"

"It would be a shame if you were out when he got here." The pink of her cheeks verifies my suspicions. Her presence here is anything but innocent, and I don't care...

"You're right," I tell her with a nod.

"I'm right? I mean, of course I am. That's me! Hannah the helpful."

"Look, would you mind covering the rest of the day? Tell Sheila if she can't be here tonight, she's fired."

"Whoa, what's going on?" Hannah circles around the front desk to narrow her eyes at me.

"Scott," I say with a smile. "I'm going to tell him."

"Wait... What are you going to tell him, exactly?"

"That I think I love him—no, that I *do* love him."

"Babe, I'm not trying to rain on your parade, and it's crazy to think I have to be the voice of reason here, but are you sure?"

"That's the thing, Hannah. I've never been so sure of anything in my entire life."

"I get that, but this is a little sudden. I mean, you've only been fooling around with the guy for a week."

"And I've *loved* every second we spent together. The thought of it ending in just a few hours... it breaks my heart. I don't want this to be over."

Hannah bites her lip in concern. She's my friend and I love her, but she just doesn't understand.

"I know to the outside observer, this sounds rash, but when you've spent an entire relationship feeling like you were always holding your breath while trying to squeeze into a role that didn't fit, only to then find someone who hugs you in all the right places... someone who, when you kiss them, the world falls away... when you go from loving someone to actually being *in love* with someone, it's like night and day. I don't need any more time to tell me what I already know, and what I know is that I love Scott Moore."

"Okay." She smiles. "If you're sure, then so am I."

My heart races as I stop in front of Moore Books and Coffee. I've been here hundreds of times before but today is different—I'm different. *We're* different.

Taking a deep breath, I open the door. As if he senses it's me, Scott looks up from the drink he's making and smiles. Everyone in the crowded room fades away, and it's just the two of us.

"Can you finish this?" he asks the girl behind the counter before he walks around to greet me.

I'm not sure what I expected, but it wasn't him crashing his mouth onto mine, then dipping me backwards as we share a passionate kiss in front of half the town. Granted, I'm not complaining about it either. No, I wrap my arms around his neck and pull him closer. I tune out the excited whispers and savor this moment, because *this is real*.

"Hello," he says as we break apart and he helps steady me on my feet.

"Hi," I say, feeling suddenly shy as all eyes are on us.

"You look amazing," he tells me as he brushes back my bangs. Then he takes my hand in his. "Here, I reserved a table for you guys this morning. I knew it would be packed and wanted to make sure you had somewhere to sit."

"Are you joining us?"

"Of course. When are they meeting you here?"

I look at my watch. "In about twenty minutes."

"Perfect. I have a few things I need to finish before they arrive, then I'll be right out." He kisses me on the cheek. "I'll be back in a minute."

I take a seat at the large set of tables Scott pulled together. I can hear the whispers, and I couldn't care less. Let them talk, because it's all true.

"Oh, before I forget," Scott says as he delivers me my usual. "Okay, now I'll be right back." He walks away but turns around to press another quick kiss to my lips. "All right, I'm going for real this time."

With a satisfied grin, I drink my coffee and savor my chocolate muffin. It isn't long before my family arrives. "Wow, this place is packed," Mom says as she takes a seat. "Actually, the whole town seems to be buzzing."

"Yeah, the day after Christmas can get busy around here, especially on a Monday morning when everyone is forced to step back into the real world."

Even though we're a small town, we still experience the after Christmas chaos of people doing returns, exchanges, gift cards burning a hole in their pocket. Plus, most shops have been closed for the past couple of days and everyone usually needs to stock up on supplies.

"Good thing you were able to snag us a table," Trisha says as she gets situated.

"Actually, Scott saved it for us." I smile at the gesture.

"He's such a sweet boy. Speaking of, where is he?" Mom glances around, looking for the man in question.

"He said he had a few things to finish up before he joined us."

"Right on time," Scott says as he walks out. "Let me grab your food."

Trisha leans in. "But we didn't order yet."

Scott returns with Logan in tow, their arms full of plates. Each one is different, and I realize it's all our favorites as he sets them in front of us.

"Waffles with ice cream and sprinkles!" Brittany cheers.

"How'd you know I liked eggs benedict?" Mom questions.

I look around and see some sort of egg white omelet in front of Kasey and crustless quiche for Trisha. Scott delivers my plate of avocado toast on whole grain bread, topped with poached eggs and red pepper flakes before taking a seat next to me.

"You're incredible, you know that? Where's yours?" I ask him.

"I prefer cooking breakfast more than eating it, so I figured I'd share with you."

"Who says I'm going to share?" I shield my plate while lifting a challenging brow.

He leans in and whispers, "Well, then, I'll just have to eat you."

Yup, I'm definitely not sharing now, and he knows it.

"When do y'all fly out?" Scott says, turning to address my family.

"Probably when we're done here," Kasey tells him.

"You don't have a set flight plan?" Scott's brows knit with his obvious confusion.

"Benefits of a private jet," I whisper.

"Oh," he says in understanding. "That must mean it'll be easy for you guys to visit again."

Kasey and Trisha share a look and smile. "That's the plan."

"Virginia Peterson?" A man stops and stares at my mom, her maiden name a question on his tongue. It takes me a second to recognize him outside his grease-stained blue overalls.

My mom studies him for a moment before recognition brings a smile to her face. "Christopher Biggs?" She stands. "Is that you?"

"As I live and breathe. What brings you around these parts? I seem to recall your parting farewell and pointed vow to never *step foot in this shithole* again." While he says it with a smirk, I get the sense the statement strikes a chord with him.

"Oh, I'm here visiting my daughter."

"Daughter?" he parrots, and Mom points to me. "Wow, I can't believe... I thought you looked familiar, but I guess I never put two and two together. I'll be damned." He scratches his head.

"And you? I assume you have a litter running around here somewhere," she asks him.

"Nope, never settled down."

"Oh..." She seems surprised.

"Yeah, I thought I found the one. But she had the sort of stars in her eyes that I could never compete with."

"Chris, your order's up," someone calls from the counter.

"Well, Ginny, it was a pleasure seeing you. But I better grab those and get to work. My boss can be a real hard-ass if I'm late."

Scott laughs, because that *hard-ass* is his big brother, Robbie.

"It was nice seeing you too," Mom says.

"Yeah, try not to be a stranger," Chris tells her, and Mom blushes at the invitation. "Scarlett, Scott, pleasure as always."

"Mom," I whisper. "What was that about?"

"Oh, nothing." She waves me off as she takes her seat.

"Didn't look like nothing from where I'm sitting," Trisha chimes in.

"Girls," Mom scolds. "Drop it, please."

We do, but only because our breakfast is getting cold.

"Hey, Scott." Gia appears at our table, with a handheld phone pressed to her chest. "I'm sorry to bother you, but there's an Amanda on the phone for you. She says it's urgent."

"Oh, sure. Excuse me, everyone. I'll be right back." He stands and I barely overhear him say, "I'm going to take the call in the office." He grabs the handheld from Gia and walks to the back.

I know I shouldn't... that I should trust him. But my stomach ties into a knot and forces me to excuse myself from the table and follow him. Everyone is so preoccupied with their meals they don't even notice. I press my ear to the door and can just make out the muffled exchange taking place on the other side.

"Amanda... I've been hoping you'd call... Oh sure, what's going on?..." Scott says, and I hold my breath as I listen. "Really! That's great... No, really, it's perfect timing actually..."

It doesn't take long for me to realize I've heard enough. *God, I'm so stupid.* Of course, he was just using me to kill time while he waited for *her*. My family is getting ready to leave, so honestly, it's best this happened now. I'd say everything will just go back to normal, but let's face it, that can never happen.

31

Scott

"AMANDA," I SAY AS soon as I enter the office. It's crazy. I've been waiting for her to reach out to me. I'm just surprised at how drastically my reason for wanting to hear from her has changed.

"I'm so sorry to bother you at work, but your profile was deleted off the app, and I couldn't find your cell. So I figured I'd try you here."

"I've been hoping you'd call," I say, clearing my throat to tamp down the excitement in my voice.

"Look, I don't know how to say this. But some things have come up, and if you have time, I'd love to talk to you about them."

"Oh, sure, what's going on?" While I can't wait to get back to Scarlett and her family, I can tell by Amanda's tone that this is urgent.

She lets out a deep sigh. "Okay, just let me get this out. After our date, as wonderful as it was, when I got home and saw my husband passed out on the couch, with our kids piled up on him, it hit me. Despite all our problems, I love him—our family—and I wasn't ready for it to end. We had a real conversation the next day, even started counseling because I think me going on a date was eye-opening for him as well. Sorry... I'm rambling. I guess the point is I know we have a lot to work on, but the fact is it *is* working, and with the new year coming, I wanted to tell you. Close this door, so we can both open new ones."

"Really! That's great." I slap a relieved hand on my desk. I really didn't want to hurt someone I thought I had a connection with at one time.

"I'm sorry, Scott. You're amazing and—wait! You're okay with this?"

"No, really. It's perfect timing actually. I'm happy that you and your husband are working things out, but even if you weren't, I found someone."

Amanda chuckles into the phone. "Of course you did. God, I feel so stupid right now. I had this fear you were waiting around for me and... yeah, just I'm stupid."

"No, you're not, because I was. But then some things came up, one thing led to another, and before I knew it, I was engaged."

"You're engaged!" I can hear her excitement for me.

"Not really. It was pretend but that was the only fake part. The rest was very much real, and her family's leaving today so we can finally get a moment to talk about what we're feeling."

"I told you someone would snatch you up. But I'm happy, not just for you but for myself. It really feels like everything worked out."

"It did."

"Well, Scott Moore, don't let me keep you. Go get your girl."

"I will, and, Amanda?"

"Yeah...?"

"Happy New Year."

As I hang up the phone, it's like the world is brighter. Not that I was feeling a certain way before, because I wasn't in a relationship with the woman, but now I have no guilt about Amanda. It sounds like everything worked out for the both of us, and I'm glad she's doing well for herself. Even if I didn't have Scarlett, I'd be happy for Amanda and her family. Though I must admit finding someone myself makes the whole thing that much sweeter.

When I walk back out to the front of the store, it's like there's an extra pep in my step. I feel different. Lighter. Ready to move on without anything from the past creeping up to haunt us.

"Hey, sorry about that." I go in for a kiss when I approach the table, but Scarlett avoids me.

Taking a seat, I can sense something's wrong—well, between us that is. Everyone else seems happy and to be enjoying their meal. I can only imagine what's going through Scarlett's head right now, but I just need to awkwardly wait and pretend everything is fine until her family leaves and we can talk. I have a feeling there are a few things I need to clear up.

"It was such a pleasure meeting you, Scott. You and your family were absolutely lovely. Please thank them again for me. It was so nice of them to allow us to crash your Christmas Eve." Ginny is surprisingly strong when she squeezes me in a tight hug.

"Anytime," I tell her.

Kasey shakes my hand. "I'll be in touch with you and Jax. Hopefully, by this time next year, we'll be putting Tral Lake on the map."

"I can't wait."

"Goodbye, Uncle Scott." Brittany hugs me.

"See you soon, pip-squeak. Make sure you take good care of Mr. Moosey."

Once the farewells are wrapped up and Scarlett's family drives off, she bolts down the street. "Hey, wait up!" I chase after her. "Scar," I call out as I run faster.

She stops in her tracks and turns around, but her gaze remains fixed on the sidewalk. "Thank you for your help this week. I appreciate it."

"Can we talk?" I grip her shoulders, but she takes a step back.

When she looks up at me, her eyes are dead. "Here." She hands me the ring. "I don't think it's appropriate I keep this any longer since our arrangement is done."

"Done? I thought—"

"Scott, let's be honest with each other. Sure, we had some fun but it was just pretend. Now we don't need to fake it anymore."

"I wasn't faking—"

"Look, I need to get back to the inn. I have a plumber coming by and need to get on the phone with the insurance company. I have a lot to deal with. Feel free to leave your key on the coffee table when you grab your stuff. I'll see you around."

"Scarlett." I try to reach out to her again, but she distances herself more.

"Goodbye."

This time I don't stop her as she turns and walks away while I stand there, stunned, until my fingers go numb. I'm not sure how long I wait, hoping she turns the corner. But when the snow starts to fall, I spin on my heel and return to the shop. I enter through the bookstore since that door is closer.

"Hey, Scott," Tilly says. "Hey... are you okay?"

I set the ring in front of her on the counter. "Here. Thought you might want this back."

Tilly grips my wrist as I walk away. "Scott, what happened?"

"What do you think happened? It's over."

"Are you sure?"

"There are only so many ways for her to say it."

"Oh no, I'm sorry. I really thought..." Tilly trails off. "Is there anything I can do?"

"Come to Chicago with me?"

"Of course." She gives me a sympathetic smile.

"Thanks, but, uh, I have to get back to work."

"Scott," she calls out again.

"Yeah?"

"I really am sorry." Tilly sighs, and I don't reply. Because there isn't anything more to say other than *you thought wrong*, and I honestly don't have the energy right now.

32

Scarlett

I FEEL LIKE SUCH an outsider as I sit with a group of women I've grown to consider friends, who for the past year I've been meeting with on a monthly basis. It used to be weekly but after the twins, Tilly cut things back. You'd think I'd be excited to discuss one of my most favorite things in the world: romance books. Without shame or embarrassment, I've been able to recommend some pretty smutty and morally gray stories, talk about them openly, and for the first time in my life, not feel like I need to hide.

Tonight, though, it feels like I'm a stranger. Not that anyone has been rude or mean. But the atmosphere feels different. Cassie isn't here, which bookwise we've become kindred spirits. Tilly said hi, has been polite, but has otherwise seemed distant. However, the most noticeable thing missing is Scott. Not that he joined our group, but he was always clunking around in the café and keeping up on our refreshments.

Is he not here because of me?

Duh, that's a dumb question. He's probably out with *Amanda.*

"Okay, can we start with the cover?" Patty kicks off the conversation. "*Meow*. I want a copy of this where the title has been removed and it shows me the goods."

"Of course, you would," Michelle teases. She still tries to play the conservative hard-ass, but this past year she's let her freak flag fly. Even suggesting a few questionable books herself.

"It makes me wish that some old crush of mine would have a major glow up and we'd get snowed in together because, seriously, Quinn and Mason were beyond hot." Mandy sighs wistfully.

"Old crush?" Effie scoffs. "If I'm ever fortunate enough to meet some tall, hunky guy, who calls me *kitten* and makes me purr, I don't care if he's an old crush, the biggest nerd from high school, or a complete stranger. We're running away together."

Her best friend Toni chuckles. They are newer additions to our group. I tried to get Hannah to join but it interferes with her schedule—plus, she doesn't exactly enjoy reading.

"They say less is more, and I absolutely loved that I was able to devour this story in a couple of hours," Sally adds.

"Yes, especially with how hectic the holidays are. This was a perfect short and spicy little read," Patty states. "I've already added all of Elyse's books to my queue. I was so excited to see that she has a ton of quick reads to help satisfy my cravings."

"What I want to know is where do people learn this stuff? Like rope play? Not judging," Michelle clarifies, and I doubt anyone thought she was. "It just seems like a very intensive kink that requires a lot of time and dedication. I'm curious how people get into it."

"I'm guessing for everyone it's different," Effie chimes in. "I was dabbling in restraints and met a guy who was into Shibari. And from there, it was a ton of research."

"You never told me you were a rope bunny!" Toni elbows her friend.

"With how vanilla you and Josh like things, I didn't think to bring it up." A weird look is shared between the friends.

"What about you, Scar?" Patty is the one to break the awkward silence. "You've been uncharacteristically quiet this evening."

"Oh..." I clear my throat. "I loved it. Elyse Kelly is a one-click author of mine. If you liked this one, I strongly recommend her Heated series."

Everyone shares a look that says *we know about you and Scott but we aren't talking about it.* The conversation quickly moves from our current read to a brief look into Shibari as Effie goes into detail about some of her favorite scenes. I keep glancing over at the café, hoping to see him, but as Tilly walks in front of me with a chair, I realize the group is over and I'm the freak sitting here staring off into the distance.

"Hey, let me help you with that." I take the chair from my friend—*at least I still hope she's my friend*—and stack it in the corner with the rest.

"Thanks." Tilly is being polite, but based on the total lack of eye contact, I can tell she's reserved.

"No Cassie tonight?" I continue the small talk.

"Nova got her shots earlier and has been fussy all day, so she stayed home to give the baby extra mommy snuggles."

"Oh, I'm sorry to hear that. Tell her I hope she feels better."

"Why not tell her yourself?" Tilly stops cleaning up and stares at me. "Look, I'm not sure what happened between you and Scott—that's your business, not mine. I've learned my lesson and I'm keeping out of it. But just because you two didn't work out, it doesn't mean we have to stop being friends." Tilly pauses. "Unless you don't want to be—"

"God no," I say with a relieved sigh. "I'm sorry. I just wasn't sure, and I did what I do best..."

"Hide away," Tilly says for me.

"Exactly." I nod and we pull each other into a hug. "I did really miss talking to you... all of you."

"Us too." She squeezes me close.

Things still feel a little awkward. But I know, with time, we can put this whole mess behind us and move on. Although I'm ready to hang out with Tilly and the girls, I'm not ready to see Scott—not yet.

Then a thought occurs to me. "Hey, do you have any New Year's Eve plans?" I'm sure she and Cassie have some sort of family-focused night on their radar, while Scott will more than likely be off spending a romantic evening with his new girlfriend and won't be there. "I'm not really feeling the big party scene this year, and if you wouldn't mind me crashing, I'd love to hang out. I can even bring some sparkling cider!"

"That sounds amazing," Tilly says, and I'm already feeling pumped for the new year. "But... I can't." She looks away and appears to contemplate before elaborating further, "I'm actually going to Chicago."

I stare at her, confused, because that doesn't sound like something she and Jax would normally do. Unless maybe he has a work thing?

"But, hey, Jax will be home with the boys, and if they're feeling up to it, I'm sure Cassie and Robbie will come over. You guys can all hang out together."

"Why are you going to Chicago? Without your husband?" My eyebrows knit together. Clearly, I'm missing something.

Tilly hesitates again. "Well, I kind of promised Scott that if you two didn't work out, I'd be his fallback date. Granted, when I agreed to it, I was certain you two were going to be a thing. Sorry... I know that's awkward to hear and, again, I'm not mad. I get it. Scott wasn't what you were looking for. Which is totally okay—"

"Why isn't he going with Amanda?"

"Amanda?" Tilly tilts her head and glares at me. "Why would he go with her? She's married."

"Yeah, but didn't she leave the guy?"

"No. Why would you think that?" Tilly asks me.

"Oh, I..." I pause, not sure I want to admit to eavesdropping on their phone call. "...just assumed."

Tilly frowns. "Why would you assume that?" she presses, and I bite my lip. "Scarlett?"

"Okay, fine. I totally listened to him on the phone. He was all excited that she called, mentioned her *perfect timing*." I wave it all off. "Anyway, I assumed that they'd be ringing in the new year together. But I guess, when you're newly divorced with three kids, running off for a romantic weekend in Chicago isn't that easy."

"Oh, Scarlett." Tilly shakes her head. "Did you break up with Scott because you thought he was getting together with Amanda?" When I don't answer her, she gasps. "You did, didn't you? You know, Scar, I expected better from you."

"What's that supposed to mean?"

"How many books do we read where the couple is happy and in love, only to break up over some stupid misunderstanding that could've been cleared up in an instant if they would've just been adults and talked to each other?"

"Almost all of them," I tell her and wince.

"Why didn't you just ask him? Confront him after the call?"

"What are you saying, Tilly?"

"It took a few shots of tequila, but Jax was finally able to pry it out of him. That call was Amanda telling Scott that she and her husband worked things out. That their date—that whole experience—as great as it was, made her realize that she still loved her husband. So, yeah, he was excited because he was already head over heels for you and didn't need to feel guilty about leaving Amanda hanging. And, as you can imagine, the timing was perfect—"

"Because my family was leaving, and we were going to talk." I collapse into a chair. "I think I'm going to be sick." I can feel my chest tightening, my breathing increasing to the point of near hyperventilation. "I ruined it, all of it. If I wouldn't have snooped or at least asked... God, I'm so stupid."

Tilly chuckles as she hands me a tissue. I hadn't even realized I'd started crying. "You're not stupid, just in love. You are, right? In love with my brother, that is?"

"Yes," I admit. "So much so that I've been a shell of myself, trying to figure out how to live in a world without him this past week. What am I going to do?"

Tilly taps a finger to her chin. "I know I said I was done meddling, but I have an idea..."

33

Scott

"Sir, I apologize but this is a couples only event," the host indicates again.

"I understand. Really, I do. I had a date lined up, but she had to cancel at the last minute."

Yeah, even my own sister flakes out on me.

Not that I blame her. If I had to choose between being home with my significant other or out with my sibling on New Year's Eve, I'd choose the former. I know I should've just called it quits, but I haven't seen Zach in years and, honestly, I really needed to get away for a weekend. Reset my mood. Then return to Tral Lake with a renewed sense of excitement. Because as it stands right now, everything makes me think of her and I don't need to bring that kind of negativity in with me next year. Nope, my focus is on me and the restaurant. Just because we're a small town doesn't mean we need to be condemned to endure small flavor.

"Again, I empathize with your situation, sir. But the event is specifically arranged with two individuals in mind. The menu catered with the expectation of two people sharing not only a meal, but an experience. I, unfortunately, cannot let you in."

I sigh. "Can I please talk to Zach? We're friends. I'm sure if I could just explain the situation, he'd understand."

The host chuckles. "I assure you Mr. Young is extremely busy and doesn't have time to come out here and explain to you what I've already stated very clearly. Now, sir, if you wouldn't mind, there are couples behind you waiting to get in." I pull out my cell phone, and the man eyes me suspiciously. "Sir, what are you doing?"

"If you're not going to get Zach for me, I'll call him myself."

"As I said, Mr. Young is very busy—"

"And instead of allowing *Mr. Young's* friend, who he *personally* invited to attend, through to his seat, you're quoting some nonsense about how my pathetic table for one will disrupt his event." As soon as the words leave my mouth and realization hits me, I hang up the phone. "I'm sorry. I have no idea what came over me."

The host gives me a sad look. *God, when did I get this pathetic?*

"Excuse me... sorry," I say as I work my way back outside. I take a seat on the stairs once I'm finally free of witnesses to my utter humiliation. "What are you even doing?" I ask myself.

"Freezing your ass off," a familiar voice says behind me before lighting a cigarette.

"You know, smoking kills your palate," I taunt.

Zach shrugs. "Hasn't stopped me from getting two Michelin stars and hopefully, after tonight's experience, a third."

"You're an asshole, you know that?"

"Me?" He looks around as if I could be talking about anyone else, then shrugs. "True, but it doesn't make my statement any less accurate. Now, what the fuck are you doing sitting out here when you should be inside, getting ready to have your mind blown?"

"Mind blown? Really?"

"What? Too much?"

"Just a little." I shake my head.

"Why'd I even invite you? I should've known you were going to rag on me harder than any of the asshole critics in there."

"Maybe that's exactly why you did it. You're tired of having people blow smoke up your ass."

Zach considers my words for a moment before smiling and clapping a hand on my shoulder. "Nope, I'll never get sick of people telling me how incredible I am." Then he leans in and speaks quietly. "Especially the ladies—fuck, do they love me."

"When did you become such a pig?"

He shrugs, finishes his smoke, and tosses the butt. "Are you coming?"

"Can't. Your bouncer turned me away."

"What? Why?"

"I don't have a date."

"Really? You couldn't find a single chick in that small town of yours who wanted to be swept off her feet, hang on your arm tonight, and get amazing free food?" He gestures across the street. "Walk into any bar and announce you need a plus-one. You'll have to beat them off with a stick."

"I found someone—the one—but somehow managed to fuck it up, and I'm so pathetic even my sister ditched me."

"Wow, man, that *is* pathetic."

"Yup. In her defense, Tilly's married now, has twin boys with another kid on the way."

"Damn, I'm really out of the loop. Who's the lucky fucker who weaseled his way into that canyon-sized hole Jax left in her heart?"

I chuckle. "Jax."

"No fucking way." Zach looks back towards the entrance. I'm sure he has a lot to do.

I stand and brush off my slacks. "Thanks for the invite, man, but I think I'm going to go back to my hotel and hope the minibar in my room can help me salvage the rest of this evening."

"Don't be stupid. Come on." Zach opens the door for me.

"I don't want to fuck with your ambiance, dude. If you're not too hung over in the morning, maybe we can get breakfast or something before I take off tomorrow?"

"You're not fucking with shit. Now come on."

Not wanting to argue or embarrass myself more than I already have, I follow my friend inside and walk past the line. The host notices me right away. "Mr. Young—" he starts while eyeing me with suspicion.

"You're doing a great job, Garret. Keep up the good work," Zach tells him.

"Why thank you, sir. But this gentleman doesn't have a companion."

"I'll be accompanying Mr. Moore this evening as his plus-one," Zach says, and I stumble over my next step while trying to stifle my laughter.

If Jake were here, he'd tell me I could do worse than Zach Young. I mean, as far as guys go, Zach's not a bad-looking dude, I guess. I shake my head at the thought.

"Very good, sir." Garret waves over a staff member and says quietly, "Please ensure they are seated in the VIP section." He smiles at me. "I hope you enjoy your evening, sir."

We walk through the heavy black curtains, and my eyes scan the opulent setup. Zach wasn't lying when he said tonight was an experience. All the tables are set for two. Everything from the tablecloth to the curtains is solid black. Then there are several gold accents sprinkled sparsely around the room, to include napkins and gold-dipped roses. Perhaps the most stunning part is the large globe hanging front and center in the middle of the open-floor plan, with a countdown clock to midnight.

A young woman seats us in one of the raised balconies that offers additional privacy, with a lacey black curtain that's just enough to diffuse prying eyes from peeping in. As strange of a turn as this night has taken, it hasn't gotten *that* strange, so I don't think Zach and I will need it. Granted, he might like not being seen by various attendees.

The server grabs a bottle of champagne from the wall, pops it open, and fills both of our glasses. "Enjoy. Your hors d'oeuvres will be out momentarily," she informs us before taking off.

"First of all, this is beyond incredible," I tell Zach while raising my glass into a toast. "But seriously, dude, you don't need to waste your night with me. I'm sure you had this seat reserved for some lucky girl and I don't feel right taking it."

"Nope, no lucky lady tonight. I hadn't planned on participating, only observing from the kitchen. But what better way to test the competency of my staff than by being one of the guests."

"Really?"

"Yup." Elbows resting on the table, he leans in. "Look, on any given day, I'd take my pick. But on holidays, it's a no-fly zone for me. Girls always get caught up in the moment and they look way more into what's happening than they should. Which, in turn, makes me have to be the asshole who breaks their heart. Even when I preface our evening with *this is just sex*, somehow the next morning rolls around and they're picking out wedding china."

Is that what I did with Scarlett? Let Christmas and our families get to me?

"Besides, it sounds like there's a lot to catch up on. What are the rest of the Moores up to?"

"Robbie, he's married with a daughter."

"No shit."

"Yup, his wife is actually Killian Murphy's sister."

Zach laughs. "Talk about a small world. I invited that bastard here tonight, and he flat-out turned me down. Fucker rather get wasted at his own bar and start an orgy."

"Sounds about right. Jake—"

"No way. Don't even tell me."

"Yup, Jake is getting married in a couple of weeks. He and Letty are flying out to Vegas."

"Letty, as in Letty Ruiz? Shit, when did those two stop bickering long enough to finally fuck?"

I chuckle. "This past summer. A tornado ripped through town, almost destroyed Harper's. She stayed at the house and, well, I bet you can figure out the rest."

"You know, it's funny. I always had this suspicion that those two were secretly boinking. There was this one summer I could've sworn I saw them making out behind the diner. But I couldn't get a close enough look."

"It wouldn't surprise me."

"Okay, who else? What about Derek?"

"Still single."

"Damn. I assumed he'd be married and five kids deep by now. Building the next Lafferty generation to rule the sheriff's station."

"Nope." I run through our short list of mutual friends. Zach isn't exactly a local. He spent his summers in Tral Lake with his aunt. So the pool of people we have in common is pretty small.

"That's cool... And Leroy?"

Ah, there it is. I've been waiting for him to ask. While I'm sure he's enjoyed catching up on some old friends, I know there's one in particular Zach's really interested in hearing about.

"He's good, still running the hardware shop."

"Good, good." Zach sips his water.

"Toni, she's doing good too," I say.

"Yeah...?" He perks up a bit but then immediately feigns disinterest.

"Yup..." I debate on telling him, but if he doesn't already know, he'll find out eventually, "...and she's engaged."

He frowns. "Oh, that's good." Based on the way he's chugging his champagne, I have a feeling that he's not as okay with it as he's pretending to be. "Who's the guy? Wait, no. I don't want to know."

"Okay," I call his bluff.

"Fine, who is it?"

"Josh."

"Fucking, goddamn it..." he grumbles as he pours himself another glass.

"Excuse me, Mr. Young. I hate to interrupt but there's a matter requiring your attention."

"Sorry, Scott, duty calls," Zach says, clearly welcoming the opportunity to escape his past the best he can. "One minute."

"I'll be here," I tell him with a two-finger salute.

It's only been a few minutes, but it feels like an eternity as I sit in almost pure darkness, listening to the soft instrumental music. I know I should be happy my friend is giving up his big night to chill with me. But, honestly, right now I feel more like a burden than anything else. I push to my feet, prepared to call it a night, when the curtain opens again. I can't make out who's standing in front of me at first, but based on the petite frame, I know it's definitely not Zach.

"I hate to be a bother, but would you mind telling Zach—I mean, Mr. Young—that I had to go?" The figure steps farther into the space, and the light from the table illuminates her sparkling gold dress, bouncing off the surface and lighting up her face. "Scarlett?"

"Hey, Scott." She bites on her lip as she wrings the small clutch in her hand.

"What are you doing here? And how'd you get in?"

"It took some embarrassing groveling with the host, but after I said your name, he made a call. I talked to this Zach guy who seemed relieved when I told him I was looking for you, and he had someone escort me back here."

"I mean... why are you here?"

Her eyes lock with mine. "Hopefully righting a really big wrong before it's too late."

"Scarlett, I don't know—"

"Please, I know I don't deserve it, but can I just say this and when I'm done, you can tell me to go away, and I'll never bother you again?"

This past week, I've fought the urge to make her talk to me. But now that she's here, I'm not sure. Despite my hesitancy, I won't lie. I really want to hear what she has to say, so I nod.

"Thank you." She takes a deep breath. "I messed up, big time. Like colossally huge! Here we were, together, and it was perfect... *too perfect*. I couldn't believe it, that everything I ever wanted was right there in front of me. I'd been so convinced that the only genuine good men were fictional, but there you were. Living, breathing, hot-blooded, and just waiting for me. I had you and I was stupid enough to let my own insecurities push you away. Because I kept thinking to myself... *how could someone as perfect as Scott want someone as messed up as me*?"

I take a step towards her, but she raises her palm and I halt.

"I followed you to the office, and when Amanda called, I listened outside the door. I heard the part of the conversation I wanted to hear. That you were excited she called, how it was perfect timing. Then I made the rookie mistake of assuming that your excitement was over her sudden availability and that timing was perfect because your obligations to me were over. Instead of asking you or letting you explain, I decided to end it first so you couldn't break my heart." She sniffles. "But it didn't work because I broke my own heart anyway."

"Mine too," I admit.

"I know, and I'm sorry. If I could go back and just talk to you—"

"But we can't go back."

Scarlett swipes a tear from her cheek. "I understand. I'm so sorry... for everything."

I grip her wrist before she leaves. She looks up at me with wide eyes. "We can't go back," I repeat as I reach up and wipe away the moisture rolling down her soft cheeks. "But we can go forward. Start over."

"Start over?" she asks with a hint of hope in her voice.

"Yes, a fresh start. Just you and me. What do you say?"

"I'd like that." She swallows hard. "You have no idea how much I'd really like that."

I chuckle. "I think I've got a pretty good idea. Here." I pull the chair out for her. "Care to join me?"

"Why thank you, sir."

I take the seat opposite her and channel my inner Zach. "Are you ready for a mind-blowing experience?"

34

Scarlett

After the most interesting meal of my life—if you can even call *that* a meal, seeing as it truly was a mind-blowing experience—we were served dessert. Which was some crazy white chocolate flower that bloomed to reveal the fluffy black mousse inside when cream was poured over the top of it. It was so soft, and I felt like I was eating a cloud covered in gold leaf. Seriously, I've never had anything like it my entire life.

Before long, the center tables are cleared from the floor, opening it for dancing. Servers still wander around the venue with champagne and canapés. I should be full, but I can't resist grabbing whatever walks by. Thankfully, Scott is just as bad as I am when it comes to overindulging.

The whole evening is magical as we dance underneath the sparkling globe, waiting for our new year and fresh start. My nerves prickle, the moment only minutes away, as a mix of excitement and fear flutter in my stomach. I'm not sure what to expect when the clock strikes midnight.

"Scarlett," Scott says. My head rests on his chest as we dance.

"Yes." I look up.

"I know this is supposed to be our fresh start, starting over."

Oh no. My heart plummets as my head drops to look at the floor.

"Wait." He grips my chin and forces me to look at him instead. "What I'm trying to say is I know we're supposed to be starting over, and I'm excited about that. But, in some ways, I don't want to start over either." Scott sighs. "They always make this look so easy in the movies. What I'm trying to say is... there's something I want to tell you, and I feel like if I don't say it before this year ends, it'll be something I regret come tomorrow. Because even if we start over, the way I feel about you hasn't changed—"

I pull Scott's mouth down to mine and stop his nervous rambling. "I love you," I say, as we break apart and he's still caught in the daze.

"Hey!" He smiles. "That was my move." This time, he's the one to kiss me. "I love you too."

We don't wait for the countdown to finish as we continue to make out on the dance floor. Everyone is cheering around us in anticipation of the new year, but for us, it's already begun. When the crowd calls out "zero," a sea of foam falls from the ceiling and coats the guests below.

Scott and I break apart, laughing as the airy bubbles tickle our skin. He licks his lips, and it takes me a moment to realize he's eating the foam. "I can't believe the bastard flavored the party foam." Scott chuckles.

I taste it myself. "Is that honey?"

Scott samples it again. "Yeah, there's some citrus there too. It kind of reminds me of ambrosia salad." We both laugh at the ensuing chaos, before his eyes meet mine and the world goes silent around us. "Do you want to get out of here?"

I smile. "Yes."

The drive back to the hotel goes by in a blur as we spend the entire Lyft ride making out in the back seat. Based on the grin the driver had on her face, I have a feeling we weren't her first or last hot-for-each-other couple of the evening. Still, we did leave her a large tip for the excessive PDA.

Hand in hand, Scott and I run through the lobby giggling like teenagers. Scott requests the elevator, then pushes me against the wall and continues to devour me. The dinging of the door interrupts us for only a moment until we relocate into the cable car. The second the metal doors trap us inside, Scott lifts me so that I'm sitting on the railing and his hands are under my dress.

"What's this?" he asks as he comes in contact with my shorts.

"It's built-in shapewear," I tell him between kisses. "But it has a—"

My sentence is cut off as his fingers find the slit in the crotch, and he slips two digits inside me. "Fuck, I've missed you." His hand pumps faster. "If this elevator doesn't speed up, I'm going to fuck you right here."

As I reach between us to undo his belt, the door opens and prevents us from putting on a show for the security folks. Our fooling around continues as we make our way down the hall, stopping every other door to attack one another.

"Finally," Scott grumbles when he finds his room. I rest against the wall as he struggles to retrieve his room key. I continue to unbutton his pants and pull down his zipper. "Angel," he scolds me.

"You're taking too long," I taunt him as my hand slides down his briefs.

"Fuck," he growls as he finally finds the small keycard and tries to open the door. But the light keeps flashing red. I give him a firm squeeze. "Come on." He tries again. When the light finally flashes green, Scott practically kicks the door open and throws me over his shoulder.

He tosses me onto the bed and I tug him down with me. "Scott, I know you love your foreplay and believe me I do too. But right now, I just need you to fuck me. After that, I'm yours to do with as you please."

He pulls me in for a searing kiss. "God, I fucking love you."

"I love you too." I yank off his pants and roll on top of him. The slit in the shapewear splits perfectly so that I'm able to glide onto his hard cock.

"And I fucking love this dress," he moans as I sheath myself on him. "Not only do you look beyond drop-dead gorgeous in it, but it's made for fucking."

"I love how sexy I look in this dress," I admit, and Scott smiles at my ability to compliment myself without his prompting. "When your eyes drink me in, I feel like I could conquer the world," I continue to say whatever comes to mind as I rotate my hips.

"That's a good girl," he encourages me.

"Oh, fuck..." I moan. "My hips... I love how they curve just right so that you can..." Scott grips my waist as he helps me keep steady. "Yes... like that. I'm so close."

"Me too, Angel." He pulls my head down to capture my lips in a kiss. As he thrusts his tongue into my mouth, he fucks me from below until I fall apart around him.

I rest my head in the crook of his arm as my lids grow heavy. Scott brushes my hair back. "Get some rest." He presses a kiss to my forehead. "We've got the rest of our lives ahead of us."

Epilogue

Scott

One Year Later

"Are you ready?" I call up the stairs of my childhood home—well, our home now I guess. Technically, we moved in six-months ago but it took Scarlett a little longer to finally settle into the space. Not that she didn't want to, but it was a big transition, going from the convenience of being onsite constantly to having to take the extra drive.

But now, with the addition of a few more reliable hands, she finally feels as though she can release the reins a little. At least that's what she says. Personally, I think when she realized that she could renovate the cabin to be a high luxury rental option and make some serious income with it, her motivation skyrocketed. Me? I honestly don't care what her motives are. As long as we're together, the logistics don't matter.

Not to mention, she wasn't the only one who was a little on the fence. It wasn't that I didn't want the house; it just felt weird for Jake to give it to me since it was left to him and Tilly. But as my siblings pointed out, my sister has her own family home, and my brother wasn't ever going to need all the extra space. Given his and Letty's lifestyle, the renovated loft apartment above Harper's is all they wanted. Maybe one day, if they settle down and get a dog, they'll look for something different. But right now, between work and travel, they're barely ever home.

"Scarlett, we're going to be late," I try again.

Bruce stands at the top of the stairs and I swear he shakes his head at me. Taking a deep breath, I trek up to our bedroom to see what's going on. Her dress is laid out on the bed and the bathroom door is shut.

"Angel." I knock. "Is everything okay?"

"Oh... um..." The toilet flushes and a flustered Scarlett appears in front of me. "Sorry."

"No need to apologize." I press my palm to her forehead. "Are you feeling okay? If your stomach is bothering you, I'm sure everyone will understand—"

"Nope, I'm fine." She smiles up at me.

"Scarlett..." I scold her. "If you're sick, we should stay home—"

"I feel great." She presses a kiss to my cheek. "Sorry. I was having an eyeliner malfunction. But it's all fixed now."

I inspect her closely but as usual... "You look flawless."

Her cheeks pinken. "Thank you." She kisses me again. "I'll be down in five."

"Are you ready?" I ask as Scarlett squeezes my hand.

"As I'll ever be." She plasters on a bright smile before pushing open the big barn door. The place is decorated with twinkling lights, pine garland, balloons, and a giant banner that says *congratulations.*

"Oh, hey!" Tilly squeals as she jogs over to us, my new niece clutched in her arms. "I was beginning to wonder if you guys were going to make it." She gives Scarlett a one-handed hug.

"Sorry," Scarlett apologizes. "Makeup crisis. Why, hello, pretty girl," she coos as she takes Callie from my sister's arms. "Aren't you just the belle of the ball?" My niece has on a giant glittery bow on her head with a matching poofy dress.

"Boys!" Jax yells just as two matching toddler terrors run between my legs. "No running!" He sighs in defeat, then turns to me. "Hey, you made it."

"You act like this is our party." I pat him on the back. "We're just here for the free food and drinks. Speaking of..." I snatch a couple flutes from a passing tray and hand one to Scarlett.

She scrunches her nose. "No thanks. I think I'll take it easy tonight."

I nod. Her stomach has been in knots for the last few weeks. As nice as it's been to have the inn packed this winter with the film crew, it's been an added stress for her as well.

"I'll take that." Tilly snatches the second champagne glass from my hands. I lift a brow at her, and she shrugs. "What? For the first time in like two years, I'm not pregnant or breastfeeding. Let me enjoy myself."

No one objects, especially not her husband.

"Scott!" Kasey calls out as he makes his way over to us. "What do you think?" He drapes an arm over my shoulder as he gestures to the barn.

"It looks great. How does it feel to have another movie wrapped up?"

"It feels like an Emmy," he says confidently. "Come on, I have a few friends I'd like you to meet."

I look at Scar, to make sure she's fine. She uses Callie's hand as they both smile and wave at me—my cue that she's good and I can step away for a bit. I follow Kasey, glancing over my shoulder one last time to find that Scarlett is surrounded by her mother, sister, and new nephew.

Trisha and Kasey have officially made Tral Lake a second home. They purchased a modest property—at least modest compared to the mansion they have in California—in one of the private communities along the north shore. It was a gift for Trisha and Kasey surprised her with it after their wedding this past spring. With the new baby on the way, Kasey cleared his filming schedule, allowing them to spend their summer with us. Even after their son was born, Trisha and Brittany have remained here, enjoying the change of pace.

As I chat with a few people I've gotten to know since filming started, plus get introduced to a few of my other favorite actors, I keep a close eye on Scarlett—waiting for the perfect moment. But it's almost as if everyone has been on a mission to keep us apart all night. Finally, she hands Callie back to my sister, giving me the opportunity I've been looking for.

"Excuse me," I say as I leave the current conversation I'm hardly paying attention to and seize my moment. Scarlett jumps as I grab her hand. "Come on." I tug her along.

"Where are we going?" she asks with a chuckle but she's already following me. I open the curtain to the small, familiar booth, making sure it's empty before shoving her inside and taking a seat next to her.

"I've been waiting all night to get a moment alone with you." I pull her in for a passionate kiss.

"Scott," she says against my lips. "I don't think we'll be able to get away with a quickie in the photo booth."

"As much fun as that would be..." The thought of the camera catching her expressions as she rides my lap has me rock hard, but I shake away the lustful thoughts because I'm on a mission. And nothing, not even her delicious pussy, can keep me from completing it. "I have something else in mind." I pull out a few bills and slide them into the machine. "Now close your eyes, Angel." She does as I say, and I quickly pull the small box from my pocket and open it just as the first light flashes. "Open them," I tell her as the clock counts down again.

"Scott," she says with a palm to her chest as her gaze locks on the object in my hands. "Is that?"

My great-great grandmother's ring sparkles back at her from inside the box. After we made *this* official, we decided not to rush things. But Tilly insisted I keep the ring for the perfect moment.

"I know I should have a big speech planned, but I'm running against a clock here. So, Scarlett Rhea Valentine, will you marry me?"

"Oh my god, yes." She crashes her mouth to mine just as the camera flashes again. And, hopefully, I timed everything well enough that I captured each moment on the strip of photo paper. Our embrace continues long after our session is done, and now, I really wish this thing had more than a little curtain for privacy.

"Let's get out of here," I groan. "I can't wait another second to feel what it's like to have you ride me wearing nothing but that ring."

"Wait." Scarlett grips my wrist. "Do you have another ten?" she asks, gesturing to the insert-cash mechanism.

"I think so..." I tell her as I grab my wallet from my back pocket. "Wanna see what naughty things I can do to you before the camera finishes clicking?"

Scarlett bites her lip. "Close your eyes," she whispers seductively, then she slides the bill into the machine. "When I count down to one, I want you to open your eyes again. Five, four, three, two..."

When my eyes shoot open, I have no words. Scarlett is smiling ear to ear with a plastic stick in her hand. My gaze lands on the little screen that flashes *pregnant*.

"You mean?" Obviously, I can read but we haven't been trying. Not that we've been *not trying*. As far as I know, Scarlett's on birth control, but my sister is living proof that it doesn't work all the time.

Scarlett nods. "Are you...? Is this okay?" She worries her bottom lip between her teeth, and I feel like the biggest ass.

I thread my fingers through her soft waves and pull her mouth to mine. "It's more than okay." I kiss her deeply. "It's perfect." We continue to make out until there's a knock on the booth.

"Are you guys finished with whatever it is you're doing in there? Some of us would really like—" My sister's words morph into a high-pitched squeal as she rips open the curtain, with photo sheets in hand. "Are you?" She looks between us. "Oh, my god!" Tilly runs off, having effectively stolen the moments I was trying to capture on film, and I chuckle and press a kiss to Scarlett's cheek.

"I hope you know what you're getting into," I tease my new but *very real* fiancée. "Tilly!" I shout as I chase after my sister. When I finally catch up to her, she's already shared our news with everyone, and I'm welcomed with congratulations all around.

And you know what? I'm too fucking hyped to care because I have the girl of my dreams by my side, and the next phase of our happily ever after is already in full swing.

The end.

Want moore Scott & Scarlett? Sign up for my newsletter to get access to bonus content.
Visit: https://bit.ly/FinallyMooreBonus
or scan

Moore By Frankie Page

The Moore Family Series:

<u>Forever Moore</u> (Tilly and Jax)

<u>Expecting Moore</u> (Robbie and Cassie)

<u>Want You Moore</u> (Jake and Letty)

<u>Finally Moore</u> (Scott & Scarlett)
Fighting for Love:

<u>Flirty at Murphy's: A Murphy's Bar Novella</u>

<u>Last Round</u>

<u>Sucker Punch</u> (Luke's book coming 2024)
Bare Knuckle (Sean's book coming 2024)
Rose's Inferno Trilogy:

<u>Retribution</u> (Book 1)

<u>Desolation</u> (Book 2

Pandemonium (Book 3)
Standalone Novella:

Learning to Love Again

New books are always coming visit

WWW.FRANKIEPAGEBOOKS.COM
to see the current list of titles available

www.ingramcontent.com/pod-product-compliance
Lightning Source LLC
Chambersburg PA
CBHW032014150726
47990CB00005B/1964